UNCOL

They are the extraordinary "forgotten" works of authors whose names are solid staples in crime and detective fiction. They are fourteen stories from yesterday and today which some mystery fans will remember with delight, and others will discover for the first time with equal pleasure.

They are packed with suspense, intrigue, and the dark motives of the criminal mind . . .

He had been sitting there for some time when the telephone rang in the darkness.

In the act of lighting a cigarette, Lonergan turned and stared at it as though it was a thing cursed.

"This is Dick Lonergan."

"This is Sally."

It was her voice. There was no question, her voice. He cupped the phone.

"Listen, if this is some kind of lousy joke—"

"Why did you kill me, Dick?" The voice was faintly sad.

"Who is this?"

"Sally. It's your Sally. Don't you recognize me?"

The horrible part was, he did.

From *I Still See Sally* by John Jakes

UNCOLLECTED CRIMES

Edited by Bill Pronzini & Martin H. Greenberg

BERKLEY BOOKS, NEW YORK

This Berkley book contains the complete
text of the original hardcover edition.
It has been completely reset in a typeface
designed for easy reading and was printed
from new film.

UNCOLLECTED CRIMES

A Berkley Book / published by arrangement with
Walker and Company

PRINTING HISTORY
Walker edition published 1987
Berkley edition/June 1989

ISBN: 0-425-11613-1

A BERKLEY BOOK® TM 757,375
Berkley Books are published by The Berkley Publishing Group,
200 Madison Avenue, New York, NY 10016.
The name ''BERKLEY'' and the ''B'' logo
are trademarks belonging to Berkley Publishing Corporation.

PRINTED IN THE UNITED STATES OF AMERICA

10 9 8 7 6 5 4 3 2 1

Acknowledgments

"Two O'Clock Blonde," by James M. Cain. Copyright © 1953 by Flying Eagle Publications, Inc. Copyright renewed © 1981 by Alice M. Piper. First published in *Manhunt*. Reprinted by permission of the author.

"Riddle of the Marble Blade," by Stuart Palmer. Copyright © 1963 by Fiction Publishing Company. First published in *The Saint Mystery Magazine*. Reprinted by permission of Scott Meredith Literary Agency, Inc., 845 Third Avenue, New York, N.Y. 10022.

"The $5,000 Getaway," by Jack Ritchie. Copyright © 1959 by H. S. D. Publications, Inc. First published in *Alfred Hitchcock's Mystery Magazine*. Reprinted by permission of Larry Sternig Literary Agency, agents for the estate of Jack Ritchie.

"Squealer," by John D. MacDonald. Copyright © by Flying Eagle Publications, Inc. Copyright renewed © 1984 by John D. MacDonald Publishing, Inc. First published in *Manhunt*. Reprinted by permission of the author.

"The Cackle Bladder," by William Campbell Gault. Copyright © 1950 by Popular Publications, Inc. Originally published under the title "The Corpse and the Cackle Bladder." Present version reprinted by permission of the author from *Ellery Queen's Mystery Magazine*, November 1960.

CONTENTS

UNCOLLECTED CRIMES

INTRODUCTION

During this century thousands upon thousands of mystery, detective, and suspense stories have been published in American magazines. A small percentage first appeared in such slick-paper periodicals as *The Saturday Evening Post, Collier's, American Magazine* and *Cosmopolitan*. A far greater percentage initially saw print in pulp and digest-size publications devoted exclusively (or almost exclusively) to crime fiction.

Prior to 1950, it was the pulps—notably, *Black Mask, Dime Detective, Detective Fiction Weekly, Detective Tales,* and *Street & Smith's Detective Story Magazine*—that provided a constant supply of mystery and detective stories to the reading public. Since 1950, when the pulps began their inevitable decline into extinction, the main supplier has been the digest-size monthlies, two of which are still flourishing at the time of this writing: *Ellery Queen's Mystery Magazine* and *Alfred Hitchcock's Mystery Magazine*. (They are "digests" only in size; the stories are published in their entirety.) Pulps and digests alike showcased the work of most of the genre's titans—Dashiell Hammett, Raymond Chandler, Agatha Christie, Rex Stout, Erle Stanley Gardner, Cornell Woolrich, John Dickson Carr, Ellery Queen, John D. MacDonald, James M. Cain, Dick Francis, and Evan Hunter (Ed McBain), to name just a few.

Much of the magazine output by these and other outstanding crime-fiction writers has been anthologized (in some cases, over-anthologized) and/or collected by the individual authors. And yet, for one reason or another, excellent stories by the best in the business have escaped notice and remain long out of print. In recent years, a number of neglected pulp stories have been resurrected for the enjoyment of the modern reader; but until *Uncollected Crimes,* there has been no anthology devoted to "lost" stories from the post-1950, digest-size mystery magazines.

This volume contains a baker's dozen plus one of first-rate tales that have not appeared anywhere since their original publication in such periodicals as:

Ellery Queen's Mystery Magazine. Founded in 1941 by the Messrs. Frederic Dannay and Manfred B. Lee (together, "Ellery Queen"), EQMM is the elder statesman among all criminous magazines. In its almost half a century of continuous publication, dozens of award-winning stories have been featured in its pages. EQMM's specialty is the traditional, fair-play detective story, though almost any type of criminous yarn can be found in a given issue.

Alfred Hitchcock's Mystery Magazine. AHMM is second only to EQMM in terms of longevity, having been established in 1956. As befits its namesake, AHMM's forte is the story with a surprise or "twist" ending.

The Saint (1953–1967). Known at different stages of its short life as *The Saint Detective Magazine, The Saint Mystery Magazine,* and *The Saint Magazine,* it was similar to EQMM in its presentation of the more traditional type of crime story—especially of obscure reprints from pulps and other sources. Named for Leslie Charteris's roguish hero, it featured a Saint adventure in each issue.

Manhunt (1953–1967). This magazine's birth and death dates exactly coincide with *The Saint*'s, although it was a source of quality crime fiction for only slightly more than half of its existence. (During its last few years it was allowed to degenerate into a mere shadow of its former self, publishing second- and third-rate originals and reprints from its early days.) *Manhunt*'s main fare was tough, realistic, and uncompromising stories of "the seamier side of life."

Mike Shayne Mystery Magazine (1956–1985). Like *The Saint,* MSMM was named for a major fictional sleuth—Brett Halliday's Michael Shayne—and featured a novella or novelette about the Miami-based private detective in each issue. It was founded by Leo Margulies, probably the most famous of pulp editors (he was editorial director of more than forty magazines in the late 1930s), and as a result it leaned toward the action-oriented, pulp-style story. As with EQMM, AHMM, and *The Saint,* however, it also presented a variety of other criminous fare.

Shell Scott Mystery Magazine (February–November 1966). Also a Leo Margulies product, SSMM headlined in each issue a new case for Shell Scott, Richard S. Prather's wild, wacky, and wench-hungry Los Angeles private eye. Its other offerings were the similar mixed bag as could be found in MSMM et al.

Mystery Monthly (June 1976–February 1977). Another regrettably short-lived publication, MM provided hard-hitting, contemporary crime stories with no taboos in terms of subject matter, language, and sexual content.

Among the authors whose stories found homes in these magazines and are being reprinted here for the first time are James M. Cain, the master of realism-in-the-raw; John D. MacDonald, one of the most popular mystery writers of our times; John Jakes, a consistent producer of best-selling novels; Ed McBain, whose 87th Precinct series has been universally praised as the finest series of police procedurals ever penned; Dorothy B. Hughes, the creator of such classic novels (and films) as *Ride the Pink Horse* and *In a Lonely Place;* and such eminent practitioners of the modern mystery and suspense story as William Campbell Gault, Helen Nielsen, Loren D. Estleman, Michael Collins, Edward D. Hoch, Jack Ritchie, and John Lutz.

Uncollected Crimes is an anthology of and for connoisseurs, as we're sure you'll agree when you've finished devouring it. *Bon appetit!*

—Bill Pronzini and
Martin H. Greenberg

When Manhunt *was in its infancy, its editor (John McCloud) and publisher (Michael St. John) had sufficient enthusiasm and clout—the magazine's first issue sold 500,000 copies—to entice some of the biggest names in and out of the mystery field to contribute stories: Mickey Spillane, Ross Macdonald, John D. MacDonald, Ira Levin, Erle Stanley Gardner, William Irish, Erskine Caldwell, James T. Farrell, James M. Cain. Cain published two stories in* Manhunt *in 1953, ''Cigarette Girl'' and ''Two O'Clock Blonde.'' Although both of these stories have the distinctive style and content of such Cain novels as* The Postman Always Rings Twice, Double Indemnity, *and* Serenade, *''Cigarette Girl'' was not reprinted until 1986 and ''Two O'Clock Blonde'' not until these pages—neglect of rather startling proportions, considering Cain's stature.*

TWO O'CLOCK BLONDE

James M. Cain

(1953)

My heart did a throbby flip-flop when the buzzer sounded at last. It was all very well to ask a girl to my hotel suite, but I was new to such stuff, and before this particular girl I could easily look like a hick. It wasn't as if she'd been just another girl, you understand. She was special, and I was serious about her.

The trouble was, for what I was up to, man-of-the-world wouldn't do it. From the girl's looks, accent, manners, and especially the way she was treated by the other guests, I knew she was class. So I guess 'gentleman' would be more like what I was shooting for. Up until now I'd always figured I was one, but then—up until now—I'd never really been called on to prove it.

I had one last look at my champagne and flowers, riffled the Venetian blind to kill the glare of the sun, and then went to the foyer and opened the door. There she was, her pale face, dark hair, trim figure, and maroon dress making the same lovely picture I had fallen for so hard. Everything was the same—except the expression in her eyes. It was almost as if she were surprised to see me.

I managed a grin. "Is something wrong?"

She took her time answering me. Finally she shook her head, looked away from me. "No," she said. "Nothing's wrong."

I tried to act natural, but my voice sounded like the bark from a dictating machine. "Come in, come in," I said. "Welcome to my little abode. At least it's comfortable—and private. We'll be able to talk, and . . ."

She looked at me again and broke out a hard little smile. "Tell me," she said, "does the plane still leave at two?"

That didn't make any more sense than the fact that she'd seemed surprised to see me. I'd told her about the plane when I'd phoned to ask her here. I'd told her quite a lot more, about the construction contract and how I had closed it, with the binder check in my pocket, and other stuff. But a nervous guy doesn't argue. "I thought I explained about that," I told her. "The plane was booked up solid, and I'm grounded here until tomorrow morning. The home office said to see the town. Have me a really good time. I—thought I'd do it with you."

"I am indeed flattered," she said.

She didn't sound flattered, but I asked her once more to come in, and when she made no move I tried a fresh start. "Don't you think it's time you told me your name?" I asked.

Her eyes studied me carefully. "Zita," she said.

"Just Zita? Nothing more?"

"My family name is Hungarian, somewhat difficult for Americans. Zita does very well."

"Mine's Hull," I said. "Jack Hull."

She didn't say anything. The burn was still in her eyes, and I couldn't understand it. After the several chats we'd had in the dining room and the lobby, while I waited for lawyers, contractors, and the rest during the week I'd been here, I couldn't figure it at all. There wasn't much I could do about it, but there's a limit to what you can take, and I was getting a burn myself.

I was still trying to think of something to say when the door of the elevator opened, and out stepped a cute blonde in a maid's uniform—short skirt and apron and cap, and all. I'd seen her once or twice around the hotel, but I'd paid no attention to her.

She smiled quick at me, but gasped when she saw who I was talking to. "Mademoiselle!" she said, in the same accent as Zita's. "*Mademoiselle!*" Then she bobbed up and down, bending her knees and straightening them, in what seemed to be meant for bows.

But if Zita minded her being there, she didn't show it at all. She said something to her in Hungarian, and then turned back to me. In English, she said, "This is Maria, Mr. Hull—the girl with whom you have the date."

"I have the—*what?*"

"Your date is with Maria," she said.

I stared at her, and then at Maria, and then at Zita again. If this was a joke, I didn't feel like laughing.

"I heard Maria's telephone conversation with you," Zita said. "I did not know it was you then, of course, but I heard her repeat your room number." She smiled again. "And I heard her say something about wine."

"Listen—" I began.

"Wine . . ." she said. "How romantic."

"I ordered the wine for you," I told her. "My date was with you, not with—"

"Yes, the wine," she said. "Where was it to be served? On the plane perhaps? It leaves at two, you said, when you told me goodbye a little while ago. You made me feel quite sad. But at two o'clock, with a smile, comes Maria."

I knew by then what had happened, and how important it is to get names straight before you phone—and to make sure of the person you're talking to before you do any asking. It put quite a crimp in my pitch, and I guess I sounded weak when I got the blueprints out and tried to start all over again.

"Please," Zita said. "Don't apologize for the maid. She is very pretty, Mr. Hull. *Very* pretty."

I opened my mouth to say something, but she didn't wait to hear it. She went off down the hall, switching her hips very haughtily. She didn't stop for the elevator, but left by way of the stairs.

I looked at the blonde maid. "Come in, Maria," I said. "We've got a little talking to do."

I had some idea of a message, which Maria could deliver when the situation cooled down a bit. But by the time I'd closed the door and followed Maria into the living room, I'd come to the conclusion that a message was not such a good idea. So I got my wallet out, took out a ten, and handed it to Maria. "I'm sorry," I told her, "that we had to have this mixup. I think you see the reason. Over the telephone, to an American, one accent sounds pretty much like another. I hope your feelings aren't hurt, and that this little present will help."

Judging by her smile, it helped quite a lot. But as she started toward the door, something started to nag at me. "Wait a minute," I said. "Sit down."

She sat down on the edge of my sofa, crossing her slim legs while I cogitated, and trying to tug the short skirt down over her knees. It was quite a display of nylon, and it didn't make it any easier for me to think. She was an extremely well-built girl, this Maria, and she had the legs to go with the short skirt. I looked the other way, and tried to figure out this point that had popped into my mind.

"There's an angle I don't get, Maria," I said. "What was she doing here?"

"You mean Mademoiselle Zita?"

I turned around to face her. "What did she come here for?"

"Didn't she tell you?"

"Not a word. Listen, I can't be mistaken. She knew romance was here—with wine ordered, who wouldn't? But she didn't know *I* was here. Until she saw me, I was just Mr. X. Why would she buzz Mr. X?"

I closed my eyes, working on my little mystery, and when I opened them Maria was no longer a maid making a tip. She was a ferret, watching me in a way that told me she knew the answer all right, and hoped to make it pay. That suited me fine. I got out another ten.

"Okay," I said. "Give."

She eyed my wallet.

She eyed my ten-spot.

She picked it up.

"It baffles me," she said.

"Listen," I told her. "I'm paying you."

She walked to the door and opened it part way. She hesitated a moment, and then pushed the door shut again and walked back to where I was standing. She looked me straight in the eye, and now she was smiling. It wasn't an especially pretty smile.

"Well?" I said.

The door buzzer sounded.

"Heavens!" Maria whispered. "I musn't be seen here, I'd compromise you, Mr. Hull. I'll wait in the bedroom."

I may have wondered, as she ran in there, just what compromising was. But as I stepped into the foyer I was thinking about Zita. I was sure it was she, back to tell me some more.

I turned the knob, and then the door banged into my face. When the bells shook out of my ears, a guy was there. He stood in the middle of the living room floor, a big, thick-shouldered character in Hollywood coat and slacks.

"Who the hell are you?" I asked him. "And what the hell do you want?"

"My wife's all I want, Mister. Where is she?"

"Wife?"

"Quit acting dumb! Where is she?"

I heard the sharp sound of high heels on the floor behind me. "But, Bill!" Maria said. "What is this?"

I looked around at Maria—and got one of the biggest jolts of my life.

She didn't have a stitch on, except those nylons and that little white cap on her head.

"You damned tramp!" Bill yelled, and made a lunge at her.

I took a seat by the window and watched them put on their act—he chasing her around, she backing away—and I woke up at last to what I'd got my foot into. When Maria had gone to the door and opened it part way, it had been a signal to this big bruiser. She couldn't have been wearing anything under her maid's uniform, or she couldn't have gotten so naked so fast. And now I was the sucker in a badger game, caught like a rat in a trap. This pair had me, and unless I wanted the house detective, and maybe even the police, all I could do was grin and kick in when the bite was made.

When the ruckus began to slacken off a bit, I said, "Okay, Bill, I get it. I don't have to be hit with a brick. What is it you're after? Let's hear your pitch." I hadn't seen any bulges on him as he circled around, and it seemed to me that a gun was the last thing he should have if his caper went slightly sour and he had to face some cops. I couldn't be sure, of course, but by then I didn't much give a damn.

But all he did was blink.

"What're you after?" I asked him again.

"Dough, Mister. Just dough."

"How much?"

"How much you got?"

I took out my wallet, squeezed it to show how thick it was, and began dealing out tens, dropping them on the cocktail table. When I'd let eight bills fall, I stopped. "That'll do it," I said.

"Hey," he said, "you got more."

"I think you'll settle for this."

"And what gives you that idea?"

"Well," I said, taking my time, "I figure you for tinhorn chiselers, a pair that'll sell out cheap. It's worth a hundred—this eighty and the twenty I already gave her, which I'm sure she'll tell you about—to get you out of here. I'll just charge it to lessons in life. But for more, I'd just as soon crack it open. You want this money or not?"

It wasn't all just talk. From Maria's eyes as she watched the bills, I knew that for some reason they worried her. She looked at them a second, and then said to me, "Will you please bring me my uniform, Mr. Hull? Like a nice fellow?"

I didn't know why I was being got rid of, but when I went into the bedroom and had a peep through the crack in the door, Maria was down on her knees at the table, holding my tens to the light, looking for the punctures that are sometimes put on marked money. Bill was grumbling at her, but she grumbled back, and I heard her say, "Mademoiselle Zita."

When I heard Zita's name, I saw red. I made up my mind I'd get to the bottom of this if I had to take the place apart piece by piece. The big problem was how. I sat down on the edge of the bed, and the more I thought about it the madder I got. I glared down at Maria's uniform lying there on the bed beside me, and called her a few choice names under my breath. And then, still glaring at the uniform, I suddenly knew I had it. That uniform was going to be good for something besides showing off Maria's legs.

I grabbed the uniform off the bed, went to the window and threw it out. Then I went back to the sitting room. Maria was still on her knees at the table.

"Lady," I said, "if you want a uniform, you tell

Mademoiselle Zita to bring it up here. Call her, and make it quick. Somebody else won't do. I want to talk to *her*.''

"But my uniform! Where is it?"

"It's gone," I said.

"Where?"

"Out the window."

She gave a little scream, and Bill hauled off with a barroom haymaker. I stepped inside it and ducked beneath his arm. Then both of them ran to the window, put their heads under the blind, and looked down in the alley. "Good God," Maria said, like there'd been a death in the family. Then she slid out from beneath the blind and ran over to me. "But my money!" she said. "You took my money! The twenty dollars you gave me! I had it in my uniform pocket!"

"Oh," I said. "That."

"Give it to me!" she said. "You took it. You—"

"Well, no, Maria, I didn't," I said. "Not that I wouldn't have taken it. Not that you misjudge my character. I'm just that greedy. And just that mean. I didn't remember it, that's all."

"Ah!" she said. "Ah!" She was standing with her feet spread apart and her hands on her hips. I'd never seen a nude woman so completely unconscious of her body as this one was.

Bill came over from the window and slapped her—to make her pipe down with the racket, I suppose—and suddenly I realized I'd pulled a damn good stunt. It was now a question of who was trapped. All three of us were, of course, except that I didn't care any more if the cops barged in or not. I didn't care, but *they* did.

"Get on that phone," I told Maria, "because you don't get out till Zita comes—unless you go with the cops."

"Call," Bill told her. "You got to."

He went to the phone in the foyer, put in the call, and gave Maria the receiver. She talked a long time in Hungarian, and then she hung up and came back into the living room. "She'll be here," she said. "She'll bring me something to wear. And now, Mr. Hull, give me that money you threw out with my—"

I clipped her on the jaw, and I didn't pull the punch. Bill caught her as she fell, which was his big mistake. I dived over her head and got both hands on his throat, and we all went down together.

I didn't hit him, or take time to pull the girl away, or anything of the kind. I just lay there, squeezing my fingers into his windpipe, while he clawed at my hands and threshed. I let him thresh for one minute, clocking it by my wristwatch, which was as long as I figured him to last.

When he'd quit threshing, and lay there as limp as Maria was, I let go and dragged him away from her. I reached in his pocket and got my eighty dollars, and then I massaged his throat to give him a chance to breathe.

His face was almost black, but he began to fight for air, sounding like a windsucker horse.

I went over to Maria and aimed a kick at her bottom.

It gave me some satisfaction, sinking my toe in like a kick from the forty-yard stripe, and listening to her groan. I did it again, and when she sat up I said, "Once more, baby—what did Zita come here for? You ready to talk about it?"

She opened her mouth to answer me, but then she saw Bill lying there and she gave a yelp and scrambled on all fours to help him.

I had to slap her around a little more to get it through her head that I was the most important guy in this room. And I had to ask her a question.

"Come on," I said. "Let's have it. What was it she came about?"

"To—warn you," Maria said. "I knew she was becoming suspicious of Bill and me, and . . ."

She moistened her lips and turned to look at where Bill was still sleeping with his noisy gasps.

"The rest of it!" I said. "And hurry!"

She shrugged. "I phoned Bill right after I talked to you, so that he'd know where to come. I spoke softly—but even so, perhaps Mademoiselle Zita overheard enough to put two and two together."

"You said she came here to warn me," I told her. "Why didn't she go ahead and do it?"

She shrugged again. "You ask her."

She moved over and took Bill in her arms, and I didn't try to stop her. I watched her stroking his face, and I was so surprised to see that a ferret like her could love that I was a second slow on the buzzer when it sounded abruptly.

I was a little groggy from all my exertion by then, but I staggered into the foyer, closed the living room door, and opened the one to the hall.

Sure enough, Zita was there again. She was holding a dress folded across her arms.

I jerked the dress away from her. "Come in, Zita," I said. "Come in and join our fouled-up little party. We're having one hell of a time here, Zita—thanks to the warning you didn't give me."

I took a breath, and was all ready to start in on her again, when she took a step toward me and fired a slap that stung clear down to my heels. Her eyes sparkled with anger.

"What did you expect?" she said. "You dated my maid! *My maid!*"

I stepped out of range and thought over what she'd just said. It could explain a lot, the warning she had expected to give some poor boob in this suite, and the warning she didn't give when she saw that the boob was me.

The way she'd reacted when she knew it was I who had made the date with Maria was just feminine enough to be compatible with liking me pretty well.

All at once, Bill started that wind-sucking sound in the living room again, a truly frightening sound. Zita grabbed the dress away from me, brushed past me, and went in there.

It wasn't more than a minute before Bill went staggering out, and after him Maria, zipping up the dress in back, and crying.

Zita came out of the living room and walked up to me slowly. She apologized then for having slapped me, and I apologized for having spoken so roughly to her, and she nodded at me and I nodded at her.

Pretty soon we were both smiling, and there didn't seem to be much point in doing any more apologizing.

And so that was that. Starting from that moment, things moved along very smoothly, and Zita's Hungarian accent never gave me a minute's trouble.

It didn't, that is, until a few afternoons later when we were faced with the novel situation of the bridegroom having to ask the bride what he should fill in under: WOMAN'S FULL NAME—PLEASE PRINT.

*Ask any knowledgeable mystery reader to name the quintes-
sential little old lady sleuth, and the response will invariably
be either Agatha Christie's Miss Jane Marple or Stuart Palmer's Hildegarde Withers. Miss Withers, the spinster schoolteacher from New York, and her friend (and sometimes nemesis)
Oscar Piper were among the most popular of sleuths both
before and long after World War II—in such novels as* The
Penguin Pool Murder, The Puzzle of the Red Stallion, *and*
Miss Withers Regrets; *in a series of films starring Edna May
Oliver and James Gleason; and in a number of short stories
published in EQMM and* The Saint, *among other magazines.
"Riddle of the Marble Blade," from* The Saint Mystery
Magazine, *is a Miss Withers adventure from the latter stages
of her long career—and good fun it is, too.*

RIDDLE OF THE MARBLE BLADE

Stuart Palmer

(1963)

In order to love her fellow man as she felt duty-bound to
do, Miss Hildegarde Withers found it advisable to avoid
humanity en masse whenever possible. Had her inclina-
tions led her otherwise, she might possibly have stood
shoulder to shoulder with a thousand or so other Manhat-
tanites in solemn conclave one bright October afternoon.
In that case, one chapter in the history of criminology
would have been considerably shorter.

But as it happened, she spent most of that Saturday in
her little West Side apartment with a stack of test papers
before her. By the time she was dragged rudely back to the
present century by the shrilling of her telephone, the fat

was in the fire. "All hell is broke loose in Central Park!" was the way Inspector Oscar Piper put it. "You see, they were in the middle of unveiling some blasted statue or other . . ."

Properly speaking, the unveiling was completely in the firm white hands of Miss Deirdre Bryan, daughter of the commissioner of parks. She had been given the historic name because of old Mike Bryan's desire to honor thus the most beautiful and unhappy queen who ever graced ancient Eire, but nobody ever called the young lady anything but "Dee."

At a few minutes before two o'clock that afternoon Miss Dee Bryan, looking better than her best for the benefit of the crowd and the massed newsreel cameras, was clutching the end of a rope. That rope, if properly and briskly tugged, would uncover from its drapes of flags and canvas the latest representation in stone of the Father of His Country. Now the statue loomed shapeless and muffled against the sky, and thus it was to remain until the last band number had been played and the last speech orated.

The minutes dragged by for Dee Bryan. His Honor the Mayor, looking even more like an angry sparrow than usual, was working himself up toward a climax. He had already told the audience what George Washington would have thought of Tammany Hall, slum clearance, the widening of Broadway, and the fifteen cent fare being raised to twenty. Now he was in the midst of a panegyric on "The City Beautiful."

When he finished, if ever, Dee would go into action with the rope, while the band struck up "The Stars and Stripes Forever," and the mayor shook hands with Dravid, the famous sculptor.

And then the almighty marble Washington, which the City of New York had commissioned for the sum of ten thousand dollars as part of its program of encouraging the fine arts, would stand in impassive magnificence above the as yet uncompleted hole that eventually was to be George Washington Uptown Swimming Pool Number Two.

Dee was only eighteen, but she had had considerable experience at public affairs. She sensed by the mayor's delivery that he was approaching the end, at last. She tightened her grasp of the rope and took a look out of the corner of her eye at the three newsreel cameras set up on the top of nearby sedans. The news director, a bored little man in a leather jacket, waved her to look up at the statue. She turned obediently, though God knows she had seen all the statues of George Washington that she wanted to. . . .

There was a sudden commotion behind her. The brisk young secretary from City Hall who was acting as master of ceremonies had caught her father by the arm and led him out of the cluster of aldermen. "Commissioner!" his voice came clearly to the wondering girl. "There's been an upset. Dravid hasn't shown up! So you've got to stand beside the mayor and let him shake hands with *you* instead!"

"Me?" Dee's father looked unhappy. It was bad enough dressed up in a cutaway and striped trousers. "But I had nothing to do with the damn statue," he protested. Then he pointed past Dee into the crowd. "That's Dravid's wife, the big handsome woman in white standing by the newsreel car. Why not let His Honor shake hands with her?"

"There isn't time to brief her!" hissed the master of ceremonies. He came over toward Dee. "Look, honey, you understand the switch? When His Honor shakes hands with your dad, haul on the rope!"

Dee nodded wearily. Her father shrugged his shoulders. "All right," said Commissioner Bryan. "But it's a shame that Dravid isn't here to take his own bows."

The mayor was at last coming to his finale. ". . . to dedicate this statue to the Father of Our Country in the spirit of reverence, and to honor a true genius, which has grown and flowered in our fair city, the great sculptor Manuel Dravid . . ."

He half-turned, with his hand out—and then caught the frantic signals of the secretary from City Hall. His Honor blinked, and managed a graceful about-face. "Manuel Dravid, New York City's own, who is unfortunately unable to be with us today due to illness—" The mayor was an old hand at ad-libbing, and his hand went to his breast pocket and brought forth a yellow sheet of paper. "—but who has telegraphed to ask that his great statue, which is shortly to be displayed before you, be accepted and understood as a true affirmation of his artistic faith! Ladies and gentlemen, in behalf of the people of this fair city, I accept the Dravid Washington!"

At this the band broke into a fervent Sousa march, and the mayor took the hand of the commissioner of parks and shook it vigorously. In the meantime, Dee's blue eyes had fallen on something that struck her curiously. It was a man standing against the newsreel truck. He was fairly young, tall, and had a beard. What she thought odd was that this man was gazing up at the statue with a weird, distorted look combining distress and fascination, as if hypnotized by a snake. Dee frowned; then the master of ceremonies murmured something to bring her attention back to the matter at hand, and as she turned to the rope she saw the bearded man fade into the throng.

The crowd held its breath as she tugged at the rope. But nothing budged. She yanked it once more. Still no response. She felt her face grow hot, like that of a salesman demonstrating a gadget that fails at the crucial moment. A nearby councilman stepped forward and they joined forces with a heavy tug. The shroud fell.

Expecting nothing but the best, the crowd burst into cheers, but these were short-lived and quickly melted into a horrified groan. It was not the Dravid Washington that caused the change of heart, for it lived fully up to its promise—a magnificent, dignified, gleaming white marble statue of the Father of His Country, twice as big as live, his arm stretched before him as though exhibiting the breadth and beauty of the nation.

But—doubled over the crook of his elbow was the limp body of a lean, sportily-clad man whose face bore the astonished expression of sudden death, and whose head was tilted at an unnatural angle. His neck displayed an ugly wound from which his blood had flooded over his wild white hair and down the marble of the statue. Dee felt her knees grow weak and thought she would surely pass out. She saw, through blurring eyes, the expressions of the newsreel men, expressions of pleased surprise that instead of just another ceremony their cameras had caught this once-in-a-lifetime moment of drama.

Dee's only thought was: "Am I going to faint? I *mustn't* faint in front of the cameras!"

Because the cameras were still rolling, she could hear them. And the expression on the faces of the newsreel men was one of pure and unalloyed delight. They'd come for just another speech and another statue—and got *this!* A newsbreak!

But it wasn't over. The mayor, caught flat-footed and speechless for the first time in his life, was pointing up at the body. He barked, clearing his throat, and finally croaked—"But that—*that's* Dravid!"

And then, for a full minute, there was no sound that Dee could hear except the widow's horrible, hysterical laughter.

"So I thought you might possibly be interested, in a screwy murder like that," the inspector finished.

"You mean, Oscar, that you're stuck with it and you want me to lend you a hand!" she told him. "But it's a fine time to get on the phone and tell me about it. The body was discovered a little after two, you say. It's five-thirty now."

"I know it," Piper admitted testily. "But there's no phone booths in the middle of Central Park. And you have no idea what it's like to try to investigate a murder with His Honor right there and screaming for an arrest. The cops on the scene haven't much of anything to report, the precinct homicide boys are up a tree. I got there as soon as I could, and it was a madhouse. I haven't had a second to slip away and call you. But I'm on my way to have a look at Dravid's studio down in the Village, and I thought you might like to come along—"

"Wild horses couldn't keep me away!" she promised. "I'll be ready." True to her word, the angular schoolmarm was pacing restlessly up and down the sidewalk outside her apartment when the inspector, for once traveling incognito, pulled up beside her in a taxicab.

"Jump in," he said, and started to give the driver a downtown address. But Miss Withers immediately vetoed the suggestion. "You can give me just five minutes at the scene of the crime," she snapped. "*You've* had all afternoon." The taxi obediently headed for Central Park West and the 72nd Street entrance.

There was still a good-sized crowd in the park, held back from the statue itself by a squadron of uniformed officers. George Washington had been shrouded with canvas again, but Piper stood on a box to lift the drape and show her the telltale brownish stain. The body had, of course, already been taken away for an autopsy.

"But he was killed with some sort of a stone hammer or arrow," the inspector told her. "Part of it stuck out of the back of his neck. Been dead at least twelve hours, so that makes it sometime in the night, Doc Bloom says."

"Between twelve and one, I should say," Miss Withers murmured.

"What? Why do you think that?"

"Because the park is quite crowded until midnight. And I happen to know there was bright moonlight from about one o'clock on—except for that one cloudy hour, when it darkened and looked like rain and then the storm blew over. The murderer would hardly risk working except in the dark. Elementary, my dear Watson. By the way, Oscar, when was the statue actually set in place?''

''Yesterday, which was Friday,'' he told her. ''Mr. Owen—Dravid's young assistant—and a whole bunch of workmen hauled it up and got it set with a crane; the newspapers took a few photos, and then Dravid was mailed his check. Today's unveiling was just the official splurge.''

''I didn't know,'' Miss Withers said. ''Unveilings are not in my line. I suppose the sculptor was in a last-minute rush to finish the thing?''

''You suppose wrong.'' Piper laughed. ''Why, the statue's been finished for weeks. It was only commissioned after a model of it was chosen from a dozen others in an open competition, you know.''

''Hmm,'' observed the schoolteacher. ''I just wonder why there are all these marble chips around the base, that's all. Unless the workmen had an accident setting it up.'' She gathered up a handful of shards. ''For my fern rockery,'' she explained.

A stepladder leaning against a pile of scaffolding told how the body must have been lifted to its oddly macabre position in the arm of the massive statue. ''Cases like this one are broken pretty easy,'' the inspector was saying. ''Contrary to usual ideas on the part of the public, the more unusual crime and the weapon, the more easily it's solved. The whole problem comes down to one point—the *how* of the crime. Why was the guy killed with a piece of sharpened stone?''

''No doubt,'' agreed Miss Withers. She was thinking of something else, as usual. For most of her short career as an amateur sleuth she had been most successful when she set her course at right angles to the inspector's reasoning. ''Well, I see nothing more here. I'm ready to go with you to the Village.''

The taxi swirled southward, with the incessant howling of newsboys at every corner. It was not often that the papers got hold of a hot story like this. "HIS HONOR FINDS CORPSE" was the way the tabloids handled it. "His Honor finds corpse and detectives find somebody to arrest, or else a lot of guys find themselves in uniform and walking a beat out Staten Island way," Oscar Piper remarked. "Maybe even me."

"They say the suburbs are much more healthful," Miss Withers comforted him. And then they pulled down a narrow street beneath the Ninth Avenue El, in a noisy, dirty world of garages, rooming houses, and lofts. Finally they stopped before what appeared to be an ancient stable. In spite of the brass plaque outside that read Atelier Dravid, the schoolteacher looked dubious. But Piper dismissed the taxi.

An exceedingly seedy-looking member of the great unemployed detached himself from a railing and shambled over toward the visitors. Miss Withers was already fishing in her purse for a dime, when the raggedy man said, "Nobody come in since I come on duty, inspector," out of one corner of his mouth.

"Swell," said Piper. He led the way to the big double door and tried a key in the padlock. It worked. "The boys borrowed it from the stiff's pocket," he admitted. "I didn't feel like waiting for a court order. Come on, it's only illegal entry."

There were mingled smells of clay, rock dust, cooking and decay, at which Miss Withers wrinkled her sensitive nose. Piper closed the door behind them and cast his flash around the rudely-furnished hall. A stairway was on the left, and a locked door directly ahead of them, which yielded to another key. "Let's just see what's in here," Piper said, and they went down a long, bare passage. The place still looked more like a barn or a warehouse than a dwelling or a studio, in spite of the signs of occasional human occupancy—overalls and rough work clothing hung on nails here and there. At the far end the corridor made an abrupt turn to the right and opened through a doorway into what at first seemed to be a starless and skyless outdoors. From somewhere came a cool little wind. . . .

Piper cast his flash curiously around, and Miss Withers squealed. Looking down on her was the face of a black and evil giant, crouched as if to spring. A second glance told the schoolteacher that the Nubian monstrosity was only cut of basalt, doomed to crouch eternally.

All around them loomed the vast, rebellious struggling creatures which spoke of the odd genius of Dravid the sculptor. He worked in the living stone only—no casts from the clay for him. A large proportion of the statues were in ghostly white marble, finished and ready for exhibition. Farther on were various projects, some of the smaller ones still little more than blocks of stone. . . .

Walking softly, almost unwilling to speak aloud for fear of disturbing the massive, brooding figures, Miss Withers and the inspector pushed farther and farther into the studio. Once the schoolteacher paused to admire a fanciful interpretation marked with a placard *The Fates;* it consisted of four crouching, female figures completely hooded in marble folds of loose drapery. A moment later the inspector, stepping back suddenly from too close a look at an unlovely figure of Judas Iscariot writhing beneath a thorn tree, lost his balance on a pile of rock chips and staggered into the outstretched arms of an over-sized, naked lady who seemed to leer back at him.

"Pardon me—," he started to say. Then he looked sidewise at Miss Withers, who was amused. In the full light of the flash, the opulent, Junoesque figure before them was almost a caricature of womanhood. The robe had just slipped to her ankles, and her face wore an expression right out of Mae West but without the saving grace of humor; her "Whyn'tcha come up and see me sometime?" had sleazy honky-tonk overtones. "Gollywhiz," whispered the inspector. "Almost makes me glad I'm a bachelor!"

"Obviously no better than she should be," agreed Miss Withers, frowning. "Poor Dravid—he must have once known the wrong woman much too well!"

But they were not meant to spend the evening in admiration of the varied talents of a murdered genius. From somewhere in the upper regions of the hall sounded the shrill ringing of a telephone. "Who'd be calling here, now?" said Piper. "I'd like to answer that! Maybe if I hurry . . ."

"Don't you leave me here in the dark!" the schoolteacher cried, and took off after him, feeling a cold draft about her ankles. "Oscar! How in the world do you think you're going to locate a ringing phone in a strange place when you can't even find the light switch?" They ran past the Fates, past the Judas and the Black Giant, and then came out into the hallway again. There was a doorway which they hadn't noticed on their way in. And the door was opening, with a shaft of light coming through.

The inspector almost dropped his flash, and Miss Withers—normally a person of considerable aplomb—gave out with her second scream of the evening. For coming toward them was the white marble woman, the opulent Juno. True, on second glance she seemed to be a little closer to actual life-size, and she was wearing a white negligee that partly concealed her voluptuous curves, but it was the same woman. Even though now she had red lips, and walked smoothly.

Somehow she didn't seem at all surprised to see them. "I'm Gretchen Dravid," she said. "If you're the police detective, you're wanted on the phone."

Piper gurgled a bit. "But my man outside said you hadn't come home!"

She pointed past them. "Perhaps your spies don't know of the side entrance—it opens on the other street. I heard you come in the front door, and I'm sure I don't mind your poking about. But I wish you'd have your telephone calls somewhere else, I've stood about all I can stand today."

Without a word, the inspector followed her up the stairs and Miss Withers, not caring to be left alone, threw her dignity to the winds and scampered after them. "The phone's in here," said Gretchen Dravid, leading the way to a chaste and modernistic bedroom. She sprawled out on the king-sized bed, where she had evidently been comforting herself in her deep grief with smelling salts, a French novel, and a jug of red wine.

"She's the sort of woman who never *sits* down," Miss Withers said to herself. "The horizontal type . . ."

"Lucky I left word at the office," the inspector was saying. "Because this must be a matter of life and death." Gretchen had to show him the phone, which was found by lifting the skirts of a demure little doll. Piper looked somewhat abashed as he picked up the instrument.

"Hello, Piper speakin'." He listened for a minute or so, during which he said, "My God!" twice, not irreverently. Then he put down the phone and stared at it.

"They've found the murderer!" Miss Withers hazarded.

He shook his head. "Wrong," he said. "It's Dee Bryan, the cute doll who unveiled the statue. She's been kidnapped!"

At which news, for no particular reason, the widow Dravid was hysterical all over again.

It was not until half an hour after the discovery of the corpse that Commissioner Bryan had been able to leave the blood-smeared statue in Central Park. Miss Deirdre Bryan had waited, in spite of his efforts to make her drive home alone without him. " 'Tis a terrible thing for a girl your age," he told her.

"It's the most thrilling thing that ever happened to me," Dee insisted. "And if you make me go home, I'll never speak to you again as long as I live!" Deirdre had wanted to remain all through the questioning of the witnesses, the preliminary examination of the corpse by the medical examiner, and the removal of the body in the morgue wagon.

But her father finally dragged her away by force, and then, and not until then, she drove him along the boulevard in a smart new roadster. They came out of the park onto Fifth Avenue and headed downtown.

"I've got to phone my office," Bryan told her. "Pull up here at the corner a minute and wait." Then he offered her his pack. "Have a cigarette. I know it's a breach of discipline, but maybe it'll calm you down a bit." He jumped out of the car and headed down 59th Street toward a cigar store.

He was barely out of sight when Dee caught a glimpse of the tall young man with the beard. He was walking very fast down Fifth. Instantly she remembered something. This was the man who had stood by the newsreel and stared up at the hooded statue with a wild and fascinated look of horror on his face. He must have known, then, what was hidden from the rest of them! And he was so good looking, too!

Suddenly she knew what she must do! Though her knees trembled and she found difficulty in breathing, she slipped from the car. Her red-stained cigarette dropped to the leather upholstery unnoticed; she left the motor running and the car door open—but Dee Bryan had no thoughts of such minor matters.

The young man who was hurrying away in the twilight was either clairvoyant—or a murderer! And Deirdre was going to find out which!

Tense as a steel spring, eager as a cat at a mousehole, Dee implacably trailed her quarry. He was walking fast, but seemingly not too sure of his directions. Finally, after making a complete circle, he stopped and looked cautiously around before he descended the stairs to the BMT subway station, but Dee was at the moment actress enough to be briskly walking in the other direction, as if there was not a thought in her pretty head except a desire to have tea and cakes at Rumpelmayer's. . . .

But she doubled back and slipped down the farther stair.

She saw the bearded young man enter the middle door of a southbound train, and by sprinting desperately she managed to slip into the end door of the same car, feeling very pleased with herself.

Her quarry leaned against a pillar, though there were many empty seats. Dee crowded between a fat woman and a couple of giggling stenographers and picked up a discarded paper, pretending to be reading the sports page, now and then peeking over the top at her handsome, romantic quarry.

Not over thirty, she decided, in spite of the beard. Hatless, dressed in rumpled clothing of expensive cut, he looked lost, appealing, and exceedingly masculine. He stared constantly out of the car windows at the bleak ugliness of the subway cavern as it flashed past. And at 42nd Street he suddenly left the car, so that she had to tread almost on his heels to get out before the door closed. But he did not look back.

"I wonder if I have the nerve to grab hold of his arm and ask him—," Dee breathed. But he was already hurrying up the stair. At the top he turned left and made for the IRT. Luckily she got through in time to see him go down the Downtown stairway of the other subway.

Here the platform was crowded with people going home, even if it was Saturday. Dee saw the bearded young man buy a tabloid and stuff it into his pocket. Then he moved restlessly along.

He was standing on the express side of the platform, but as a local train pulled in he turned suddenly and slipped in through a closing door. For a moment Dee imagined that he cast a triumphant glance back at her, and then she realized that if her suspicions were correct he was running away not from her, but from everybody.

She managed to get her arm in the door of the last car, and the automatic release flung it open and held the train just long enough for her to crowd inside. The young man with the beard was two cars ahead, and there was too much of a crowd for her to force her way forward even if she had dared to risk being noticed again. But she thought of another idea. There was room on the rear platform, and she paid no attention to signs warning passengers not to ride there. Shoving the door open, she took her stand at the back tailgate, where she could at least lean out and see if her intended victim got out anywhere.

Penn Station . . . 28th Street . . . 23rd . . . 18th . . . 14th . . . slowly the train emptied, and was refilled, but still no sign of the man with the beard. Maybe it was only a disguise, and he'd taken it off! Sheridan Square came next, in the heart of Greenwich Village. Beards wouldn't be so noticeable there. . . .

Then, as the train started forward with a jerk, she saw him! He had managed to slip off the train and conceal himself behind a pillar on the platform. Now he was hurrying toward the stairway that led to Sheridan Square!

He knew, then! Yet he was not looking back toward Dee. It must be a police tail that he was afraid of, she thought. There was nothing for it now—he was gone, with his terrible secret. Yet Dee's Irish was up. No—she had followed him this far, and she wasn't going to lose him now.

The train was under way and gathering speed. But she climbed up on the gate, balanced herself a moment and then sprang to the platform, well aware of the deadly third rail lying just beneath her if she tripped. . . .

But she landed sprawling, overturned a tin container full of old newspapers, and then rose dizzily to her feet. The train roared off into the tunnel. "Me and Tarzan!" said Dee Bryan proudly. And then, as people began to gather, openmouthed, she ran briskly past them and up the stairs.

Her quarry was luckily still in sight, walking fast in the direction of the North River. "Now to see where you live, big boy," said Dee, not without triumph. "And then a phone call to daddy and the cops . . ."

He went on, with Dee keeping as close behind as she dared. One block—two, three, and yet another. They were coming now into an odorous and unsavory region, the borderland of the Hudson River waterfront.

The young man with the beard hurried past a building where he glanced at the sign on the door that said Atelier—something, and went briskly on. There was a lounger in a raggedy jacket across the street, casually examining an old cigar butt he had just picked up, but Dee took him at face value as a bum—to her all policemen wore bright cheerful brass buttons and carried nightsticks.

Around the corner and along a side street went the bearded man—and then suddenly he disappeared into thin air. Dee stopped, stared all around and even up into the narrow lane of sky, but there was no sign of him. She went ahead softly, and then she saw the door. It was a large door, big enough to permit the passage of a truck, and it was not completely closed. Everything would have ended right then and there if it had been shut, but it wasn't. And now it offered untold possibilities.

Dee bolstered up her courage, and walked briskly up to the door, shoved it a little wider, and slipped through. Nothing happened! Yet the man she was following must have come in here, there had been no place else for him to go. As her eyes adjusted to the semidarkness, she saw looming figures all around her, marble figures. "A studio!" she whispered. Intrigued, excited, overconfident, she tiptoed forward. . . .

She knew that it was madness as soon as she heard the closing of the door behind her. She turned, and her young mouth opened in a silent scream as the darkness engulfed her, rising like mighty waters over her head so that she went down . . . down . . .

Miss Hildegarde Withers was looking at Inspector Piper. "So the girl was kidnapped. What next?" she demanded. "Don't just stand there!"

"Blanked if I know what to do first," he admitted.

"But I've got to drop the murder case and do what I can on the Bryan girl snatch. That girl has to be found quick! I suppose the Federal men will be horning in any minute . . ."

"Fiddlesticks!" said the schoolteacher. "Can't you see? The kidnapping of the girl is part of your murder case! She must have been grabbed because she knows something or saw something!"

"What?" demanded Piper, not unreasonably.

Miss Withers admitted that she didn't know and didn't care to guess. "But when Miss Dee Bryan was holding that rope at the unveiling ceremony, she must have got herself involved somehow, or this wouldn't have happened!"

"But what could she see that a thousand others didn't?"

"I wasn't there, worse luck. If I had been, I could no doubt tell you. Saving that, I'll have to have a talk with an eyewitness. Can you suggest anybody?"

The inspector leaned against the block of uncut marble, and rubbed his chin. "There's the mayor—but he was involved with his own eloquence. Her father—but the commissioner is so upset at losing his daughter he can't think straight. Says he left her in her roadster and came back five minutes later to find the car deserted and her disappeared off the face of the earth."

Miss Withers shook her head. "No, I don't want to talk to any of the official personages involved. You don't happen to know any of the newspapermen who were there? They usually have a way of seeing what there is to be seen—"

She was suddenly cut short by a bellow from the inspector, who turned back, leaped up the stairs again, and burst back into Gretchen Dravid's bedroom. Rudely he seized the telephone from beneath the skirts of the silly doll and barked a number. It was all settled in a matter of minutes. "I've got us an eyewitness that *is* an eyewitness," he announced to Miss Withers.

As Gretchen Dravid, widow of the sculptor, watched with wide and slightly bleary eyes, the two oddly matched sleuths went scurrying out of the studio and into the street, to finally find a cruising taxicab. Fifteen minutes later Miss Withers was hustled into the Times Square offices of the Paradox Pictures Newsreel Service, whisked to an upper floor, and elbowed into a pitch-dark room that seemed to be well provided with leather chairs. After a few moments the inspector plunked himself down beside her.

"The film's just out of the drying racks," said a voice somewhere above them in the darkness. "It hasn't been cut yet or anything."

Then a great white square appeared on the screen before them, and a moment later the projection machine presented them with a faintly flickering picture of a public gathering. With a gasp Miss Withers recognized the mayor, who was beginning his speech. He looked more like a comic, angry sparrow—or a robin redbreast—than ever now, all in pantomime. Just beyond him was the looming, draped figure of the statue, and there was a pretty dark-haired girl holding the release cord.

"That's Deirdre Bryan," said the inspector unnecessarily.

Everywhere else in the view of the camera were people, crowding against the base of the statue, even a line of heads before and below. In the background were the trees of the park and, far off to one side, the spires of Manhattan.

Miss Withers and the inspector watched the mayor's speech—they noted the last-minute bustling of the master of ceremonies and saw him giving his hurried change of instructions to Commissioner Bryan and his daughter. They watched, spellbound, while Dee Bryan nodded to show that she understood her instructions. They saw her glance at the camera and turn hastily away—then she looked up at the muffled statue.

The mayor made his clever recovery toward the end of his speech, and then took the "telegram" from his pocket— the message supposedly from Dravid saying that he was sorry but must send regrets. "That was a quickly thought-up lie on the part of His Honor," said Piper.

But Miss Withers was staring at the screen, not missing a single detail. When it was over—all too soon—she asked that it be repeated. "Notice, Oscar? That's the back of Gretchen Dravid's head. It couldn't be anybody else, with that neck and shoulders. But see—she doesn't expect anything, she has no guilty knowledge."

"So who said she did?"

"But watch Deirdre! When the time comes for her to pull the rope, she is looking off to the right, out of the camera, past Gretchen! There's a funny expression on her face, as if she'd seen a ghost. She almost missed her cue." The schoolteacher wanted the film run a third time, and then held at one spot—but the weary projectionist explained that was impossible. He could, however, have some stills made—but it would take time.

Inspector Piper and Miss Withers killed time by grabbing hamburgers and coffee, one of their favorite little restaurants being nearby. When they returned they found not only some prints, still wet, made from newsreel footage, but the man in charge had another exhibit for them. "There were a couple of still photographers here, and I sent over and got their prints, just in case."

Miss Withers could have kissed him! "Look, Oscar! Here are various different angles of the crowd! We can time the thing by what is happening on the stand. Remember, it was just before she was supposed to pull the rope that she saw something. If we match the pictures—that little boy there was licking his ice cream cone in this one, and here it's half gone—"

"We're wasting time barking up the wrong tree," said Piper.

"Wait! Deirdre was looking off here, past Mrs. Dravid. She must have seen *this*. But the crowd looks perfectly normal to me. There's a young couple, and the boy with the cone, and the two women just behind Gretchen Dravid—"

"And the guy with the trick beard," said Piper, staring down at the print. "Maybe she never saw a man that age with whiskers before." He sighed. "Only Deirdre could tell us—and she's gone."

"It must be the man with the beard!" insisted Miss Withers. "But put him aside for a minute. The answer to this puzzle isn't so much Who, or Why, as it is *Where!*"

"You mean the setting for the murder? But maybe Dravid was killed somewhere else, and brought to the spot." Piper shook his head. "No, because the blood was on the marble, and bodies don't bleed after death. So Dravid was actually killed while climbing on his own statue. But I don't see—"

"I think you will," Miss Withers told him. She started to gather the pictures together, to return them. Then she stopped. "Oscar, here's the last shot. The ice cream cone is gone—the little boy is wiping his mouth. And notice—the man with the beard isn't there anymore!"

"So he left!"

"At the moment the body was discovered? Come, now!"

They came out of the projection room, and Piper thanked the newsreel men. "Only hope we can release that film tomorrow," said the director. "Biggest scoop since we caught the death plunge of those men from the Macon."

Down in the lobby the inspector said he really ought to call his office, and Miss Withers suggested another call he might make. "But that was only a dodge of the mayor's—he didn't really get any telegram!" he protested.

"Ask him anyway," she insisted. He hurried away, and for the first time that day the schoolteacher had an opportunity to study the marble fragments that she had been lugging around. It was very much like working a jigsaw puzzle, one of her minor vices, and by the time the inspector was back she was surveying her results with considerable triumph. The results were spread out on the floor.

"What you got there?" Piper demanded. "Playing house?"

"The weapon," she told him.

"Weapon? But I just talked to Doc Bloom. Dravid was really killed with a marble blade, the doc just took it out of his neck. . . ."

"And that blade fitted right into the end of this!" She pointed to her joined fragments, with a few gaps, representing a stone hammer and sickle with the end of the blade missing! "When Dravid was struck, the blade broke off in his neck, and the rest of the contrivance fell to the base of the statue and shattered. The murderer didn't have time to search for the pieces, or thought they didn't matter."

"I don't get it. The statue was complete as it stood, wasn't it? Anyway, I just talked to His Honor, as you suggested, and he says yes, the telegram *was* on the level, he'd clean forgotten about it. But it really was delivered to him this morning. So Dravid never meant to be on the scene!"

"*If* he sent the wire."

"But he did! I called Western Union at Penn Station office and got a description of the sender. It was Dravid. Luckily the night staff have just gone on duty again, and one girl remembered seeing Dravid write the wire while a young man with a beard stood in the doorway and waited, holding a bundle. They left together."

Miss Withers nodded. "And when was Dravid seen alive, after that?"

"By nobody. His wife says he left the studio late in the evening, after ten-thirty, with a bundle under his arm. Without saying where he was going. But he seemed excited—almost gay. As if he was up to something."

"Which he was," Miss Withers agreed. "Let's get going. I don't suppose there's any news about the girl?"

"Oh, she's been reported seen in various places. Nothing definite, the usual thing."

"There's nothing about this case that is unusual," Miss Withers told him. "I'm beginning to put the pieces together, just as I put together the pieces of the hammer and sickle. But it's that girl who worries me. And another thing—I don't remember my mythology as I should. According to the ancient Greeks, how many Fates were there?"

"Huh? Four, I guess. Yeah, four. . . ."

"And their names were?"

"Athos, Porthos, Aramis, and—" the inspector surprised her by answering. "Or something like that, anyway."

"Oscar! That's the three musketeers," she snapped back. "The Fates were Atropos, Clotho, and Lachesis, if I'm not mistaken. But I know there were only *three* Fates!"

"Four!" insisted Piper. "Why I remember clearly. There were four figures in the statuary group in Dravid's studio!" He stopped short. "Hildegarde, what's the matter?"

For Miss Withers was having trouble keeping her teeth from chattering. She leaned against a lamppost. "Three Fates," she repeated. " 'One who spins, one who holds the thread, and one who cuts it off with the dreadful shears. . . .' "

"Hildegarde, you're hysterical!"

She shook her head. "Not hysterical, Oscar. Just a blind, silly woman." She turned suddenly and started to run, like some strange, long-legged bird of prey. "Come on!" she cried.

"But where?"

Miss Withers told him, grimly.

"In that case, we need the boys," said Oscar Piper reasonably. There was a police signal box on the Times Square corner and he unlocked it and spoke briefly into the mouthpiece. "Emergency," he said. "And I mean emergency."

It seemed that he had hardly hung up and closed the box when the howl of sirens sounded, increasing in pitch. And then two squad cars came roaring up with a screech of brakes. They tumbled into the first one, and were off again. But at the inspector's order the sirens stilled as they approached their destination, racing down Ninth Avenue toward the studio of the late Manuel Dravid. When they stopped, Miss Withers was the first one out.

But the inspector caught her arm and pointed out a light in an upper window. It was the widow's bedroom. "I know!" said the schoolteacher. "She doesn't matter, though I suppose she was really the cause of the whole trouble. You'll never get anything on her; women like that take care of themselves. But have your men break down this door, quick!"

"We'll find the girl," Piper promised grimly.

"Or what's left of her!" The door was breached, and they were running down the long hall, with much pounding of heavy brogans. And they came into the high-vaulted studio with its grim, looming figures.

Even a hard-boiled copper might well wince as his flashlight struck the grinning face of the black giant, or the tortured figure of Judas beneath the thorn tree. But it was beside the statue group marked *The Fates* that Miss Withers paused.

"I'll be something!" gasped Piper. "There were only three figures, after all!"

"There *are* only three figures," Miss Withers corrected. "Which means that we are too late!" Then she felt a draft across her ankles—just as she had done on her other visit to this world of stone figures. But this time there was the faint sound of a closing door. "Quick," she gasped. "There's another way out of here! Find the door!"

Blue-clad policemen scurried like a pack of hounds who had lost the scent, or perhaps more like frightened fireflies, among the great implacable figures, their torches slashing the darkness in frenzied and futile endeavor. It was five minutes, at least, before the big doorway was discovered and flung open. They plunged out into the street, and stopped short. Across the way was a lounging figure in an old overcoat.

"Mullins!" yelled the inspector. The plainclothes cop snapped to attention. "You're supposed to be at the other door, what are you doing here?"

"Why, nothing. But I had an idea that maybe this studio place had a service entrance on the side street here, so I was just having a look—"

"Did you see anybody leave by this door?"

Mullins shook his head. "Why, nobody, Inspector. Nobody that doesn't belong here, that is. . . ."

"Did you see *anybody?*"

"Why there was nobody but a guy named Owens, who identified himself okay. He works here, a nice young fellow with a beard."

"You saw him leave, just now?" Miss Withers put in.

Mullins nodded. "He come out of there with a big statue, all wrapped up, and dumped it into an old car that he had waiting at the curb. Said he had to deliver it somewhere, and showed me the order."

"Remind me to recommend Mullins for promotion to the Sewer Department!" gasped Piper as he led the way in a race back to the squad cars. "If we only had an idea which way the guy went—"

"North—to the bridge!" Miss Withers moaned. "Can't you see? He'll throw it over the rail!"

"Can't you go any faster?" Piper demanded of the driver, who was already doing seventy through crowded West Side streets. They picked up speed. . . .

At the foot of 57th Street a ramp leads up to the elevated auto highway, later connecting with Riverside Drive. As the cars raced up this ramp Miss Withers screamed, and pointed.

There, ahead of them in an open touring car, she had glimpsed a bearded man who was driving like a maniac, and there was a white bundle in the back seat. The squad car leaped forward, sirens howling—and the lone driver knew that the trail had come to an end. He turned back for one quick, despairing glance, face paper-white above his beard, and then suddenly jerked the wheel toward the thin wooden railing and the street fifty feet below. . . .

There was a crash of wood as the car plunged through. The police car slowed, skidding to a stop, and Miss Withers closed her eyes. But she opened them again—for the fugitive car was hanging awkwardly half through the railing, tangled in cables that the power company or somebody had left, front wheels foolishly spinning in thin air. The driver was clutching the wheel, at an awkward, impossible angle. Then suddenly he pulled himself free, shouted something incoherent, and dived deliberately down toward the pavement far below.

"Best thing he could have done," the inspector was saying, as he and the schoolteacher watched as the squads of officers, aided now by the Rescue Squad, gingerly pulled the old touring car back from its precarious position. "With two murders on his conscience. . . ."

Deft hands were unwrapping the cleverly draped sheets which had given the soft young form of Deirdre Bryan the semblance of a draped marble statue. Then somebody yelled, a shrill exclamation of amazement and glory. "She's breathing!"

And so she was. "You can't kill the Irish with one whack on the back of the head," Piper told Miss Withers proudly, after the ambulance had borne Dee Bryan away. "She's in a coma, but she's young and she'll pull through."

"It may teach her not to follow strange murderers home," Miss Withers agreed. "Well, Oscar, it wasn't as bad a tangle as I had feared. Quite run-of-the-mill, in fact."

"Huh? Well, I'm still tangled. I catch on that this Owens killed Dravid, but why?"

"You didn't study these sufficiently, Oscar." They were now sitting in a convenient little Coffee Pot, and she produced her rock samples again.

"Just broken pieces of some statue or other."

Again she arranged them, so that the head of the hammer came inside the curve of the sickle. "Does this mean anything more to you?"

"Huh? No—why, yeah! That's the symbol or whatever you call it of the Communist Party!"

"Right!" Miss Withers nodded in approval. "Well, I think Dravid was trying to perform a practical joke on the city by slipping a stone hammer and sickle into the hand of his own statue of George Washington! It would be great publicity for him, too, on account of the newsreels and the mayor's speech. But he couldn't risk being there at the unveiling, so he sent a wire begging off, and then sneaked up to the park last night with his assistant to help him. It was no easy job to get those extra pieces into the outstretched hand."

"And this Owen, being superpatriotic and all that, hit him in the back of the neck with the sickle blade. And then just walked off and left the body there, to be discovered at the unveiling?" Piper slowed down, suddenly dubious. "Who'd kill over a silly thing like that!"

"I told you, Oscar, that the important angle of this case was the place where the murder happened. Why was Dravid stabbed while mounted on his own statue—unless he had come there to make a last-minute change?" Miss Withers took a large bite of ham and eggs. "But as for motive—I wonder, Oscar, if that wasn't the big woman who was married to Dravid? Remember the statue that her husband did of her? It was a terrible revelation of her true nature—and I'm very much afraid that, whether Owen admitted it to himself or not, that woman was really the reason why it happened that a great surge of hatred swept over him when he was alone with Dravid at the statue last night."

"Jealousy? Just the old triangle situation." The inspector finished his coffee, reached for a toothpick, and then hastily threw it away under Miss Withers's disapproving stare. "So all's well that ends well," he observed philosophically. "Dee Bryan, when she gets out of the hospital, will have a rousing good story to tell about it all. And the woman really responsible for it goes free—"

"She does, Oscar. Unless somebody remembers that she admits she heard us when *we* came into the studio, and asks her and keeps asking her why she *didn't* hear Mr. Owens, who must have made a lot more noise than we did! You pick her up, Oscar, and you might find she was an accomplice! See if I'm not right!"

And they did. And she was.

For more than thirty years, Jack Ritchie was one of the two or three best writers of the criminous short story. He published several hundred between 1953 and his death in 1983; eighteen of the most accomplished can be found in his only book, the 1971 paperback collection A New Leaf and Other Stories. *He was the leading contributor, both in terms of quantity and quality, to AHMM from that magazine's inception in 1956. An early AHMM story, ''The $5,000 Getaway,'' is not only vintage Ritchie and not only a neglected gem; it is the only mystery story to utilize the infamous federal prison on Alcatraz (albeit not by name) as its setting.*

THE $5,000 GETAWAY

Jack Ritchie

(1959)

O'Hanlon and I were in the guard's dining room having a cup of coffee with Lieutenant Farley before going on duty.

"It's impossible," Farley said.

I lit a cigar. "You mean it hasn't been done."

He shook his head. "I mean it's impossible. Nobody ever got off this rock unless we let him."

"What about Hilliard?"

Farley snorted. "Maybe he got off, but what good did it do him? His little wooden flippers didn't do much to improve his swimming. The current and the cold finished him and he drowned."

I grinned slightly. "For two weeks, until we found his body, we thought he made it."

"Not me," Farley snapped. "I would have bet plenty against it."

O'Hanlon looked pained, the way he always does when I argue with the lieutenant.

I watched a fleck of cigar ash drop to the floor. "It's only a mile and a half across the bay to the city. Or about two and a half to the point. A good swimmer shouldn't have trouble."

"There's the fog and the cold, Regan," Farley said. "Don't forget about them. And the current is tricky and strong."

"That's what the newspapers say."

Farley pounded the table. "That's what I say, too. I been here since the place opened and I know what I'm talking about."

I rolled the cigar in my mouth. "I read about Henderson and Wallace in '37. Their bodies were never found. Some people like to think that they crawled out of the bay on the other side and went on to a happy life in South America."

Farley's voice rose. "Their bodies were carried out to sea."

I rubbed my jaw. "We'll never know."

Farley glared at me. "We never heard a thing about them."

O'Hanlon glanced at his watch. "It's nearly four, Regan. Time for us to go."

He sighed as we left the room. "You're just a rookie guard, Regan. He's the lieutenant. It isn't smart to make him sore."

I knocked the light off my cigar when we reached the cell house. The gatekeeper waited while the armory officer checked us through his vision panel.

O'Hanlon's eyes took in the tool-steel bars. "Farley's right. Nobody gets off this place and lives."

The armory officer pressed his buzzer and the shield pulled off the lock.

"People sure go through a lot of trouble to get out of

some places," O'Hanlon said. "Like a break I read about in Kansas City. This guy was in a cell on the sixth floor of the police station waiting to go to trial. He'd been there a couple of months, and then one night he sawed through the window bars and climbed down the side of the building."

Inside the first gate we waited until the keeper opened the door.

"It seemed like something impossible," O'Hanlon said. "But when the police got him back later, he told them how he'd done it. For six weeks he practiced in his cell for hours every day strengthening his fingers with exercises. Finally, he could actually support the full weight of his body for over half an hour with just his fingertips. He went down the side of that building just that way, with his fingertips and using every crack and joint for a hold."

We relieved Gomez and Morgan in Cell Block C.

The late afternoon sun made the place bright, and two orderlies were polishing Broadway between the three-tiered cells. One of them was Turpin.

The rest of the men were at the shops, and the cell doors were all open. I walked along the shelves, glancing inside each cell. Some were plain and bare, with no more than the bed, the toilet bowl, the sink and fountain, and others looked like miniature law offices, art studios, or chapels, depending on the nature of the men who occupied them.

I stopped at Turpin's cell on the second tier and went inside. It was one of the plain ones, not a thing that wasn't issued, except for Volume 18 of the library's encyclopedia. I riffled through the pages, and the book still opened to the same place, the same subject. The pages were a little grimy. Turpin really should have memorized that section by now. The article was short and clear.

When I came out of his cell, Turpin was looking up. He went back to polishing the floor.

During the break for the orderlies, I went down to talk to him. "Not smoking, Turpin?"

"No, sir. I gave it up."

"Now, I wish I could do that," I said. "Tobacco's bad for the wind."

There was the faintest flicker in his eyes. "Yes, sir."

I looked through the incurved bars at the window to where buoys marked the forbidden zone two hundred yards off shore. "This is a lot better than Dog Block, isn't it, Turpin?"

His tone was expressionless. "Yes, sir."

"At least you get more sun and air," I said. "The walls are a little farther apart and you get a chance for exercise." I studied him. "Just be a good boy and you might even get more sun and air. Maybe a job with the garbage crew or the wharf gang."

"I think I'd like that, sir."

I looked out at the bay again. "Look at all that water, Turpin. I'll bet you never saw anything like that in Arizona. That's where you were born and raised, isn't it?"

His eyes were on the bay. "Yes, sir."

"Nice place," I said. "But dry." I looked back at him. "I'm a little worried about you, Turpin."

He was startled. "Why, sir?"

"Your hour in the recreation yard," I said. "Real healthy. Keeps you in condition." I pursed my lips. "You ought to keep your mind occupied too, Turpin. Take correspondence courses and stuff like that."

"I'll think about it, sir."

"We got a guy here who made himself a world authority on canary birds," I said. "Just imagine that. From books. And some of the boys in here have been making out so many writs and petitions that they know more about law than most lawyers." I smiled slightly. "A man can do almost anything if he sets his mind to it."

I walked back down the hall and joined O'Hanlon.

He watched Turpin. "That man used to give us a lot of trouble, but it looks like he's tamed."

"He doesn't care much for the isolation cells or solitary," I said. "Not much opportunity there."

O'Hanlon grinned. "He didn't much want to come to this rock in the first place. He made a break for it before the launch even got here."

I looked back down the corridor at Turpin. "That right?"

"It was before you came here, Regan. About three years ago when Farley was bringing him here from the mainland, he tried to get away. Just as the boat pulled away, he slipped his cuffs and made a jump back for the dock."

O'Hanlon chuckled. "I guess he waited a second too long because he landed in the water instead of on the dock. Went down like a stone. If Farley hadn't fished him out, he would have drowned."

At five-thirty, the prisoners were marched from the dining hall into the cell block. After the count bell, we locked them up for the night.

At eight, Lieutenant Farley came around to see how things were. He looked down the lines of closed cell doors. "Quiet," he said. "Just like always."

I covered my smile. "Not like always. This place can get noisy. Like the time seven were killed."

He scowled. "But nobody got out of the cell blocks."

"That's right," I said. "This isn't the place to try anything."

"Maximum security," Farley said. "Minimum privilege. No radios or newspapers. Correspondence and visiting restricted. No commissary. And the silence system."

"Not much to live for."

He grunted. "But only one ever took the easy way out. Everybody likes to live, no matter how hard things can get."

I looked up toward the skylights in the cell block. "I keep wondering what happened to Henderson and Wallace."

Farley scowled. "Stop wondering. The sharks chewed them up twenty years ago."

"We just don't know. Maybe they do their thinking in Spanish now."

Farley glared at me.

I smiled a little. "Did you know that a year before this became a federal pen, two women swam out here from the city, bucking those awful currents, went all around the island, and back to the mainland. Did you ever hear about it?"

Farley's face was mottled. "Sure I heard about it. But I don't believe it. And if they did, I'll bet they were like those professionals. Like the ones who swim that channel over in Europe."

"It takes a lot of practice to do something like that."

He slapped the railing and grinned. "That's it, Regan. Hours and hours of practice. Years maybe. And where are these cons going to practice swimming? We ain't got a pool here, you know."

"That's right, Lieutenant," I said. "No pool."

Farley was still pleased. "Nobody here could make it across."

I nodded. "Especially if he couldn't swim in the first place."

He patted my shoulder. "Let me know if you see anybody in the water."

I made my round of the tiers at eight-thirty instead of nine-fifteen that night. On the second shelf I walked softly and stopped in front of Turpin's cell.

He was doing push-ups.

They were easy for him now. He wasn't breathing hard at all.

I watched the number on his back, 1108-AZ, until I counted fifty push-ups, and then I made a noise with my heel.

Turpin stopped and got to his feet, slowly.

"Letting off steam?" I asked.

"Yes, sir. Letting off more steam."

"That's fine," I said. "Real intelligent."

On Tuesday, after the noon meal, O'Hanlon and I went

down to the beach for our monthly target practice. I scored a 197 with the .45 automatic.

O'Hanlon shook his head. "How come you're so good with that thing?"

"I put in an hour a day at it."

He thought that over. "You don't get a bit more practice than the rest of us. Once a month we all come down here and fire twenty rounds."

"But I still put in an hour a day."

He regarded me skeptically. "The government don't give you that many free bullets."

I lifted my empty automatic in line with the target, expelled my breath, and squeezed the trigger. "That's the way I practice, Pete. I don't need bullets."

O'Hanlon was dubious. "It can't be as good as the real thing."

"Some people think it's better," I said. "And it works."

We walked over to the truck and waited for the others to finish on the range.

"Maybe you got something," O'Hanlon said after a while. "I once saw a movie short where some diving coach was training a couple of girls for the Olympics. Instead of using a pool, he had them jump off a springboard, do their twists, and land feet-first in a pit of sand. They didn't need water at all."

Three weeks later, the deputy warden assigned Turpin to the wharf gang. That meant that every morning, Turpin and a half a dozen other prisoners unloaded the supply boat at the dock.

That evening when I made my nine-fifteen tour everything was the way it was supposed to be; the single fifty-watt bulb burning in every cell, and the prisoners in their bunks. Including Turpin.

A half an hour later I went up to the second tier again, this time on tiptoe.

Turpin was on the floor, face down. He was kicking his legs rhythmically, toes pointed.

When he knew I was there, he stopped and got to his feet.

I smiled. "Sick?"

He licked his lips. "No, sir."

"I thought you might be having convulsions."

"No, sir."

I kept smiling. "Maybe I ought to get the medical orderly?"

"No, sir. I feel all right."

"Then why aren't you in your bunk?"

He looked worried. "You're not going to put me on report?"

"I don't know," I said. "Not if you're sick. I don't like to be hard on anybody."

He nodded quickly. "Sort of sick, sir. Stiff muscles. I was just loosening them up so that I could get some sleep."

I nodded. "How do you like your new job?"

"Just fine, sir."

"I notice you got a little sunburn. A few more nice days like this and you ought to be able to get yourself a tan."

"Yes, sir."

"We get a lot of nice weather here," I said. "Bright, sunny, and clear. Most people seem to think we have nothing but fog."

Turpin said nothing.

"But when we get fog," I said, "we really get it. Can't see your hand in front of your face."

A week later at two in the afternoon, I was in my quarters when the siren began its two-minute wail. I went to the window and cursed softly. He can't be that much of a fool, I thought fiercely. This isn't the time. There isn't enough fog, and what there is will clear up soon.

Along with the other ~~guards not on duty,~~ I reported to

the armory where I was issued a rifle. Lieutenant Farley got the launch keys from the board and we began making our way to our emergency stations down at the dock.

"It's Will Stacey," Farley said.

I could feel the tension leaving me. "How did he do it?"

"Sawed his way through one of the bars in the laundry and managed to squeeze through," Farley said. "The laundry officer figures he hasn't got more than a fifteen minute start, but that was enough for him to scale the wall and get through the cyclone fence and barbed wire on top. The tower man didn't see him because a patch of fog moved in. As far as we know, Stacey was the only one who made the break, but we'll be certain after we take a count."

On the way down to the dock, we passed the men being marched from the shop building back to the cell blocks. The wharf gang's truck came through the sally gate. Turpin was on one of the side seats in the bed, and he was watching the fog thoughtfully.

I grinned and almost waved to him.

At the dock, I cast off the lines and Farley eased the boat into the bay. The fog was wispy and drifting. Clear spots were beginning to appear.

"If he decided to swim," Farley said, "he can't be out too far."

We cruised out almost to the mainland and then turned and made our way slowly back to the island, sweeping far to the right and left as we went.

Farley grinned. "You look thoughtful, Regan."

"I was a little surprised," I said. "I didn't think anybody would try it at this time of the year."

"I'm never surprised," Farley said. "I know they can't make it, but I'm never surprised when they try. Most of them got nothing to lose but their lives."

We turned up our coat collars against the chill breeze and kept our eyes on the water.

Inside of half an hour we found Stacey floundering in the water, and Farley turned the wheel toward him.

I stood up with the rifle, but O'Hanlon chuckled. "There's no fight in him, Regan. Put that thing down and save the man."

Stacey was taking desperate gulps of air when we got to him, and his eyes were wide. He was just about dead exhausted.

I pulled him aboard and slipped the cuffs over his wrist.

Stacey's lips were blue, and he shivered uncontrollably.

Farley felt generous. "Give the fool a blanket and a cigarette."

After he radioed the island, Farley watched Stacey take deep puffs of the smoke. "You were a damn fool, boy."

Stacey kept his eyes on the floorboards. "I didn't count on the fog lifting."

Farley laughed. "You were glad to see us. You didn't get one-quarter of the way across and you were about to come to pieces."

Stacey was silent for a few seconds, then a tired grimace came to his lips. "Drowning is a terrible way to die," he said softly.

Farley winked at me. "The trouble with Stacey is that he's out of condition. He needs more practice in our swimming pool. A couple of hours a day. I'll see if I can arrange it."

A detail of guards met us at the dock and took Stacey back up the hill for a medical examination and dry clothes. After questioning, he would be put in one of the solitary cells in Dog Block.

Farley and I went to the mess hall for some coffee.

He chuckled. "Disappointed, Regan?"

I shrugged. "Why should I be disappointed?"

He grinned. "I just thought you might be."

I sipped my coffee. "If the fog hadn't lifted, a good swimmer would have made it."

Irritation came to his face. "I'd bet a thousand it can't be done."

"All right," I said quietly.

He glared at me. "All right, what?"

"I was just thinking," I said, "that if anybody gave me odds, say five to one, I'd be willing to put up a thousand that somebody will make it across within the next year."

Farley frowned. "You know what you're saying?"

I put a little more sugar in my coffee. "It would have to be kept quiet, a bet like that."

Farley watched me for a half a minute. Then his eyes went over the room. A couple of off-duty guards were drawing coffee from the urn at the far end of the hall. Otherwise the place was empty.

"I got the thousand," I said softly.

Farley watched the flame of his match as he lit a cigar. "Suppose somebody was stupid enough to make a crazy bet like that with you. How would anybody know whether a man made the swim or not? If he didn't make it, his body might be washed out to sea and never recovered. Like with Henderson and Wallace."

"I'd lose the bet," I said. "We'd have to know for certain that he made it."

Farley glanced at the guards again. "But suppose he did make it and then skipped off to South America? How would we know? He isn't likely to phone us."

"That's why I get the five-to-one odds," I said. "We'd have to know for sure. I'd be counting on the fact that he'd be seen on the mainland by responsible witnesses or that he'd be picked up by the police within a year." I put down the coffee cup. "But we'd be betting only on the fact that he did or didn't make a successful break from the rock. What happens after that doesn't matter."

Farley was thoughtful. "You're betting in the teeth of a lot of things."

"That's why I want the odds."

His eyes met mine. "Like you said, the whole thing

would have to be kept quiet. The government wouldn't like to hear about it.''

"There's one other thing I'd have to worry about," I said. "If I win, would I get paid?"

Farley's face got glowering red. "I never welshed on a bet in my life. Just be sure you got a thousand."

That evening I stopped in front of Turpin's cell.

He was sitting on the bunk, idly paging through a magazine.

"That's it," I said. "Improve your mind."

He looked up.

"Stacey should have done that," I said. "Spent his time improving his mind instead of trying to escape." I shook my head sadly. "He was plain stupid. Even if he had been able to go the distance, he should have made it his business to know about the fog."

Turpin waited.

"He should have figured it would clear up and we'd be waiting for him when it did. The fog's a tricky thing here. When it rolls in from the southwest you can bet it won't stay around long. It's different when it comes from the north."

Several days later Turpin came back from the wharf wringing wet.

The guard bringing the detail back to the cell block grinned. "Turpin got too close to the edge of the dock and fell off."

I looked at one of the windows. The day was bright and clear. "How was the water, Turpin?"

There was no expression on his face, but there was a gleam of what might have been triumph in his eyes. "It was a little cold, sir."

I talked to the guard. "Going to put that on report?"

He looked surprised. "What for? It was just a little accident."

"Just wondering," I said. "Did you have any trouble fishing him out?"

He shook his head. "No. It was only a few feet from the dock. Turpin swam back himself, grinning like a monkey."

In September, Turpin was transferred to the garbage crew. It was still outside work. Every afternoon he was down at the incinerators at the beach.

And the fog weather began.

I was in my room in the guards' quarters when I saw the first heavy concentration coming from the northwest—from the sea. This would be the time he would try it. I could almost feel that.

The siren cut through the fog at two-thirty. I put my cigar in the ashtray and made my way to the armory.

Lieutenant Farley was assigning the search details. "This time it's Turpin. The fog came down on the garbage gang so fast that the guard was caught by surprise. He started herding the prisoners to the truck, but Turpin slipped away and disappeared into the fog."

Farley grinned at me. "Relax. You're not winning any bet today. I happen to know for a fact that Turpin can't swim a stroke."

I shrugged. "Then why would he run away?"

Farley chuckled. "He lost his head when he saw a chance. He wasn't thinking. Now the best he can do is to hide out in some cave or corner of this island for a couple of days and hope that we'll think he's gone out and drowned himself. He probably figures that when we stop looking for him, he can smuggle himself aboard the supply boat."

I pocketed two clips of ammunition. "Then it won't be much good to take out the launch?"

Farley showed his teeth again. "No good at all. But we take it out just the same. That's our job."

A half a dozen more guards reported, and Farley began giving them instructions.

I picked the launch keys off the board. "I'll wait for you down at the dock."

Outside, it was like walking through smoke. Every object was shrouded and strange, and the trip down to the dock took me almost fifteen minutes.

I checked the boat compass and headed the launch northeast, out into the bay. The fog misted my face, and nothing was visible more than a few feet from the bow.

I could imagine what Farley would say when I got back.

"Why the hell didn't you wait for me?"

"I'm sorry, Lieutenant. But I thought I heard something out in the water."

Farley would probably grin. "You got some imagination. Why didn't you come back when you found he wasn't out there?"

I would look embarrassed. "I couldn't find the dock, Lieutenant. The fog was too thick."

"And what about the radio?" Farley would demand. "Why didn't you get in touch with us?"

"But the radio doesn't work, Lieutenant."

Now I kept the launch going until I was about halfway across the bay and a few miles north. Then I cut the motor and let the boat drift.

I wouldn't have been able to do that if Farley were with me. We'd be cruising back and forth and there would be a chance that we might find Turpin.

I didn't want that.

I disconnected a lead-in wire on the radio and sat down to wait. The current would bring me back near the island in a few hours.

The sea was calm, with just enough swelling to let you know that it was still alive. I tried to figure how long it would take a man to swim a mile and a half. It was difficult to know how good all of Turpin's practice had made him.

The time passed slowly. It was silent except for the

breathing of the ocean and the faint foghorn of the coast guard boat searching near the mainland.

The cold and damp began to get into my bones after an hour. I checked my watch and decided to wait at least another half an hour before I started the motor and went back to the island.

And then I heard the sound, muffled in the distance.

I held my breath as it came again.

It was the hoarse cry of a man calling for help.

I cursed softly. Turpin had gotten himself lost in the fog. Instead of going straight, he had veered to the left. He was swimming parallel to the coast.

His calls were closer now, desperate in the emptiness.

I shook my head savagely. If he drowned here, the current would carry his body back to the island. It would be found in a few days, a week or two.

I started the motor and kept the launch slow as possible while I searched. It was hard work, but I kept at it, shutting off the power now and then to listen.

When I found Turpin he was treading water and taking deep gasps for air.

His eyes met mine, and I saw the same thing that I'd seen in Stacey's when we picked him up. There was defeat because his try had failed and relief because he would soon be out of the water.

I pulled him aboard and put him in the stern.

His face was dead white and he shivered with cold. I tossed him a blanket and watched him huddle inside it.

Turpin's teeth chattered. "How close did I get?"

"Not close at all," I said. "You were headed straight for Seattle."

Turpin sighed. "I was in the water a long, long time."

"An hour and a half," I said.

"I could have made it," he said softly. "If only I'd kept going straight. You knew what I was going to do, didn't you?"

I grinned, but said nothing.

"You were waiting for me to make the break. You wanted a little fun to fight the dullness of life. You knew what I was going to do, and where, and when. Maybe you even wanted to use that rifle."

I ignored what he'd said. I studied him for a half a minute, thinking it out. Then I searched through my pockets until I found an old letter. I carefully tore off a blank section at the bottom of one page. It would have to do.

I handed it to Turpin and gave him my fountain pen. "I want you to write the warden a little note."

His mouth gaped slightly.

"Go ahead," I snapped. "Write what I tell you."

He hesitated and then shrugged.

"Dear Warden," I said. "It was a cold swim, but it was worth it."

Turpin looked up, trying to figure it out. Then he shook his head, and moved the pen across the paper.

"Now wish him a Merry Christmas and a Happy New Year."

Turpin's mouth dropped again.

I glared at him. "Write it and sign your name."

He did what he was told.

I took the paper from him and examined it. The handwriting made it good enough, but I wanted more. "Put your fingers in some of that grease on the floorboards and let's have ten little fingerprints under your signature."

When that was done, I folded the paper carefully and put it in my wallet. It was worth five thousand dollars to me.

"Stand up, Turpin," I said. "And turn around."

He got up wearily and turned.

I brought the rifle stock down hard on the back of his head and he dropped without a sound.

After I made sure that he was dead, I got the anchor from the bow locker and tied it to him.

I took the launch three miles west, out to sea, and dumped Turpin's body overboard.

Then I lit a cigar, checked with the compass, and headed back for my chat with Farley.

In a month or two, when I got to the city on one of my days off, I'd mail Turpin's note in a plain, typed envelope.

The postmark ought to make news, and it would start all the world looking for the first man to escape from the rock.

The creator of Travis McGee and of such splendid nonseries suspense novels as The Damned, Murder in the Wind, *and* The Executioners, *John D. MacDonald, who died in 1986, was a major force in crime literature for more than forty years. His mystery and detective stories for the pulp magazines of the 1940s and early 1950s are well known as a result of his collections* The Good Old Stuff *and* More Good Old Stuff. *Less well known—undeservedly so—are the criminous tales he penned in the later 1950s for such publications as* Manhunt, EQMM, *and* Justice. *"Squealer" is one of these, from* Manhunt—*a story about cops and kids as only MacDonald could write it.*

SQUEALER

John D. MacDonald
(1956)

When Browden came off duty he stopped by the hospital on his way home to find out how the boy and the girl were doing. It was not out of his way. The girl's father was near the main desk, and Browden was. They crossed the lobby and sat on a bench to talk. The father was named Nichols and he was an accountant. There was a sickness in his eyes.

"Sergeant, I don't understand how a thing like this can happen," he said. "They gave Betty Lee a sedative. She's asleep now. Her mother's with her."

"Do you know how the boy is?"

"I don't care how that damn Reilly boy is," Nichols said hotly.

"Maybe you should care. I saw his hands. He put up a good scrap. There were three of them. He did what he could. They put him out by hitting him with a tire iron or something."

"He shouldn't have taken Betty Lee there."

"Maybe it wasn't smart. But they're kids. He has a car. They go to a place to park. That's normal. They go to the place where other high school kids go. You don't get anywhere blaming the Reilly kid."

Nichols looked down at his tensely clasped hands. "All right. I'm sorry. I heard he's okay. Maybe a concussion. And he lost some teeth. How can a thing like this happen?"

Browden felt tired. It was a question he had heard many times. It was a question that never failed to move him. How can this happen *to me?* How can this darkness come into *my* life?

"It happens, Mr. Nichols. It happens all over the country. It has probably happened everyplace since the beginning of time."

"Betty Lee's life is ruined."

"If you and your wife get all dramatic about it and go around wringing your hands for the next few years and telling her her life has been ruined, maybe it will be. You know the policy on this sort of thing. Her name won't be in the paper."

"Everybody will know. We ought to move away. I can get work some other place."

"I don't want to give you advice. That will just make it that much more important to your daughter. The best thing to do is get her back in school just as soon as you can and go right on as though nothing much happened. Then it will all blow over. And that's the same thing your doctor will tell you."

"But suppose she's . . ."

"Don't ask for trouble. If she is, it can be fixed. It can be legally fixed. Listen, I know kids pretty well. I know this is a terrible and shocking thing for a young girl, but it's up to you two as her parents to keep her from making too much drama out of it. Keep your wife under control. Be balanced about it.''

"That's easy for you to say," Nichols said bitterly.

"And it'll be damn hard for you to do, I know. But people can do very hard things when it's for their kids.''

After a long time Nichols said, softly, "Thanks, Sergeant. We'll try that, I guess. I guess that makes the most sense. But, what kind of animals could do that?''

"We've got a pretty good hunch it was high-school kids.''

Nichols raised his head sharply, his voice going shrill. "High-school kids! Not some kind of criminals?''

"Criminals, yes. High-school kids, yes. There have been other incidents.''

"But you mean boys that go to school with Betty Lee?''

"Maybe, Mr. Nichols, you've got a pretty glamorous idea of what high-school kids are. There are all kinds. There are over six thousand in that high school. This is an industrial town. We get the kids of a lot of transient families. The law says they have to go to school. There's no law that says they have to be like the Boy Scout oath. The vast majority are good kids, but there are some rough monkeys in that place. We get knifings and we get a little dope peddling, and we get sex offenses. I'm a big husky guy, Mr. Nichols, and I know how to take care of myself, but believe me, there are some kids in that school I wouldn't want to meet in any dark alleys.''

"Are you going to be able to find out who did this?''

"We've got a lead.''

"What will happen to them when you catch them?''

"Depends on how old they are. If they're old enough, they get a man's punishment. Otherwise they go to juvenile court.''

"They ought to be electrocuted.''

Browden looked at Nichols without expression. "I got to be running along. Try to handle it the way I said. Go explain it to your wife."

"I will, Sergeant. And—thanks."

After he reported for duty the next afternoon, Browden checked with the hospital by phone, then drove there with Lieberman, his working partner on the detective squad. When they got to the hospital they found that, as Browden had suggested, the Reilly boy had been moved temporarily into a private room so that they could question him more readily. Reilly tried to smile at them. Browden liked the kid. He had a reddish brush cut, bright hot blue eyes.

"Have you seen Betty Lee? How is she?" He frowned. "I can't get used to talking without my front teeth."

"We haven't seen her yet, but she's coming along okay."

"Did you get them?"

"Not yet, but we're going to. It will help if you give us a run-through on what you did last night."

"It was the usual Friday night date, Sergeant. I picked up Betty Lee about seven, I guess it was. We went to the drive-in movie over on Ridge Boulevard. It was a double feature, and we got out about ten-thirty. From there we drove on out to Sandy's for hamburgers. Some of the other kids were there and we circulated around from car to car, you know. I have to get Betty Lee home by midnight on weekends. By ten o'clock when we date during the week. We left a little after eleven I think it was, and we drove around by Proctor Park." The boy blushed hotly. "We usually stop by there. You know. Park for a while and we have to leave by ten of midnight to get Betty Lee home under the wire. Jerry Traybor and Ann Hawks followed along in Jerry's car and we parked near each other. They're not good friends. It just happened that way. When I get up out of here, I'm going to work Jerry over good."

"Why?"

"Here's the way it was. They were parked on our left, maybe twenty feet away. We both had the car lights out. We could hear Jerry's car radio. Mine is busted. I had my arm around Betty Lee. I didn't hear a thing and all of a sudden the door on my side is yanked open and somebody grabs me by the arm and pulls me right out onto the ground and kicks me. I yelled. I got up and started swinging. It was an awful dark night. I don't know who it was. I heard Betty Lee screaming on the other side of the car. I yelled to Jerry to help. I heard his motor start, heard him race it as he started to back out. Then something smashed me in the head, and when I woke up I was in the ambulance going right through the middle of town. I think if Jerry had piled out and jumped in, we might have been all right. Except for my teeth. It was the first kick that did that."

"Were there any other cars there?"

"Not near us. Not near enough."

"You didn't recognize any of the three?"

"I didn't even know there were three. How do you know that?"

"We got a report from a car that was parked about a hundred feet away. They heard the trouble. They saw the headlights on the Traybor kid's car sweep across yours as he turned. They saw three men, and saw you on the ground. One of the men was struggling with your girl. They were too far to see faces clearly. They drove away, too, and then they got worried and phoned the police from down the road."

"My father told me he brought my car in. He drove out with my sister and got it. They wouldn't let him see Betty Lee."

"She's pretty upset, Dick."

"Did they . . ."

"Yes."

Reilly's hand clenched and unclenched. "I figured so," he said quietly. "Damn them. Damn them!"

"She's going to need a lot of patience and—I guess the word is tenderness, Dick."

"I know, Sergeant. I keep thinking like it was my fault. I should have locked the car doors. But we've gone there a lot. You wouldn't think a thing like that would happen."

"I don't think it was your fault. I told her father that."

"Thanks."

They questioned him further, but he could provide no clue as to the identity of the attackers. They then talked to the girl in the presence of her mother. The girl, still drowsy with sedatives, could not help them in any way. Browden talked with Mrs. Nichols in the hall. She turned out to be more cooperative than he had hoped. She agreed to visit Dick Reilly, and she understood that it would be healthy for the two young people to see each other as soon as it could be arranged.

From the hospital they drove to the residence of Jerry Traybor. His mother was alarmed that two police officers should be calling on Jerry. She was partially reassured when Browden told her that there were no charges against the boy. She said he was up in his room, and since he so seldom stayed in on a Saturday afternoon, she had wondered if he felt all right. She called him down to the living room, and she was reluctant about leaving the room when Browden said they wanted to talk to the boy alone.

Jerry Traybor was a tall, gangly boy in khakis and a T-shirt, a dark-haired boy with restless eyes and a high, unpleasant nasal tone of voice.

"Sure, we ran into them at Sandy's. Ann and me had spent most of the evening just cruising around like. When we figured they were headed for Proctor Park, we followed along. I don't know what for. What do you do anything for? We just went along, that was all, and we parked near them. I guess it was maybe sort of a gag because everybody knows those two like to be alone. They're real tense about each other."

"You heard the attack."

"We heard something. The car radio was on. There was yelling and screaming and I figured we ought to get out of there. I didn't want any trouble. I backed out."

"Did you hear him call to you for help?"

"I didn't hear anything like that. I figured it was a private fight. Anyway, why should he call me? I don't know him so good. I just see him around the school, like."

"You felt you had no obligation?"

"Obligation? What do you mean by that? It was his fight. How did I know he didn't maybe start it?"

"You turned your headlights on, didn't you?"

"I guess I did. Yes."

"And when you backed out, turning the wheel as you did so, your headlights showed you what was going on, showed you the people involved."

"It was all kind of confused. I didn't see anything."

"Did you see two boys standing over Dick Reilly, and see another boy struggling with Betty Lee Nichols?"

"I didn't see anything like that."

"That's pretty strange, Jerry, because a couple in another car parked a hundred feet away saw all that, and they saw it in the light of your headlights. And you were a lot closer."

"I guess I wasn't looking. I guess maybe it was like this. I was backing the car, see. And when you back up, you look out the back."

"You had no curiosity about what was going on?"

"I didn't say that. I said I just didn't see anything."

"Did you recognize any of the boys?"

There was no more shiftiness of the eyes. Jerry Traybor lifted his head and looked directly at Browden. His eyes were wide and bland. "No, sir. I didn't recognize anybody. Like I said, I didn't see much of anything."

Traybor was a remarkably unskilled liar. Browden glanced at Lieberman and saw the disgust in his eyes.

"You're following the code, Jerry?" Lieberman asked gently.

"I don't know what you mean."

"You recognized one or more of the boys. You know them. But you're a big, brave fellow. You won't answer a yell for help. But you've got too much courage to snitch to the cops. Isn't that it?"

"I didn't see anything. I keep telling you."

"You keep telling us and we keep not believing it. Maybe you don't want to tell because these are rough kids you saw. Maybe you tell us and they stick a knife between your ribs."

"I'm not scared of anybody," the boy said sullenly.

Browden said, "You know what happened to the girl, I guess."

"It was in the paper. It didn't give any names. But from where it happened and the time I guessed it was Dick and Betty Lee."

"That doesn't mean anything to you?" Lieberman asked.

"I'm sorry about it, sure. That was a tough thing to have happen. It certainly was."

"They could just as easily have jumped your car, Jerry."

The boy swallowed. "I guess they could. It was Dick's bad luck they picked him."

"If they'd picked you, Dick would have helped you."

Jerry stared at them. "You don't know that. You can guess, but you don't know it. I figure he would have driven off too, like I did."

"Who did it, Jerry?" Browden asked.

"I tell you and I tell you, I don't know. I didn't see anything."

Lieberman said gently, "You live in the world, Jerry. You can't shut your eyes all the time. What happens to your friends is your business, and it's ours. You have an obligation."

"I don't see as I got an obligation. I never got close to

Reilly. He takes himself serious. He's a wheel. Student council and all that stuff. And he's got a stuck-up girl. What business is it of mine?"

"Then you did recognize the boys?"

"You're trying to mix me up. I didn't say that."

"First you said it was a private fight and that's why you didn't jump in. Now you say it was because you didn't know them well enough. You imply that you knew what was happening."

"It could have been a private fight. How do I know? We didn't see anything, either of us."

Browden glanced at Lieberman and said, "Come on, Mose."

As they walked down the walk to their car they heard Jerry call after them, "I'd be glad to help if I could. You know that."

They didn't turn or answer. As they drove away Lieberman said, "Worth a dozen of that one."

"The Reilly kid?"

"Who else? A code they've got. Fine. Don't tell the cops the right time. Comic book ethics. Maybe the girl will be easier."

"I have my doubts. She'll have had her instructions from Traybor."

Ann Hawks, daughter of a construction worker, lived in a large maroon trailer in a park on the south edge of town. She was alone in the trailer. She wore blue jean shorts and a tight yellow sweat shirt. Her blonde hair was tied back in a skimpy ponytail.

"Gee, I can't tell you any more than Jerry did. Like I guess he told you, we just didn't see anything. It was— you know—all confusing."

"You're a little bit better liar than he is, but not much, Ann."

"How come you think you can come in here and talk to me like that?"

"Don't get lippy, Ann," Lieberman said in his customary gentle tone. "We won't talk about what you saw or who you recognized or anything like that. Let's talk about your father for a minute."

"So what about him? I don't get it."

Lieberman, sitting on a couch in the cramped, cluttered trailer, leaned forward, his face intent. "Honey, suppose somebody was getting beat up and they yelled to your father for help. What would happen?"

"He'd jump right in, swinging."

"I guess your father is a man, isn't he?"

"Sure he's a man."

"But, honey, you go out with a punk who runs like a rabbit. It doesn't figure."

"I tried to get him to help out."

"But he didn't want to get mixed up in anything."

"That was it, I guess."

"Six thousand kids in that school. Three thousand boys. Out of three thousand you pick yourself a real tiger."

"Jerry's all right," she said sullenly.

"Too scared to help out and now he's too scared to tell us who did it."

"He can't tell you who did it. Gosh, you don't know the score. They'd maybe kill him."

"Honey, I want you to think real hard about something else. Just what would Jerry have done if they'd picked your car?"

"He'd fight."

Lieberman smiled. "Would he? You think he would? Or maybe beg for mercy? Or maybe run down the road and all the way home and hide under the bed?"

"He isn't a bad kid."

"Not bad, honey. Just weak as water."

Browden sensed it was his turn to come in again. "Mose, I think if we take them both down and put them in separate cells, we can get an answer in a day or two."

He sensed at once that it was a bad estimate. The girl's gray eyes seemed to darken. "Go ahead. You do that. Have fun. You could keep us in there forever and you won't get a damn thing."

Lieberman gave Browden a quick glance of regret. When they were back at the car Lieberman said, "I was getting close, Ed."

"I know. I sensed it. I tried to push, but I pushed too hard and spoiled it. I'm sorry."

"Okay with you if I try her alone tomorrow?"

"It's okay with me."

"There's more there than with the Traybor kid. Same bad sense of values, but more underneath. More decency. She's the one to work on."

On Monday afternoon Lieberman reported failure. "I think I got close, but not close enough. She understands what the word obligation means. But she feels it's to the Traybor kid first. She recognized those kids, same as Traybor. But . . ." He shrugged. "They got a date tonight, Ed. You want to play a little game?"

"I've heard that before, Mose. Do we, as officers of the law, exceed our authority?"

"What else?"

"I got to get me a new partner, or I'll never end up with a pension."

"Think of how I keep your life bright and exciting."

They used Lieberman's own car, a dark, elderly, asthmatic sedan. They used the patience that had been trained into them. Browden, as the better driver, waited behind the wheel. At midnight they picked up Jerry Traybor's distinctive chopped-down Ford as it turned out of Sandy's and headed toward town. Browden followed without lights. If it showed signs of turning into a chase, he was going to break it off. They had agreed on that.

"Traffic is okay, Ed, and this looks like a good place," Lieberman said, betraying his excitement by his casualness of tone.

Browden accelerated and passed the Ford. When his back wheel was even with the Ford's front wheel, he bore gradually right. There was one small thump and clash of metal. Both cars dipped down through the wide, shallow ditch and the Ford stopped with its nose against a barbed-wire fence.

They swung out of the sedan into the night shadows. Traybor had vaulted out of the open Ford. He ran down the road, shoes slapping the asphalt, a thin, frantic, receding figure in the faint starlight.

The girl had gotten out of the car and she was backing slowly away, ready to panic, aware she had no chance against the two figures.

"Relax, honey," Lieberman said, stopping. "It's me again." Browden stopped too.

Her voice was tremulous in the dark. "The cop?"

"That's right. Don't be afraid."

"I—I don't understand."

Browden got in the back. Ann Hawks sat up front with Lieberman. He said, putting the old sedan into gear, "Honey, it could have been your friends, you know. Those ones you won't identify."

"He—he ran." She began to cry. Lieberman dug Kleenex out of the glove compartment.

"Like a big rabbit," Lieberman said.

"This time it could have been you instead of Betty Lee Nichols."

"I—I know. I thought it was going to be."

They waited in silence.

"Ricky Wyostek," she said. "He was standing by Dick. Junky Turner was holding Betty Lee. I think his real name is Ronald. I don't know who the other one was, but it was probably Skip French. Those three run around together. Skip carries a switchblade."

"I know French and Turner," Browden said. "They got off on a stolen car rap over a year ago. They must be nineteen. They still in high school?"

"Not any more. Ricky Wyostek is real old. He's over twenty."

"I think I am a sadistic cop," Lieberman said softly, "and I think I am going to dearly enjoy picking up those little playmates. Let's go get 'em, Ed."

They took the girl home and then they went and got them.

William Campbell Gault has been a distinguished writer of criminous, sports, young adult, and science fiction for more than half a century. He sold his first story to a pulp magazine in 1936, was a mainstay in the pulp marketplace until its decline and fall in the early 50s, and then turned to novels (his first book, Don't Cry for Me, *won a Mystery Writers of America Edgar as Best First Novel of 1952) and to novelettes for such publications as EQMM,* Manhunt, *and* The Saint. *Originally published in a pulp, ''The Cackle Bladder'' was reprinted by Ellery Queen in edited form in 1960 as part of EQMM's ''Black Mask'' series of outstanding stories from the mystery and detective pulps. It is the edited EQMM version that follows.*

THE CACKLE BLADDER

William Campbell Gault

(1950/1960)

The last time I saw Paris, he didn't look like this. He'd always been a snappy lad when it came to clothes, and he'd never been at a loss for words, as they say.

This gloomy Monday I was sitting in Monte's, watching the rain hit the front windows and trying to find a mudder in the Form. I was low on scratch, and drinking beer when this—this apparition walked in, wringing wet.

I figured Monte would give him the heave, but good. Monte don't like no bums cluttering up the place.

But Monte just sighed and said, ''Morning, Paris.''

If this was Paris, I was Pittsburgh Phil. Then I looked

more closely. No teeth in this wretch, pale as snow, wearing stinking rags, but it was Paris, all right.

I looked at him and thought of the last time I'd seen him. He'd been with Joe Nello, then, working the short-con together. Paris had taught the kid everything he knew.

He was looking at me now. "Hi, Jonesy," he said.

"Hello, Paris," I said, and nodded to the chair across the table. "It's been a long time. Sit down and have a drink."

He sat down, and Monte brought over a big tumbler of fortified wine. I knew then that Paris was on the way out. That comes just before your toes curl, fortified wine.

I took the chance and said, "How's Joe Nello?"

He wasn't looking at me. "Would you really like to know?"

I nodded. "That's why I asked."

This is what he told me. . . .

Joe and I, he began, were pretty thick, as you know. I mean, we worked all right together. I made the guy; he wouldn't have been nothing without me. He had the looks, sure, but he was kind of soft, you know, at first. He had a lot to learn about taking care of himself in this damned world.

Times I was discouraged about Joe, but he knew what was important, really. I mean, down deep, he understood there's nothing like a few bucks to make people notice you. Lot of talk about the worthwhile things, but name me one you can't buy.

Anyhow, we were working Iowa with the short-con, everything from hog cholera tonic to three-card monte, and Joe was catching on. So many honest people in that state, they should have a closed season on the suckers. Begging to be taken, those rubes.

And the girls? They believe anything you tell them. *Anything*. Few tears when you leave them, but you don't always have to tell them you're going, not when you're on the move all the time.

We made a small pile in the tank towns and holed up in Des Moines for a while. We bought a convertible and enjoyed life. We didn't work the town; it's a wrong town. We just had ourselves a time.

That's where this Judith comes in. That's the babe that almost kept Joe from amounting to anything. I met her first, in the lobby of the hotel where we were staying.

She was a hostess for the tearoom in the hotel, and in town on her own. Her folks had a farm about eighty miles into the tall and uncut.

She was maybe twenty-two, and slim, but not slim where she shouldn't be. She had blue-black hair and deep blue eyes. An innocent, if I ever saw one. But ready, I could tell. Bored, and ready.

She was sitting near the front windows, watching the traffic, a magazine in her lap, the first time I saw her.

I took a chair nearby and said, "Things can't be that bad."

She looked over, startled, and she smiled. She seemed about eighteen when she smiled. "Was I looking as bored as I feel?" she asked.

"I don't know how bored you feel," I answered. "Haven't I seen you around here before?"

"I work in the tearoom," she said. "I'm the hostess. I went to school, and now I'm a hostess in a tearoom and I can write testimonials for the school. I'm a success."

Then Joe came along. Her eyes went past me, and they seemed to come alive when she looked at Joe. He was staring, too.

He grinned then and said, "Is this gentleman annoying you, Miss? And if he is, can I help him?"

Joe was going under the name of Jim Kruger at the time, and I said, "Jim, I'm sure you have something to do. There are lots of interesting things to do in this town. Goodbye, Jim, old pal."

"Now I know he's annoying you, Miss," Joe said. "He has evil intentions, despite his age. And if there are so many things to do, can't we do them together?"

That crack about age wasn't so hot, I thought.

Joe said, "Run along, now, Don, or I won't give you any more of my old suits."

Sharpie, he was getting to be. I said, "Why don't the three of us go out together? Then the lady will be safe, and we'll all have a good time."

"All but me," Joe said, and looked at her. "However, if that's the only way, I'm for it. You don't think we're too bold, do you?"

"I think you're fun," she said, "and my sales resistance is at an all-time low. I'm sold."

I never had a chance; this one was Joe's right from the start. We went to a spot on the edge of town where the lights were low and the liquor bonded.

They danced, and I drank. They danced and danced until you'd think Joe would develop a charley horse. Young they were, and graceful, and they danced awful close, but good. People gave them room, and some stopped to watch, and this Judith ate it up and got flushed and prettier than ever.

Joe's old man had been a hoofer, and Joe had started dancing when he was four. He was really going good that night.

I drove, going back. The car purred along, and I kept my eyes on the road ahead, and they didn't say anything.

In the room, while we were getting ready for the hay, Joe said, "This Judith, she's different, Paris."

"Not in any place I could notice," I said, "though my eyes aren't so good, now that I'm *old*."

"Aw, Paris," he said, "you know what I mean."

"I wish I did," I said.

"I mean, she's—she's a decent kid, and only a kid. She's different."

You see what I mean? I'd worked on the boy. He knew the difference between a wolf and a lamb, I thought, and now he gets all mixed up with a lamb who's ready and he's got to go soft. What could I tell him, if he wouldn't learn?

Love—How many pitches have gone wrong because some guys think it's love? Love's all right, if you want to call it that, but you don't have to buy a ring to prove it.

And that's what this punk meant to do. All the babes he'd run around with, and he's talking marriage.

"Her dad," he says one night, "has got three hundred and twenty acres of the finest corn land in Iowa, Paris."

"That's the guy you should be hanging around, not the daughter, then," I said. "Maybe we can touch him for a couple grand."

He didn't even seem to hear me. "She wants me to settle down. She wants me to take a winter course at Iowa State and learn to run those three hundred and twenty acres."

"That's the wrong side of the fence, Joe," I told him. "You're no yokel, and you couldn't learn to be one."

He laughed at me. "What have we got? A couple grand. Small-time grifters, working the short-con. I could have done this good in the five-a-day."

I was glad, then, that I had the telegram in my pocket. Lou Pettle had sent it from K.C. and I hadn't shown it to Joe yet. I did, now.

He read it and said, "Lou Pettle . . ." like a yokel would say "J.P. Morgan." Lou was just as big a man, in his field.

"Lou Pettle," I agreed. "The biggest operator in the country. This is the chance we've been waiting for. This is where we move up, Joe."

He shook his head and blew out his breath. "A fortune. Lou Pettle. Golly, Paris."

"Well," I said, "are you going to buy the ring?"

He laughed and shook his head. Then he grinned at me. "But give me a couple days. Let me get her out of my system."

I couldn't blame him for that. He could have a lifetime without meeting another like Judith. I said, "I'll wire Lou we've some unfinished business, but to expect us."

He did buy a ring, though. Nice big Mexican diamond that must have cost him well over two bucks.

He spent most of the two days with her. She had a vacation coming and she took it, and where they went I couldn't swear to in court. I know I didn't see much of Joe.

Then, one afternoon, he comes into the lobby looking like a cat that has just polished off a quart of Grade A. "When do we leave?" he said.

"Congratulations," I said. "Any time you're ready."

"Now," he said. "Judith's gone out to bring her dad to town. He wants to meet me." He seemed a little nervous. "We haven't got too much time."

We had less than that.

Joe was getting the car gassed up when Judith comes into the lobby, this stout gent in tow.

He didn't look like a farmer. He looked like a banker—that's the kind of moola there is in that Iowa soil. She introduced us and asked, "Where's Jim?"

"He'll be back," I said, watching her face.

Her face was thinner, but her eyes were starrier than ever. Golly, she was a looker! I'll never forget it.

Her dad went over to buy a paper, and she said, "He will be back, won't he, Don? I don't suppose that's a silly question, but he's so—I mean, it's hard to believe, even now, that he's all mine. Oh, you must think I'm a perfect idiot. Only—"

"Easy, baby," I said. "Of course he'll be back. You go over and sit in that big chair, and I'll try and locate him."

She was trembling like a bride at the altar.

I got hold of him at the service station. "You'd better steer clear of the hotel. There's no shotgun in sight, but there could be one around. I'll pack your stuff, and you pick me up near that restaurant where we ate the first day. Got it?"

I came out of the telephone booth, and she was standing about five feet away. I walked over, and she put a hand on my arm.

"Don, there's something wrong."

"Nothing, nothing," I said. "Jim's trying to land a customer that will net us eighteen thousand dollars, Judith, and I'm not going to bother him now. He'll be here at six to clean up. Or, if you'd rather, he'll meet you at the Golden Pheasant. He's arranged a dinner for the four of us out there. He said this is the biggest evening of his life."

She smiled. "Did he say that?"

"His exact words."

Now she looked calm. "I'm going out and buy the nicest dress in town. We'll meet you here at seven, Don."

"We'll be here," I said.

They went out, and I went to the desk. I paid our bill and told the clerk, "Any mail that comes to either of us, you could send to General Delivery, in Kansas City."

He grinned at me. "Sure thing. Don't tell me Mr. Kruger is walking out on our Judith."

I was glad, now, we hadn't used our right names. All these squares work together.

I said, "Your memory isn't much good, is it?" I laid a twenty on the desk.

"I don't know from nothin'," he said, and that twenty just disappeared.

"Send for the cab then," I told him, "and have the cabbie come up for our luggage."

Joe was waiting with the car in front of the restaurant, and we piled the luggage in the back.

Joe said, "How'd it go?"

"We're taking them to dinner at seven," I said. "Judy's out, buying a new dress."

Joe chuckled and shook his head. "Squares," he said. "Kansas City, here we come."

I was proud of him. I'd got him past this one, and I knew he wasn't going to get on the wrong side of the fence again. That was his graduation, you might say. From then on, I knew there was no danger of Joe getting simple. We were going places.

Two days after we started to work for Lou, I went over to the post office and picked up our mail. There wasn't much—a couple letters and a copy of the Des Moines paper. That was probably the clerk's idea, sending that paper along.

There was a picture of Judith on the front page. It didn't say it had been suicide. It just said she'd taken an overdose of sleeping tablets that had proved fatal. There was an unfounded rumor of an unhappy love affair, but neither of her parents would comment on that. She'd died clutching an immense imitation diamond ring in her left hand.

That's a square for you. I mean, he hadn't taken a nickel from her. As a matter of fact, he'd spent his own money on her and she hadn't lost a thing. What'd she have to beef about?

I threw the paper away. I didn't want to annoy Joe when he had his big chance, like this.

Kansas City was right. Lou was an operator and the fix was solid, and he ran enough steerers to keep him busy. Lou handled the inside, of course, and I watched him close. That's what I wanted, the inside job. That's where the moo was.

Lou had ulcers and was due to retire soon. I watched and learned, and we salted it, Joe and I. I rode the trains in from the West and he rode them in from the East, and Lou plucked them clean as a whistle, those marks we brought in to the store.

Store is just a con-name for the front we were using, an imitation bookie joint that could have been staged by a Broadway producer, it was that authentic. Lou had shills that looked like millionaires and he had shills that looked like playboys and shills that looked like retired farmers, but none that looked like shills.

Lou's ulcers got worse, and Joe and I began to take him out on parties, here and there, and raise hell with him generally.

Then one day Lou said to me, "Paris, I can't take any

more. The fix is still solid, and the store is a mint, but a man has got to think of his health. You wouldn't be interested in the inside job, would you?''

"Not for me," I said. "I'm a simple, happy man."

"There's no one else could handle it in the organization," he said. "I wouldn't expect you to shell out; all I want's a percentage. And you'd be handling the money, Paris, remember. You'd get yours."

"And you'd get yours, with me handling it," I said, "but how much?"

We finally agreed on what I should send him. I argued so long he must have thought he was actually going to get it.

So we didn't use a dime of our money. We had seventy grand, Joe and I, in a joint account. That's how I trusted him.

Well, Judith had been one milestone, and this was likely to be another. The inside man, you know, is the boss and not always popular, because he's got the chance to knock down some personal moola at the expense of the others. If Joe and I got through this, we were solid; there wasn't any limit to the long green we could garner.

It was Joe who brought me my first mark in the new job. Joe phoned me from the Alcazar and said, "Kind of a young guy, Paris. But he's got forty grand salted, right here in town. He wants to go into business here." Then he paused. "Husky, though. Might be rough to cool out."

"We'll use the cackle bladder," I said. "I've got a new poke already made, and I'll send it over to you. I'll get a suite at that hotel, and you can bring him up right after lunch tomorrow." And then I said slowly, "No mistakes, though, Joe. The gang all thinks nobody can take Lou's place, and we've got to show them how wrong they are."

"Lou," Joe said, "was a piker and an amateur."

I got the best suite in the house, and I was sitting in it the next afternoon, smoking a dollar cigar, when they rapped at the door.

I went to the door and opened it. I said, "Well?" sounding annoyed.

Joe said, "Are you Mr. Walters?"

"And what if I am? I suppose you—you gentlemen are reporters?"

"No, sir," Joe said.

"Well then, speak your piece. You're selling something? A man purchases privacy, you know, when—"

"You've got us wrong," Joe said. "We're here to return something of yours, Mr. Walters, something we found in the dining room." He had the poke I'd sent over yesterday.

I threw the door wide open. "Gentlemen," I said, "forgive me. You've found my wallet."

While I said this, I was sizing up the mark. He must have been about twenty-six, a scrubbed-looking guy in a neat blue suit. He sure didn't look like forty grand to me.

"I *think* it's your wallet," Joe said. "You'd be willing to identify it, of course, Mr. Walters."

"A few hundred dollars," I said, "and some membership cards. One for the Pegasus Club, one for the Civic Betterment Club, a couple telegrams, and"—here I paused—"and a code sheet."

Joe nodded and handed it over. "Correct, in all details. Mr. Walters, this is a recent acquaintance of mine, Mr. George Apple. And my name is Delsing, Carlton Delsing."

I shook their hands. "It's a distinct pleasure and a memorable occasion," I said. "I insist you have a drink on me."

"Don't mind if I do," Joe said, and Mr. Apple nodded and sat down. He wasn't missing a thing; he watched me like I was the president.

When I handed them their drinks, Joe said, "There was one thing you forgot to mention, Mr. Walters. You mustn't be so modest."

I looked blank.

"That newspaper clipping in your wallet," Joe went on.

"It described you as the Pittsburgh Phil of our era, the greatest plunger the track has ever known."

"Oh, that," I said. "You mustn't believe everything you read, Mr. Delsing." I smiled at him. "Income tax, you know. The less publicity, the better."

The mark sort of stirred in his chair. "You mean—this money you win isn't taxable? I mean, it really is, but you don't declare it. Isn't that dishonest, Mr. Walters?"

That wasn't good. A guy should have a little larceny in him to make the perfect mark. There's an old saw that you can't cheat an honest man. But this was important, this fish, and I barged ahead.

"Dishonest?" I said. "I have certain expenses, and the possibility of loss in other lines. Is it dishonest to build up a reserve against that contingency, Mr. Apple?"

"Well, no," he said. "I see what you mean. I'm all for the private enterprise system, myself, Mr. Walters, and I know that we have to protect ourselves against government greed, but, well, I mean—"

"We aren't under the private enterprise system at present, Mr. Apple," I told him coolly. "But there'll be a change, one of these days. There's got to be a change, or the system is dead." I sighed. "I don't worry about myself. I've made mine. This track plunging is a sort of hobby with me. It's the young people I worry about, the young lads with gumption enough to go out on their own."

He sort of flushed, as though I'd been talking about him, which I had.

I smiled at him and said, "What's your line of business, Mr. Apple?"

"Well, nothing right now." He sure was an easy blusher. "I came out of the service and bought some land in the Everglades. I put it all into celery, and I—well, I did all right. I put away forty thousand dollars in three years, and then decided to come up to Kansas City and get into business here. Mom's waiting down in Florida until I can get established up here."

"Beautiful climate, Florida," I said.

He nodded. "I liked it. But it's kind of hot for Mom in the summer, and that's one reason I'm moving north. If I don't find what I want here, I'm going up to St. Paul."

"Forty thousand of risk capital," I said, "is a nice little sum for a young man to have, and a war veteran to boot. You're one of a kind I thought was missing in America these days, Mr. Apple."

"I've always made my own way," he said, and looked at his hands. "I don't mind work, but I sure hate a time clock."

Now Joe came in. "Speaking of risk capital, Mr. Walters, I guess you've found a way to take the risk out of it."

I gave him a knowing smile. "I don't quite understand you, Mr. Delsing."

"That code sheet," Joe said. "I'm no gambler, but I've played the ponies enough to know a code tip when I see one."

"You're an astute young man, Mr. Delsing," I said. "Have a cigar."

He shook his head, and Mr. Apple declined, and I changed the subject. "I was in Washington just last month on some legislation and . . ."

I went on and on, tossing the big names around, giving this punk a picture of corruption and finagling that was bound to turn his stomach. A veteran, see, and still with some old-fashioned ideas in him, and I had to make him see it wasn't cheating, keeping the money out of the hands of those power-mad, greedy, corrupt officials.

I had to get him partly on our side of the fence and make him forget mama, sweltering down in Florida. I had to make the rube forget all those things Mom had told him.

They both listened, Apple politely, like he'd been taught, and Joe with evident irritation. Joe was starting the switch right then, the sense of allegiance from him to me. Joe was to be the goat, and the mark was going to have to dislike him, or the blowoff might go sour.

When I'd finished, Joe said impatiently, "To get back to that code sheet, Mr. Walters—"

The apple looked at him, and then at me. "I suppose we're prying, but that remark of Mr. Delsing's—I mean, am I to assume that some horse races are . . . fixed?"

"Some?" I smiled at him. "Quite a few. Though very few that I don't know about, Mr. Apple. I think I can honestly say there are none at the major tracks that I don't know about—and well in advance of the running."

The square jaw of this young mark was set, and I could see the wheels turning in his thick skull. He was remembering the picture I'd painted of Washington, and at the same time the fine words about my generosity he'd read in that newspaper clipping. Here I was, an esteemed man, and a wealthy one, not looking like a crook at all. I could almost see his ideas change.

He nodded, and his voice was quiet. "Well, as Mr. Delsing said, that certainly takes the risk out of it."

I puffed the dollar cigar and shrugged. I frowned and picked up my wallet. "Which reminds me, gentlemen. I'd like to give you a little token of my gratitude." I pulled out the three hundred from the poke. "This you won't need to declare in your income tax, and it might pay the hotel bill."

Both of them shook their heads, and Apple said, "It's enough of a reward for me just to meet a man of your caliber, Mr. Walters." He looked uncomfortable. "How do you know in advance which races are fixed?"

I smiled. "That's almost an impertinent question, young man. But if I'd lost that code, and those telegrams . . ." I took a breath. "I know in advance because I work with the organization that fixes them. As I said, it's just for fun, and most of the money I make goes to various charitable organizations. And it gives me an excuse to travel from town to town, seeing this country I love."

Now Joe said, "If you really feel indebted to us, Mr. Walters, we'll settle for the name of a horse."

"I'll do better than that," I said. "I'll make a small wager for both of you this afternoon." I rose. "And now, gentlemen, if you'll excuse me, I have to make a call to Washington. How about dinner tonight in the dining room here? I'll have your winnings with me."

"It will be an honor, Mr. Walters," Apple said. He was still looking thoughtful.

They left, and I stayed there, waiting for Joe's call. He called at three.

"You sold the jerk, I think," Joe said. "Made to order, isn't he?"

I thought of that square jaw and those wide shoulders, and a punk that could take forty grand from Everglade muck. I said, "He could wind up a beefer, Joe. He might be rough to cool off, once he gets a chance to think it over. It'll be the cackle bladder, for sure."

"Right," Joe said. "Mama's boy and I will see you at dinner. He's beginning to get bored with me already, after your personality, Paris."

At dinner I gave each of them a hundred and fifty dollars. I gave Joe a card to the Pegasus Club.

I said, "If you'd like to risk that capital again, gentlemen, this is as good a place as any. You won't be bothered by riffraff."

Joe looked at the card, and Apple looked at the money, as though wondering if it was right to pocket it.

Joe said, "If we're going to wager, it would only be on your advice, Mr. Walters. Nothing I love more than a sure thing. But we won't ask any more favors."

I could see the apple was about to say something, but he must have changed his mind. He pocketed the hundred and fifty. I could see he was starting to simmer. This was better than celery.

Joe kept yak-yakking all through the meal, and I could tell the apple didn't like it. Joe can talk awful damned foolish when he puts his mind to it.

When we were finished, I excused myself. "I have a rather important engagement with Senator Cormack," I apologized, "or I'd break the date." I looked thoughtful. "It so happens I'm going over to the Pegasus Club tomorrow afternoon. If you're both there, I might have something for you."

Joe called me that night. "I've been telling him what a gang of racketeers these bookies are. I've got him convinced it wouldn't be dishonest to take advantage of them. He's getting to think he's Robin Hood, instead of Galahad."

"I'll see you at the club," I said. "I think he's ripe."

Lou had really done a job on that Pegasus Club. It was a super streamlined, high-class bookie joint that would have fooled anybody. And the shills could have stepped right out of the Blue Book. The wire service was the regular service—with one small change.

Lou had records made of the results as they came in, and it was the records that came out of the loudspeaker—a half hour after the race was over.

That way, if any mark happened to check the race results in the paper next day it would all be the quill.

I had the results of the third at Tanforan when the pair of them came in next afternoon.

The apple's eyes got big and bright when he saw the fancy company around. Some of them were lined up laying their bets, and the thousand-dollar bills were like pushnotes in that big room. Old Judge Brewer stepped up and laid down a stack an inch high.

What the apple didn't know was that all the bills were singles on the inside. It looked like a good half million in cash being waved around that room; there was really about twenty thousand.

They came over to me, and I gave them the winner of the third at Tanforan. "He'll be odds-on," I told them, "so a small bet isn't going to do you any good."

"There's nothing small about me," Joe said. "I'm betting the whole hundred and fifty."

Apple's look was full of scorn. "Mr. Walters's gift. I'm willing to bet some of my own money on his word."

Joe looked away.

"I'm going to bet two thousand," Apple said, "of *my* money."

"Gentlemen," I said, "let's not quibble. The line is forming."

The announcement was coming through the speakers, and the winners of the second had been called off.

Joe managed to get in line before Apple did, shoving him as he did so, and not apologizing. It was a long line, but moving pretty well—until it got to Joe.

Joe mumbled and fumbled when it came his turn. The apple fidgeted and I could almost feel him burning. Joe finally stepped away from the window, and the cashier shrugged as the PA barked, "They're off!"

"Sorry, sir," the cashier said to the mark, "but the betting closes with that." He turned away and didn't even glance at the crummy two grand lying on the counter.

I thought Apple was going to swing on Joe right there. And when the horse came home, the horse I'd given him, I waited for the melee. He'd paid three for two, and Mr. Apple had been stalled out of a fast thousand dollars.

He just stood here, white in the face for a second, and then he began to use some language he must have picked up in the fields under that Florida sun.

Joe took it, and a few of the shills gathered around to see what was going on and the manager came over.

Horny Helmuth is the manager, and he made it look like the McCoy. "I'll have to ask for your guest card, sir," he said quietly to Apple. "We don't tolerate that kind of language in the Pegasus Club. This is a gentlemen's club."

"Gentlemen?" the apple said evenly. "I can see that most of them are, sir, but I think you're making a mistake in this—this—" He couldn't finish.

"Mr. Apple," I said soothingly, "you have a just complaint, but I'm sure you don't mean to lose your temper.

You've been robbed of a few dollars, but there'll be other days."

Horny says, "These men are known to you, Mr. Walters?"

"I'll vouch for both of them," I said.

Horny practically crawled into the thick carpeting. "I—I didn't mean to intrude in a personal misunderstanding. I'm sincerely sorry, Mr. Walters."

He walked away.

Joe said, "I guess I am kind of a jerk, at that. I only bet him to show. He certainly won't pay much to show."

"To show," I said, and smiled at the apple. "To show." I started to chuckle and slapped the apple on the back. "Isn't he terrific?"

The apple half-grinned. He looked at Joe and then over at the windows where the judge was collecting what looked like a quarter million, at least.

The apple said, "You'd better get over there, Mr. Delsing, before they run out of money."

We both got a laugh out of that, as Joe went to the window.

I said to Apple, "The pikers we will always have with us. The men who haven't the guts to take a risk. He's a good example."

Apple nodded. "Well, he's young, and maybe he never had to make his own way, like I did." He smiled. "I guess he'll never be bothered with income tax, like you, Mr. Walters."

"No," I said, "he sure won't."

Now the rube blushed again, and said quietly, "I—it's not right for me to ask it—but you wouldn't have another winner for today, would you?"

I shook my head sadly. "Not today, no." I frowned. "I—ah—shouldn't mention it. But call me this evening, around seven-thirty."

He said humbly, "Thank you, sir. I certainly will."

"And another thing," I cautioned him, "don't antagonize your young friend. After all, Mr. Delsing does know about me now, and he could cause me some trouble in New York. I made nearly a million dollars in undeclared income last year, Mr. Apple, and it's not a source of revenue I'd relish losing because of a personal animosity. You can see how it is.''

''I'll get along with him,'' he said. ''I'll stay right with him and see that he doesn't blab to anybody. But I wish he wasn't always running everybody down.''

''Including me?'' I suggested.

''Let's forget it,'' he said. ''I should shut up.''

I shook his hand and left him. I was a little leary of his temper. We'd had some trouble with a couple of widows I'd brought in for Lou, and he'd cleaned them all the way, and the fix was kind of wary of any big beefs right now. Forty grand would make a big beef.

I knew how I was going to play him. He wouldn't need the big convincer; he believed in me now. I knew just how the ''mistake'' was going to be made, and how I was going to cool him out after the touch. Cooling him out right would save the fix a lot of trouble.

With a temper like young Apple's, the cackle bladder was the only sure way.

He phoned at seven-thirty, this Apple did, and I said, ''Can you shake Delsing for an hour? I'd like to talk to you here.''

He was over in ten minutes. I mixed him a drink and put him in a chair away from the light. I wanted the light on me, so he could see how sincere I was.

I took a sip of my drink and looked at him for a couple seconds. ''Tomorrow night I'm leaving for Denver. Tomorrow afternoon I'm hitting the Pegasus Club for the Allenton Stakes, and I'm hitting them hard. I don't think they'll be happy to see me after that. I've won quite a lot this past week, and they don't like consistent winners.''

He was staring at me. "You've got the winner of the Allenton Stakes tomorrow?"

"Not yet," I said. "But I'll have it in the morning. I'm not going to be a pig. I figure to bet fifty thousand, collect my winnings, and take the first train out."

"And make a big profit in a few minutes." He must have been thinking of the difference between this and a celery farm.

I nodded. "In cash money. Now, because of the—the unfortunate bungling of our mutual friend this afternoon, you were cheated out of a tidy sum. Mr. Delsing seems to be something of a piker, so I prefer not to tell him of this. However, I'll be glad to wager any amount for you that you care to. Frankly, Mr. Apple, young men of your stature are rare these days, and I have a great regard for you."

He said softly, "But won't the organization find out about it if you bet more than you declare to them? Won't they be suspicious?"

"Of a few extra thousand? Why should they?"

He gulped and looked at me hard. "I—I wasn't thinking of just a few thousand. I was thinking of betting it all, the whole forty thousand. Then I could buy the kind of business I want."

I frowned. The phone rang, and I went to answer it. Joe was always a good man on his timing. He told me who he was and didn't say another word.

"New York?" I said. "I'll hold the wire." Then after a couple seconds, "Hello, hello—P.J.? I can hear you fine. Sure, everything's under control. How's your asthma, P.J.? Too bad. And the kids? Fine. No, no, not yet. Well, no later than noon. By the way, I'd like to take a little flyer myself on that one tomorrow. Need some traveling money, you know, and I eat pretty well."

A pause, a long pause, and I said, "Oh, maybe an extra forty or fifty."

Another pause, and I laughed. "No, not millions. I

haven't got your kind of money, P.J. Okay? Thanks. It's a pleasure to work with you, P.J. Remember, it's Denver, tomorrow night. And my regards to your wife."

When I turned from the phone, I said, "That was New York. That was a man who really has trouble with his income tax."

"He said it was all right?"

I nodded. "Now, not a word of this to Delsing. He could spoil the whole deal, you know."

"Not a word," he agreed. "I'll stay with him. You'll be here the rest of the night, Mr. Walters?"

I nodded. "Why?"

"I'll want to phone you, in case Delsing gets out of hand. I wouldn't want him to cause you any trouble with his talk."

"Well," I said, "I'll be here." I finished my drink and shook his hand. "I'll see you in the morning, down in the grill."

He went out.

I checked my money, stacking it to look like fifty grand. I checked the revolver I'd inherited from Lou. It was clean and loaded—with blank cartridges.

I started to get sleepy, and I couldn't figure it. I don't usually hit the kip before two, and it wasn't even nine now. I was sound asleep by nine-thirty.

I was still pounding the pillow at eight, next morning, when the phone rang. It was the apple, and he was waiting in the grill.

I told him I'd be right down.

Over ten hours, and I'd slept like a baby all through it. This one was working like a dream.

When I came into the grill, the apple looked unhappy. "I don't know where Mr. Delsing's gone to," he said apologetically. "You don't think he's out somewhere—"

"Shooting off his mouth? We can hope he isn't. I wish I

hadn't given him that guest card to the club. You and he . . .
quarreled?''

He nodded. ''Nothing serious. He talks and talks and
talks.''

I sat down at the table. ''Well, I'm not without influ-
ence in this town. It isn't as though we were cheating any
honest citizens, you know. The authorities would like to
see the Pegasus Club out of business.'' Which was no lie.

After breakfast we sat in the lobby for a while, and then
I went with him to the bank. He drew out the forty grand,
and we returned to the hotel.

We sat there, waiting for the code telegram that was
going to make us our pile. He didn't have much to say.
He'd sweated for that forty grand, and he might have been
thinking of the risk, even on a sure thing.

The telegram came just before lunch, and I excused
myself while I decoded it.

At lunch he said, ''Well, Mr. Delsing hasn't appeared
as yet. It looks like we'll be spared his company.''

''It looks that way.'' I chewed my lip. ''There's some
trouble in New York. We may have to settle for second
place today. We know what horse is going to finish second, and that should give us a reasonable return, if we bet
to place, but I'm still waiting for word of the winner. Of
course, it will depend on the final odds. The second place
horse may even pay better. We'll see what develops.''

Mr. Apple said earnestly, ''All I expect is a reasonable
return, Mr. Walters. It's very seldom a fellow gets a sure
thing.''

''We'll wait,'' I said, ''and see.''

We waited and waited and waited after lunch. Finally, I
went to the booth and pretended to put in a call to New
York. I really put in a call to Horny, at the club.

When I came back, I said, ''We'll have to settle for
second. I hope it's going to be all right with you, Mr.
Apple, if we make only an ordinary profit today.''

He nodded, watching my face.

I let him simmer for a few seconds, and said, "Honey Boy to place, and it's in the bag."

Outside, I gave the cabbie a twenty and said, "Don't spare the horsepower."

He didn't. We got to the Pegasus Club in five minutes and hurried up to the second floor.

The place was as busy as ever. They were calling off the entries for the Allenton, and the line was forming. At the board the results of races all over the country were being chalked up.

The line was starting to stretch out, and Horny was there, getting it orderly. He smiled at me and said, "Some of you aren't going to make it for the Allenton, I'm afraid, Mr. Walters."

I could see the impatience in the mark's eyes. I could see him remembering yesterday and how he'd been robbed of an easy grand.

His eyes moved along the line, measuring it, and then he said quickly, "There's Delsing, right up near the front. Do you think? I mean—"

"Let him place it?" I asked. "Is that what you mean?"

Joe saw us and waved. I waved back and looked at the punk. "I guess we'll have to. I'll make it clear to him that he's not to increase his own bet too much. That wouldn't sit well with New York."

Apple said, "He hasn't got the money to hurt us. We'll just have to take the chance, Mr. Walters. Of course, it's really your decision."

I stepped out of the line. I had the apple's forty grand and my phony fifty. I handed it to Joe and said clearly, "Here's ninety thousand dollars. On Honey Boy, to *place*. Have you got that straight?"

"I certainly have," he said. "Only I'm going to add my hundred dollars to it now."

The apple and I went over to sit down. He had the shakes, and his face was like snow. He said, "It's only justice that he helps us out now, after what happened yesterday.''

Joe just made it. The PA started to bawl right after he left the window, bringing the tickets with him. He'd bought two, one for him and one for us.

He showed us his first. ''I still haven't got the faith I should have, Mr. Walters. I bet him to place, for myself.''

''For yourself?'' I said. ''How did you bet him for us? I said to *place*.''

Joe looked stubborn. ''You said straight, Mr. Walters.''

I held my breath until my face was good and red. ''I asked if you had it *straight*. But I distinctly told you to bet Honey Boy to place. You damned fool, you—''

My voice was loud, and Horny came over. ''Gentlemen, gentlemen,'' he said quietly.

''Mr. Nelson,'' I said in a lower voice, ''a mistake has been made and I'm sure it's not too late to correct it. I asked this young man to purchase a place ticket on Honey Boy, in the Allenton, for me. He misunderstood and purchased one to win. I'd like to exchange it.''

Horny frowned and said, ''There really isn't much time. However, for you, Mr. Walters—''

And then the call came over the system, and he smiled and said, ''I'm afraid your request came just a few seconds too late, Mr. Walters. Well, perhaps Honey Boy will win.''

He walked away and I looked at Joe, and he backed away a step, looking belligerent.

''Ninety thousand dollars,'' I said. ''Young man, that horse had better—''

Apple was white and talking to himself, and I thought he was going to hang one on Joe. Then the account of the running came, and we stood up. In the excitement I saw Joe slip the cackle bladder into his mouth.

It's a rubber dingus, you know, like a syringe, filled with blood, usually chicken blood, and it's the big part of the act.

Honey Boy was leading at the five-furlong post, and he was going away, and the apple almost looked human for a change. I started to talk to myself, and then the challenge came.

Into the last turn it was still Honey Boy, but Velveteen was coming up now on the outside, making the big bid, and Velveteen was the odds-on favorite in this one.

Velveteen was moving, moving up, moving past, going away in first place as she hit the wire. It was Honey Boy second, paying a bundle to place.

I saw Apple look at Joe and start to get up, but I was there in front of him, and I had Joe by the neck, shaking him, and his face started to get blue.

The shills were hollering and Horny was making his way through the crowd, and Apple was trying to get in with a slug or two of his own.

I slammed Joe's jaw, and he went to his knees. I stepped back, pulled the gun from my pocket, and now the apple looked scared.

I fired three times, at point-blank range, and it made one hell of a racket in the noisy room. The chicken blood just squirted from Joe's mouth, and he crashed forward on his face.

A couple of the shills started hollering, "Police!" and Horny had me by the arm.

"My God, Mr. Walters, you've killed him! Here, follow me!" He turned to Apple. "You too, sir. This will ruin us." Now he had us both by the arm and was pushing through the room toward his office.

He closed the door behind him there and took us to another door, leading out the back way. "I wouldn't do this for anyone in the world, but you, Mr. Walters. Go—hurry."

The apple and I clattered down the steps and through the short alley to the street. There was a cab waiting, one of our shills.

I put the apple in and handed him a couple hundred

dollars. I said, ''The Rockland Hotel, in Denver. Don't even go back to the hotel. I'll meet you there.''

"But you—" he said, scared.

"I've got to see our local attorney," I said. "Remember, if I'm not there tomorrow, don't wire. I'll get in touch with you. Take a plane. Goodbye."

In Monte's, the rain was still hitting the front windows, and Paris finished his fourth glass of the fortified.

"Smooth as silk," I said. "You've got the touch, and you've got him cooled out and blown off. In Denver he gets a wire to go to Frisco, because the law is hot and he's an accessory. In Frisco he gets a wire telling him you're leaving for Europe to avoid the chair, because Mr. Carlton Delsing, alias Joe, is dead.''

Paris was staring past me at nothing, the same thing he'd been staring at when he came in.

"Joe was dead," he said, without looking at me. "He lived for two hours, and I didn't go up for murder, though I got quite a jolt. But he had three slugs in him—three slugs *I* put there." Now he looked at me. "My boy, you understand. I made him. I killed him."

Monte was listening to it all. He came over and filled Paris's glass. "On the house," Monte said.

"The mark," Paris went on. "That night in my room, while I was pretending to talk to New York, he drugged my drink. While I slept, he changed the bullets from blanks to real slugs. He knew enough about the big con to guess we'd use the cackle bladder. And Joe was the boy he wanted dead.''

"But why?" I asked. "Forty grand he drops, and gets involved in a murder. Why?"

Paris reached a dirty hand into a pocket and pulled out a torn, much-folded piece of paper that had once been a letter. I read: Dear Grifter: You'll want to know why, and maybe you won't remember back those years to Des Moines—and Judith. But I'll remember her. That wasn't

Florida money I flashed, that was Iowa money, from selling my farm. I knew Judith since she was twelve, and we were engaged before your buddy came along. She sent me a picture of him when he gave her that phony ring, and I studied it a long time until I knew it. I learned the big con from Mike Joaquin, and I rode the trains for a long time waiting for the guy in the picture to pick me up. I figured you'd use the cackle bladder, and I was glad he was the outside man. Because you made him, grifter, and you should destroy him.

"A nut," I said. "Forty grand, but because he was sold on the dame. Of all the lop-eared—"

But Paris wasn't listening. Paris's head was on the table; the fifth glass of fortified was empty near his dirty, outstretched hand.

The rain was letting up a little, and I went back to the Form, trying to find a mudder.

Well known for her superb suspense novels—among them The
Fallen Sparrow, The Blackbirder, Ride the Pink Horse, The
Delicate Ape—*Dorothy B. Hughes has published only a very
few criminous short stories. All are excellent, however, as
one would expect from a writer of her ability; and "Everybody Needs a Mink," which appeared in* The Saint *is argu-
ably the best of the lot.*

EVERYBODY NEEDS A MINK

Dorothy B. Hughes

(1965)

One was dusty rose brocade, tranquil as an arras in a
forsaken castle. One was a waterfall of gold, shimmering
from a secret jungle cache. And there was, of course, the
stiletto of black, cut to here and here—the practical one, as
it would go everywhere—and she had the black evening
slippers from last year, like new for they went out only to
the New Year's Eve and Mardi Gras dances at the club,
and the annual office executive dinner at the Biltmore.
With her pearls, single strand, good cultured, Christmas
present two years ago from Tashi—black and pearls, always good.

She selected the gold. She'd dash down to Florida and
pick up a copper tan before the Christmas party, or maybe
Hawaii. Or a week in Arizona, quite chic. She could buy
gold slippers and hunky gold jewelry. When you were
selecting, you didn't have to think practical, you could let
yourself go.

And the only fun on a shopping tour to the city for

underpants and sox and polo shirts for second-grader Ron, and two jumpers and calico blouses and sox for fourth-grader Stancia, in the before-school sale at Randolph's— the only fun was in selecting. For when the Tashman ship came in, when the long-lost uncle in Australia left them his fortune, when in the someday, never-never land future, they became rich, astronomically rich. . . .

And now for a fur, because Meggy Tashman, that soignee young socialite of Larksville-nearly-on-the-Hudson, could hardly be expected to appear in a waterfall of gold with her old black velvet double duty raincoat and evening wrap. She moved the few steps from the French Room entrance arch to the Fur Salon entrance arch. And there it was. Like a precious jewel impaled on the arms of an emerald tree. The perfect mink. A deep brown, exquisitely matched, full-length mink.

She didn't have to look further. This was it. Practical too. Something to cover the beat-up terry jump suit when she drove the children to school. Something to sling over the faded blues and Tash's old shirt on the dash from the vacuum cleaner to the supermarket. Mink was so durable. A lifetime investment. So rich, so utter, utterly rich.

"Miss." The voice came from the Louis XV chair near the mink. In the chair was a small, elderly man. Near him, smoothed into black crepe, towered one of those living store dummies who sold furs, hair and face lacquered in gold and red and lavender.

"Miss!" the voice said just a little louder. A stubby forefinger beckoned. The button eyes held in place by a network of weathered wrinkles seemed to be looking directly at Meg. The finger seemed to be beckoning to her.

She half-shifted her position in order to glance over her shoulder. There was no one behind her. She looked in at the man again. His hat bobbed; he was wearing his hat and overcoat.

"She's just the right size," he was saying to the saleslady. He gave a very small and very timid smile at Meg. "Would you mind modeling it, Miss?"

Meg advanced through the arch to the man and the mink.

"Model this?" she asked, not quite believing.

"If it isn't too much trouble."

"You're the right size, Modom," the saleslady intoned through her haughty nose. Then she tried to smile, because after all Meg was a customer, too, witness the bulging, sage-green paper sacks with the legend "Randolph's" spelled out on them in paler green. It wasn't much of a smile, but you had to be careful with lacquer.

"It's no trouble at all," Meg gave the little man a real smile. "I'd love to."

She deposited on the ocher satin love seat, the paper sacks, her own coat, and her scuffed, tan leather purse. The saleslady helped her into the mink. Exactly the right size.

As it settled on her shoulders, Meg breathed, "Ohhh!" She had meant to be sophisticated about it. As if she had a mink for every day of the week; as if she only wore the old brown and white checkered wool for sales shopping at Randolph's.

"You like it?" the man wondered.

"Ohhh!" Her voice sounded like a silly teenager but she didn't care. "It's the most beautiful thing I've ever seen." She swooped the fur about her and half-turned, mannikin style. "It is simply—simply supernal."

The old man smiled. The salesperson smiled. She ought to, with the commission she'd make on this sale.

"I've got to see it," Meg exclaimed. She half-danced to the pier mirror supported by gilt plaster cupids at the rear of the salon. When she beheld herself in the coat, she stopped breathing. She erased the young joyous excitement from her flushed face and posed in elegance, simple $10,000 mink elegance. She wished Stancia could see her. She

wished Tash and Ron could see her. But she didn't wish
for the coat. There was a point where wishes were too far
out.

The saleslady's reflection came up behind her in the
mirror. Smiling all over this time. She'd made the sale.
Meggy slipped out of the coat and said, woman to woman,
"It is gorgeous."

The woman placed it reverently on another Louis XV
chair. "You'd like your initials in it?" Her pencil pointed
on her sales pad.

"But certainly," Meg said, playing the game. "M.O.T."

"Old English? Or Modern?"

"Old English, of course," Meg said, just as hoity-toity.
She went back to the love seat and retrieved her good old
checkered.

The woman followed her. "May I have your name,
please?"

This was carrying the game too far. "What for?" Meg
asked. She wasn't about to get on any special mink list;
there was enough junk mail to dispose of. She'd had her
moment.

"For delivery," the woman suggested. And added, not
quite so sure of herself, "You'd like us to deliver it,
wouldn't you?"

"Deliver what?" Meg shouldered her oversize handbag,
tried to heft the sacks into a better carrying position.

"The coat."

"That mink coat?" Meg gestured with her free elbow.

"Yes."

Meg began to laugh. "I couldn't afford a coat like that
in a million years."

"He bought it." The saleslady spoke plainly. "He bought
it, for you."

Meg's eyes slipped to the chair where he'd been sitting,
but he wasn't there anymore. She returned her gaze to the
face of the woman. Speculation in it now.

"He asked me to have it delivered, to whatever address you gave."

"Are you nuts?" Meg demanded flatly.

Sliding off her rarefied perch, the woman returned just as flatly, "No, I'm not nuts." Then awe came into her mouth. "He paid cash. Eleven one thousand dollar bills. Cash!"

Meg shook her head. "It must be a gag," she said slowly.

"I'd like to be on the receiving end of a gag like that." The pencil poised again, "Your name and address?"

Meg gave her name and address.

She went down the escalator, outside, down the subway steps, train to Times Square, shuttle to Grand Central. There was time for a coke and to buy the children each a sack of gold-covered coins. She didn't think about the mad, mad episode at all. It kept galloping through her head like a steeplechase, but she didn't think about it.

She caught the fourish, well ahead of the commuter crowds; time to get home, gather the children from neighbor Betts (look after hers next week); get dinner, pack the children to bed, wait for Tash to come home from his upstate appointment.

It was a gag, of course. One of those TV things. Instead of the coat would be delivered a toupeed, not as young as he thought he was man, who'd burble, "So sorry, Mrs. Tashman, but you made a mistake. However, we are giving you absolutely free this frying pan and one dozen eggs." She'd throw the eggs right in his toothy teeth. She decided she wouldn't tell Tash about it. Not that she'd accepted or expected the coat, but being the butt of a practical joke was too humiliating. Anyway, by now the little old man's keeper would have caught up with him and his play money.

The coat arrived on Monday. In the green van from

Randolph's with a driver who couldn't care less, just sign here, Mrs. Tashman, and here's your receipt. Not like when you sent sheets or underwear; they were dumped on the doorstep.

It was the same mink. The absolute same mink. Only the initials M.O.T. were now embroidered in the satin lining. She didn't put it on. It was a firecracker ready to explode. She stroked it and looked at it and then stashed it at the deep, dark rear of her closet.

She didn't mention it until the family was at dinner. Then she said, "The funniest thing happened to me when I was shopping in the city last week."

"Like what?" Tash asked, dutiful husband, his mouth full of meat pie.

She told the story. Just as it happened. Ron couldn't have cared less. A coat was a dull coat at six and three-fourths years, something you had to wear in winter. Stancia's face shone with acceptance of all the magic in all the fairy tales. Tash queried, "You mean he gave you a mink coat, just like that?" He was a modern, intelligent young husband. Not one of those old-fashioned, suspicious, my-wife's-got-a-secret-lover guys. "The broccoli, please, Stancy."

"What'll I do?" Meg wanted to know.

"Wear it," Tash stated practically. "Everybody needs a mink. Eat your salad, Ron."

The telephone rang. It was Betts, could Meg take her children Thursday instead of Friday? Meg could. She went upstairs, unstashed the coat, put it on. She returned to the dining room.

Ron noticed first. "Is that it?" Uninterested.

Stancia and Tash popped to attention.

"It wasn't pretend?" Stancia asked.

Tash echoed his daughter. "You mean it really happened?"

"It did," Meg assured them.

They all thought up reasons. Ron settled on Superman.

"But this was an old man."

"Disguised." Ron was shrewd.

Stancia dreamed. "You reminded him of his dear daughter who died young and who never had a mink coat."

"Must have been a crook—getting rid of some dough he couldn't be caught with. Counterfeit." But Tash himself nixed that idea. "No. The store would have checked." He tried again. "Income tax write-off. You know, a gift."

Stancia was carried away. "He had only a week to live. Leukemia." Nine-year-olds knew about everything. "He was all alone. He wanted to make one beautiful gesture before joining his loved ones."

"Zrrp!" cried Ron. "Into the secret room. Put on wrinkles. Overcoat and hat. Zrrp to Randolph's."

But Meg and Tash worried it seriously. For at least a month. Tash had to have answers to problems.

Then the picture was in the paper. An old-time gangster, off to prison on income tax evasion. At first she thought it was her man. The same pulled-down hat, the same type overcoat. It wasn't of course. Her man had a sweet, secret smile not a tight-lipped glare.

But she told Tash, "It could be." And when he looked so hopeful, "It really could be." And, finally, her fingers crossed for what must be a lie, "It really is." She relaxed in his relieved sigh. Tonight he would enjoy TV. She warned, "Don't tell the children!"

"Don't tell anybody," he stressed.

The temperature dropped sharply that weekend.

Tash said, "You might as well get the good of it while you have it. Just in case Uncle Jabez decides to turn it into a pumpkin."

She wore the coat to the school dinner, explained to friends, "A gift from my uncle."

"The rich one," Tash abetted. "Lives in Australia."

She wore it to the PTA and the supermarket and the parties and the executive dinner and everywhere. Always with joy and tenderness. And a little feather of sadness.

Because she could never say, "Thank you," to the little old man. Because he could never know what it meant to her. Unless. Unless he remembered her face at that first moment when he chose her to wear mink.

Before he achieved best-seller status with his intricately plotted and meticulously researched historical novels, John Jakes was a regular contributor to the mystery and detective (as well as science fiction, fantasy, and Western) magazines of the 1950s and 1960s. He also published a number of criminous novels during that same period, among them A Night for Treason, The Devil Has Four Faces, *and* Johnny Havoc. *"I Still See Sally," which was featured in an issue of the short-lived* Shell Scott Mystery Magazine, *is the suspenseful and chilling tale of a man whose late wife returns from the dead to haunt him.*

I STILL SEE SALLY

John Jakes

(1966)

On the second Tuesday in April, Lonergan saw Sally again. She had been dead sixty days.

The time was around half-past six. Most of the commuters had rushed for their Connecticut trains. Lonergan was one of half a dozen people left in Fingal's, a stamp-sized bar of leather and amber lights. Around him was the smell of smoke and the cheddar cheese kept in small crocks at regular intervals on the bar.

He heard the automatic door opener hiss slightly and turned as though, at this late stage of the game, something better might step into his life. From the jukebox jingled an updated version of an old tune.

His right hand, holding his third double Scotch, grew so slippery he nearly dropped the glass.

A diamond of glass inset into Fingal's front door some-how caught the red sunset far off in Jersey as the woman held the door open and looked into the bar. The diamond of sun dazzled him, and illuminated her face briefly. She was blonde, slender, with nice legs, dark shoes, a spring-weight cranberry jacket, and smart hat.

She was—Sally. The music honked and shook, upbeat and meaningless.

He stood up. His heart was hitting hard. As he stood, his elbow hit the glass, which he had set on the bar. The glass spilled. Automatically he turned to catch it. Doing so, he cursed the distraction.

Before he turned he saw her face a moment as she bent forward, looking into the bar. She looked directly at him and her face turned hurt. The dark eyes seemed to leap out of her face, immense, accusing. Then the split second was over and he was turning and picking up the spilled glass.

When he looked around again, the door was hissing shut. He cursed out loud.

"That's okay, Mr. Lonergan," the barkeep said. "It's just Scotch."

"Did you see that woman in the door a minute ago?"

The barkeep frowned. "No, Mr. Lonergan. I wasn't looking, though."

That helped alleviate the edge of terror. Lonergan swallowed and smiled as best he could. "Here." He shoved four singles on the bar top and bolted.

He ran out the door into the street, just off Fifth, colliding with a fierce-eyed office boy running for the subway. The boy snarled. Lonergan apologized. He looked both ways into the crowds.

The woman was gone.

He started west, into the swordlike blaze of orange sun slicing down between the shadows. Why did he think of her as the woman? It was Sally.

That couldn't be, of course. Sally was buried in Connecti-cut. He had left her there in early February. To forget her he had taken an expensive apartment off the park. He had plunged into work at the shop. He couldn't forget her.

Lonergan put his hands in his pockets and walked head down in the crowd-streaming loneliness of the dirty streets.

What was it, a case of nerves? In a shop window he looked at himself. There were gritty half circles under his eyes. His hair was pure white. He was dressed expensively, but the rest of the image was a joke. He was a shell, that was about the size of it. Completely gray-haired at forty-one. He was Richard Lonergan, creative director of the ninth-largest advertising agency in the U.S., Dunham & Sheffield, and he was paid $72,000 a year.

Today had been a bad day. Imperial Sportswear was a big account, with several millions of billing in consumer and trade media. At two o'clock in the afternoon, the firm's advertising committee had looked at the fall's campaign in the D & S conference room. Lonergan had gone forty-eight hours with only catnaps, supervising the last-minute work on the presentation.

The session had lasted only twenty minutes. The clients had expressed displeasure and hinted of seeking another agency. Lonergan had left at six. He was getting too old to go under the thumbscrews every other day. But he was always put there when a creative angle went wrong. . . .

At the corner of Sixth, Lonergan glanced up. He thought he saw a woman in a cranberry suit. His mouth went dry.

It was only a high school girl in a dark red athletic jacket. Lonergan rubbed his eyes and started searching for a bar. It mustn't get hold of him. It was the guilt again, pure and simple. The doctor had made him talk it out.

He hadn't been responsible for killing the woman he loved so much. That the station wagon's brakes failed on the hill as his wife was driving to meet him at the train was an act of God. . . .

He could have had the brakes checked. He had neglected it because of time. At $72,000 a year, you put first things first.

Of course he wasn't responsible for killing her.

Then why did she look into the door of Fingal's small bar, accusing him?

She didn't. That was a trick. A deception of the light. The effect of fatigue and the setback with the client.

Lonergan found a small French restaurant and proceeded to eat and drink away as much of the fear and confusion as he could. A taxi let him off in front of his apartment at ten past eleven. He lived on the tenth floor. Lights from the park sprinkled the carpet as he stepped into the darkness, tired and sweaty in his Brooks tweeds. He slumped onto the couch, trying to keep Sally's face out of his mind.

He had been sitting there for some time when the telephone rang in the darkness.

In the act of lighting a cigarette, Lonergan turned and stared at it as though it was a thing cursed. It would be Bruce Shapiro, the account executive on Imperial Sportswear. Bruce always had brainstorms at night and phoned to discuss them. Lonergan swallowed. He picked up the phone as some of the cigarette smoke got into his eyes and stung. The light from below in the park swam, and coalesced and seemed to dissolve, but it was only his eyes watering.

"This is Dick Lonergan."

"This is Sally."

It was her voice. There was no question, her voice. He cupped the phone.

"Listen, if this is some kind of lousy joke—"

"Why did you kill me, Dick?" The voice was faintly sad.

"Who is this?"

"Sally. It's your Sally. Don't you recognize me?"

The horrible part was, he did. "Sally, it really isn't—"

"Why did you kill me? I wanted to live as much as you do."

"Sally, I didn't mean it. I swear before God I never wanted anything to happen—"

The line was dead.

Lonergan replaced the phone. He thought about the police and instantly dismissed the idea. He was in enough trouble at D & S as it was. A man was only as good as his last campaign, and his last campaign had been rejected. Back in February old Charlie Sheffield, the board chairman, had suggested, with no ulterior motive, that he take two months off.

For the sake of his nerves, Sheffield had said. And because of what he had been through. If Lonergan so much as hinted right now that something was happening to his mental processes. . . .

He stumbled to the built-in bar. He mixed a tall double Scotch over ice and drank it faster than was good for him. Then he crawled onto the couch with his clothes still on and tried to sleep. In his mind he saw the burned wreck of the station wagon. Then a scene with the coroner standing by as he identified unburned scraps of clothing.

The remembered room reeked of ether and the smell of the hideous seared lump that had been a lively, charming woman. The lump was unrecognizable, with the smell of corruption rising from it. Lonergan had turned away with guilt already biting at his vitals.

"Yes, I identify her things. Mrs. Sally Lonergan—"

With his cheek pressed against the fabric of the couch he tried to forget it. He couldn't. And he couldn't sleep. The phone rang again at three in the morning.

He stared at it, dry-mouthed. His belly constricted into the start of the heaves. He couldn't answer it. He couldn't move his hand. Finally, after eight or nine minutes of ringing, it stopped.

He knew it had been Sally.

At three-thirty the next afternoon, Lonergan was sitting in his paneled office on the fifteenth floor of the building on Madison Avenue. Across from him, with his imported English shoes cocked on the corner of Lonergan's desk, was Mitch Anderson.

Mitch was the agency's associate creative director for radio-television, a dark, slender, flamboyant man several years older than Lonergan. He was the opposite number of Stu Hadley, director for print. Of the two, Lonergan relied on Mitch Anderson. Mitch knew his field. He had started as a floor director in the early days of television. Now he made $56,000 a year, and was worth it, Lonergan thought. Except for a tendency to drink a bit too much, Mitch was a mainstay.

"Can we translate these okay, do you think?" Lonergan said. He was in shirt-sleeves, slumped in his chrome and leather chair. The filtered air units hummed.

Mitch got up and walked around behind Lonergan. He stared down over Lonergan's shoulder at the half dozen print roughs that Lonergan had penciled this morning, behind a shut door and a barrier of held phone calls.

"I recognize the Lonergan touch, baby," Mitch said. His breath smelled of gin, as did a lot of other breaths in the shop at this time of the afternoon.

"Will they work for TV? On radio we can make the gal a voice, but for TV we'd need a model who can act—"

Mitch waved a cigarette. "I can dub another girl so you'll never know the difference." He walked around in front of the desk again. "Did you show these to Stu?"

"No, I just did them and called you."

A dark grin lifted Mitch's mouth. "You're learning, Dickie-bird."

"It's just a matter of time being short, Mitch."

"It's just a matter of Stu Hadley lousing things up, and you know it."

Lonergan studied the layouts. This was one of the few things he didn't care for in Mitch—the man's tendency to blast the reputations of men he disliked, behind their backs. A certain amount of ambition was laudable and necessary. But in Mitch, it sometimes seemed to be . . .

Lonergan started mentally. It was a cool relief to realize that he had forgotten Fingal's and the telephone calls. Actually forgotten them for a short time.

"You're looking rocky," Mitch said.

Lonergan felt the twinge of insecurity. "I hope it doesn't show."

"Only to your friends. As soon as we save Shapiro's bacon, if you'll pardon the ethnic paradox, you ought to hit Sheffield for a month in Europe."

Lonergan said too quickly, "There's nothing wrong with me."

Mitch held out his hands, palms down. "Easy, baby. I didn't say that. You lost Sally and she meant a lot to you, and nobody expects you to go around whistling sunshine songs. A guy can only take so much. You deserve a little holiday. And I know what you must be going through. I lost a wife too, you know. Voluntarily. But sometimes I think the fact that my first is still around and bugging me is even worse than—sorry. That was crude. Mouthy Mitch, they call me."

Mitch smiled in an apologetic way. He glanced at his watch. "I hate to ask you this, but could you take the layouts down to Jerry Disney and explain what you want? He'll need your feel of it. I'm twenty minutes late for a recording date."

Lonergan got up. It was good to stretch. "Sure, Mitch. How's Debra?"

"Driving me crazy with her frantic energy." Mitch leered and left. He had been referring to his second wife, twenty years his junior. Mitch and Debra had moved to Connecticut last summer.

The Andersons and the Lonergans had enjoyed a pleasant six months as neighbors, even though Lonergan never cared much for Debra. She had been a model. Small, brunette, vulgar-mouthed. Mitch's first wife had been sexy looking too, with a terrible temper. She and Mitch had had one child, and she had custody. She was a second-string vocalist somewhere in the West now.

Walking out of his office, Lonergan realized the train of thought was unhealthy. It reminded him of his own childless marriage, which had been all the more poignant, somehow, for that very reason. It reminded him of Sally. . . .

He took the elevator down to the thirteenth floor, where he intended to discuss the print roughs with Jerry Disney, one of the TV copywriters. Lonergan stepped off the elevator, spoke absent-mindedly to a time buyer from media, and turned down the brightly lighted hallway.

A half dozen secretaries in perfume and high hairdos rushed past from the opposite direction, murmuring his name politely. Suddenly, from a door further down, a girl in a cranberry jacket emerged.

She looked over her shoulder at him. Time stopped. Lonergan's stomach hurt.

The upper part of her face was shadowed by her hat. But her features were unmistakable. It was Sally, hurt accusation in her very posture.

"Sally, wait a minute," Lonergan called. He started to run.

An art director from the TV department came out of a door. Lonergan nearly knocked him down. The man recognized Lonergan, called his name in surprise, but Lonergan raced on. The girl had gone through the door to the stairway. Lonergan pushed through the steel door after her.

He listened in the faintly chilly gloom of the well. Tick-tacking heels sounded, below him. He ran down the stairs two at a time. The door leading back to the twelfth floor was shutting. Lonergan plunged through into a pleasant hallway richly furnished in Early American. This was the D & S executive floor.

Far down on his left, past the corridor branch that led to the offices of the senior account men, Sally was turning into another door. Lonergan followed. His frustration and fear grew when he realized the door led into the women's rest room.

Just as he reached the door, a short, gray-haired woman in a gray uniform came out, carrying a ring of keys.

Lonergan gestured. "The woman who just went in there—"

The older woman looked puzzled. "Nobody's in there, sir."

"You're lying. A girl in a cranberry suit went in there just a minute ago."

"I don't know what you're talking about. Nobody's in there."

Lonergan almost lunged at her, checked himself. He stared at the woman.

"You work here?"

"Yes, I work for the managers of the building. My name is Mrs. Reynolds." Her small, blue eyes met his, almost as though she intended to defy him with the name. "I don't know what you're all excited about, sir, but there's no woman in there right now. I know, I've been straightening up and—"

"You're lying to me! I saw her go in there! I saw my wife go in there, God damn you!"

At that moment Lonergan realized two things. He had been shouting. And a rich oak door along the wall had opened. A number of men—clients Lonergan recognized— had walked out, preceded by the chairman of D & S, Charlie Sheffield.

Lonergan's gaze locked with Sheffield's. He realized the chairman and the visitors had heard the outburst. Sheffield was staring at him with a mixture of anger and pity.

Desperate, Lonergan said the first thing that came to him: "Charlie, I was on my way to the TV department with these layouts . . ."

He realized his hands were empty. He had dropped the layouts somewhere.

"Charlie, Charlie, you've got to believe what happened. It did happen! I saw Sally go—"

"Mr. Lonergan," Sheffield said for the benefit of the clients, "please take your hands off my arm."

Lonergan turned and ran.

•   •   •

The rest of the day disappeared at the bottom of a glass.
Of many glasses.

At half-past ten the next morning Lonergan walked out
of Charlie Sheffield's office on the twelfth floor. Sheffield's secretary, a pretty ash blonde with a fashionable
British accent, gave him a friendly nod.

"Terribly sorry I had to disturb you at home this morning, Mr. Lonergan. I hadn't realized you weren't coming
in. But Mr. Sheffield did wish—"

"That's all right, Miss Poole." Lonergan waved vaguely.
"We—had a few things to talk over." Lonergan found he
was revolving his hat brim nervously in both hands. Across
the reception area, bright green ivy spilled out of a brass
planter. The ivy was plastic. Its unnaturally bright color
sickened him. It was garish, like a scream of taunting
laughter.

Coughing, Lonergan moved toward the elevators. He
walked briskly even though he had nowhere to go now.

Miss Poole's phone call had come at nine-thirty that
morning, as he was swimming up out of the empty-
stomached delirium left by yesterday's binge. He had shaken
with fright before he answered and discovered who it was.

When Miss Poole reported that Charlie Sheffield ur-
gently wished to see him, Lonergan had suspected something bad. A stiff reprimand, certainly. Perhaps even an
insistence upon medical help. At the extreme, a leave of
absence ordered.

But now he was completely out.

Though Sheffield hadn't said as much, or showed it this
morning, plainly he had been murderously embarrassed
and angered by the exhibition yesterday. Now Lonergan
stood in a clutch of secretaries waiting for the down car.
He thought he heard his name whispered. He even thought
he caught the word crazy.

It was probably all over the shop now. They knew.

Facing Sheffield, Lonergan had tried to begin an explanation but had found himself unable to continue after a few incoherent sentences. How could he explain that he had been responsible for Sally's death? How could he explain that she had come back from the dead to haunt and accuse him?

He felt light-headed as he stepped into the car. He wiped his forehead with his fingers. They came away cold and slick. Of course Sally hadn't come back. That was impossible. As a rational man, he knew it was impossible. Yet he had seen her.

Perhaps he wasn't a rational man any longer.

As the car descended, Lonergan felt himself on some kind of shifting border line. On one side lay the normal world. On the other was a similar world, but with slight differences. Shadows out of place. Lights discolored. Voices off-key. Street signs wrong. In that world Sally walked, and he was slipping over into it.

Clearly Sheffield had believed as much, because he had requested Lonergan to—as the expression went—look around. The process did not need to be rushed, of course. The shop would allow a minimum of six months for Lonergan to find a new position. In extreme circumstances, they would suffer him to go a year. But for practical purposes his career at D & S had ended in Sheffield's office.

Stepping out into the mild sunlight, moving like a sleep-walker through the loud crowds, Lonergan knew it might take longer than a year. It might take forever. No shop would hire a psychopath who saw ghosts.

As the day wore on his self-torture sharpened. He drifted from cocktail lounge to bar, from bar to grimy saloon. In a place on Seventh he almost got in a fight with a greasy character in a dark purple suit. Later, a cop blew a whistle at him as he stepped into an intersection on a red light. Somehow the hours passed.

The shadows grew longer. The spring dusk came on. Lonergan kept wandering, hiding himself in the crowds because he did not want to return to familiar places.

He might see Sally there. Or she might telephone him. He couldn't get her face out of his mind, but at least she could not find him in the anonymous joints where he drifted, drunk all day.

The low point came around nine-thirty that night. He partially woke up in a Third Avenue beer joint with his hand in his rear pants pocket. The pocket was empty.

"Bartender," he said in a drink-blurred voice, "I had my wallet—"

"You're not going to give me that old bull, are you, Mac?" the thick-set man said.

It angered Lonergan. "Before I came into this crummy place, I had my wallet in—"

"So my customers are pickpockets, huh? It's a lousy dodge. Get out of here, college, before I knock that fancy tie six feet back into your belly."

Over the bar a TV set was turned on. The volume was down, drowned in the noise of customers who ignored Lonergan's argument. Lonergan grew belligerent. The bartender came around the bar.

Lonergan saw a double head on the man's shoulders. Then the bartender shoved him.

On the TV screen a situation comedy was ending. A robust announcer held up a cleanser can. His mouth worked. The bartender hustled Lonergan to the door. Lonergan turned and tried to struggle. His right arm roundhoused without aim. As he spun he caught a glimpse of the TV screen. The crawl at the program's end was on. The bartender brought his fist in under Lonergan's aimless punch and belted him hard.

The crawl on the screen split into multiple images. Lonergan was hauled around and booted out the door. He slammed past a walking couple, the woman in furs. The woman exclaimed as though she'd touched something dirty. Lonergan fell and hit the sidewalk. His cheek grated cement.

Blood leaked warm inside his mouth and over his tongue. He lay with his right cheek on the curb, staring at a scrap of wet newspaper and some dark-colored filth a few inches down from his nose in the gutter. He hated the bartender, he hated Charlie Sheffield, he hated himself worst of all.

His mind was a clutter of pictures. He saw Sally's face in the door of Fingal's. He saw old Charlie Sheffield's face, ponderously bland as he requested Lonergan to look around. He saw the furious scowl of the bartender as he swung, and in the background the unreal, silent rectangle of the TV screen like a white wound, idiotically revolving the program credits past the lens . . .

A foot tapped the small of his back. "All right, pal, get up."

Lonergan turned his head. He saw a polished boot. Superimposed over it was the TV screen. Something was trying to penetrate the fog of fear and self-pity and drunkenness his mind had become.

"Get up out of there and let's go along to the station," the cop said, reaching down.

Suddenly Lonergan was revolted at the thought of himself lying in the gutter. Worse, he was revolted at the thought that he wanted to lie there. He stumbled to his feet. The tough-eyed young cop reached for him. Lonergan smiled apologetically and pulled back as though to brush off his suit. He felt sober. He saw the TV screen flashing in his mind. He wasn't going to lie in the gutter. That's where someone *wanted* him to lie.

"Let's see some identification," the cop said.

Turning, Lonergan jumped off the curb. The taxi hit its brakes and slowed. The cop blew a whistle. Lonergan reached the other side of the avenue, running with his lungs already hurting. But he didn't stop.

He ran for a dozen blocks before he slowed down. His chest burned. But that was nothing compared to the low, blue anger beginning to burn away his confusion. Although his wallet had been lifted, he found a quarter in his pants pocket. At a candy store he made a collect call to Connecticut.

Debra Anderson answered. She accepted the charges
when Lonergan identified himself and said it was urgent.
Mitch was not at home. He had stayed late in the city for a
filming. He was spending the night at the apartment D & S
maintained for the use of clients and agency personnel.
Debra called Lonergan sugarpie and said he sounded gassed.
He put her off and said he was fine.

The apartment was located on Park. It took him thirty-
five minutes to reach it because a chill that was the result
of nerves, liquor, shock, no food, and fear shook him so
violently several times that he had to stop and rest. Finally
he arrived in front of the building. The doorman at the
entrance gave him a suspicious glance. Lonergan called
the man by his first name and muttered something about
needing to use the electric razor in the agency apartment.
The man appeared satisfied.

Lonergan slumped in the elevator. He raked his palms
with his fingernails to waken himself. He was still shaking.

The number of the apartment was 17-B. The corridor
was carpeted in white. There was a gold-leaf ornamenta-
tion on the woodwork. The hall seemed as dead as the
setting for a commercial. Lonergan pressed the buzzer of
17-B. He felt like turning to run. He managed to stand
where he was.

It got worse as the door was opened and he saw Sally
standing there, framed against a darkened living room and
huge windows overlooking the city's lights. Sally stared at
him. She wore the same cranberry jacket. Her pink mouth
pursed, hurt, accusing.

Everything revolved wildly, dizzily, in Lonergan's mind.
He wanted to yell in fear.

Then he noticed a mole on her chin, and other details
that were wrong.

"Where's Mitch?" he said. "I want to see him."

"Right here, Dickie-bird," Mitch called from the dark.

Lonergan walked past the girl into the faint splatter of
lights thrown by the big buildings beyond the glass. He
heard the door close. A security chain clicked in place.

"I knew you'd be coming around," Mitch said. He was over there on the left, Lonergan thought. "Right after you phoned Debra, she phoned me here. She said you sounded drunk and upset. She's a protective little slut. Only the two of us know what you're so upset about, don't we, Dickiebird? Make that the three of us."

A click, and a table lamp with a huge gourd-shaped orange ceramic base flashed on. Beside it on a couch, shoes off, feet up on a coffee table, sat Mitch. He drew his right hand away from the lamp switch. Then he transferred the gun from his left hand to his right.

"You bastard," Lonergan said.

Mitch grinned. "Who ever said otherwise?"

"It won't work."

"It already has."

"What do you mean?"

"At three this afternoon old man Sheffield called me in and made me acting creative director. At an additional twenty thousand per. Sheffield didn't like putting a drunk in your spot—"

"A drunk? You aren't—"

"Shut up and pay attention while I'm talking. Sheffield didn't have much choice. He hasn't got anybody else inside. And the shop is in enough trouble with Imperial and some of the other clients so the old jerk couldn't risk any trade rumbles by going outside."

Lonergan swiped his sleeve across his mouth. His shirt at the base of his back was wet with sweat. Mitch's eyes were squinted down. His speech was slurred. There was a very dark highball beside the lamp. He managed to hold the gun steady, though. The gun terrified Lonergan. Before this, he had lived in a world where guns were used only by people he didn't know. The gun, plus Mitch's fixed smile, told Lonergan this was not a charade that would end with a joke all around.

"Why did you want my job, Mitch?" Lonergan asked. "The money?"

Mitch nodded. "You catch on fast for a guy who's basically a self-centered hick. Do you know how much my first wlfe takes out of my skin in alimony every month? And how much Debra costs me? I'll just barely break even at the new salary. And now that I've found Sheilah—little old Sheilah. Sheilah, have you met your husband?"

The girl walked around into the light. Her step was unsteady. She was smoking a cigarette in quick puffs. Lonergan realized that she was not over twenty-one or two. But basically she resembled Sally very much, and from a distance, or in shadows, the resemblance would be wholly adequate to frighten a man who was so tired and so guilt-ridden that every thought was distorted. Lonergan felt he was emerging from a fog, stepping back across the line.

But on the normal side of the line sat Mitch with his ridiculous gun.

"You do look a lot like her," Lonergan said to the girl. "Especially in that suit."

"Thanks," the girl said with an inane grin. She was frightened.

"But you don't sound too much like her," Lonergan said.

"Enough so that a little electronic fiddling at a recording studio produced a fair match to Sally's voice on tape," Mitch said. "I know an engineer who owes me a favor."

"Where did you find her?" Lonergan asked.

"Sheilah's from Newark. She's just dying to get into TV, aren't you, sweetheart? There are a million like her, hanging around the talent agencies—"

Lonergan nodded. "That's what I figured. That's why I woke up that it probably had to be you, Mitch. I was in a bar tonight. I got thrown out of it like a bum because of you, Mitch. A TV set was on, with the crawl, the credits, at the end of the program.

"Just before the bartender slugged me and threw me out I looked at the credits that were on right then. The program gave a credit to the talent agency that did the casting.

I saw that one word, Mitch. Casting. You're the one man I knew who could search through hundreds and hundreds of model resumes, and even interview girls until you found the right look and voice, because you're the radio and TV director and that's your job.''

"My," Mitch said, "aren't you getting bright? What else have you figured out?''

"Not much. I don't know how you worked it with the woman attendant on the twelfth floor.''

Mitch shrugged. "Fifty bucks. It was a sort of open-end deal. I had Sheilah all set up to let you see her in the building, and then lead you to the twelfth floor and disappear into the john. Mrs. Reynolds is usually in there. She runs the floor setup from a little office inside.

"So the minute she saw Sheilah come in, she was to run out. It just meant she had to stand by for a period of two or three hours while Sheilah hung around waiting for me to get you out in the hall. The old Reynolds dame is as greedy as the rest of us. I planned it for the twelfth floor because that's the executive floor. A scene there would be better than a scene anywhere else. Sheffield walking out of the conference room—that was pure coincidence, but it couldn't have been better if we'd written a storyboard first.''

"So much trouble—'' Lonergan shook his head in wonderment. "So much planning—''

"They won't fire me at D & S unless I make a scene in front of a client like you did. And besides, being a drunk isn't as bad as being loony. It was either go up at D & S and get more dough, or go out. Out like you're out, Dickie-bird. People in the business know I'm a drunk.''

Lonergan blinked. "You drink heavily, but—''

"Oh, for Christ's sake.'' Mitch sounded tired. "You're so wrapped up picking your own sores all the time you can't see anybody objectively. That's what made you such a beautiful psychological mark. I'm a lousy drunk, and everybody in the business in town but you knows it.''

It was like a shower bath of cold water. Something went tick inside Lonergan, and he realized that what Mitch had said about him was true. He realized it, it was that simple. And like a sleeper waking up to discover his room as though it were wholly new, part of the agony of the past went away. Lonergan almost wanted to smile.

Then Mitch stood up. He made a slight motion with his gun hand. "You're getting so bright it's positively frightening. What happens now, can you guess?"

"I'm going to call Sheffield and tell—"

Mitch's laughter made Lonergan realize how foolish he sounded. The customary laws weren't operating. He realized the full significance of the gun.

"I wish you hadn't shown up here, or guessed," Mitch said. "Now I can't leave you around to blow the whistle on me, Dickie-bird. I can't have you anything but a despondent suicide."

Lonergan felt compelled to say something to the effect that it was impossible for a civilized man like Mitch Anderson to think of murder. Then Lonergan understood again that he was in an entirely new kind of game. Mitch's eyes were cold.

"We won't do it here," he said. "We'll get the car and drive—"

Lonergan made a lunge. Sheilah let out a squeak of fright and tripped him. Lonergan sprawled, knocking his head on the corner of the coffee table. Mitch kicked him in the side.

Lonergan rolled over onto his back. Mitch towered, the gun muzzle in the foreground, pointing downward, Mitch's head in the background, smile fixed. Lonergan knew it was all over. He couldn't win against the two of them.

"I guess we'll have to do part of it here," Mitch said.

His right hand grew white as he squeezed on the trigger.

The door chimes sounded. Sheilah squeaked again. Mitch jerked his head up.

Mitch whispered, "You hold this. Watch him. I'll answer it."

In a few seconds the security chain clicked. Lonergan heard a voice. He thought he recognized it. The voice spoke politely to Mr. Anderson, sir, about a man who had looked familiar, from the agency, maybe. The man had come in a while ago and said he was going up to the apartment.

But the voice had been thinking about it, and this man—the voice couldn't remember his name, but he'd needed a shave and his clothes were torn—well, it had occurred to the voice finally that this man looked sort of wild and dangerous. The voice hoped he wasn't butting in, but after all it was his job to keep an eye out for—

"Thanks, thanks, that's all right, Warren," came Mitch's voice distantly.

"He is one of your people, then, sir?"

"That's right, Warren, a pal of mine from the shop. He's sleeping one off."

"Oh, that's why he looked so bad."

"Yeah, right, right."

"I thought it was something else. I can spot 'em when they've had too much, but—"

"Well, he was carrying an extra big load tonight. He'll be okay. Good night, Warren."

"Well, good night, sir," said the doorman. His voice receded. "I'm sorry if—"

Lonergan knew he wouldn't have another chance. He rolled over and kicked Sheilah in the shin and jumped up.

Sheilah stumbled backwards, screamed. Lonergan twisted the gun out of her hand. He backed into a corner as Mitch appeared at the edge of the light from the lamp.

"Doorman," Lonergan shouted, "doorman, come in here."

"You stupid bastard," Mitch said. He took a step forward, raising his hands to grab the gun.

Strange spasms wrenched Lonergan's face. Mitch halted suddenly. His smile melted. His eyes flared wide. He backed up a step, two. The doorman looked into the room.

Mitch kept backing up. Another step. Another. His shoulders shook.

Lonergan's facial muscles seemed to possess a life of their own, jerking. He heard a raw sound and realized it was his own laughter. It drowned out the sobs of Sheilah lying on the floor.

Abruptly Mitch collided with the wall at his back. He peered hard at Lonergan. He shook violently. Then the tension left him and he said, "I thought for a minute, from the look on your face—thought you were going to kill me, Dickie-bird."

"I was," Lonergan said. "I almost did. But I'm carrying enough guilt around already."

"What?" Mitch said.

"I still see Sally, Mitch. I'll always see Sally."

"What the hell does that have to do with—"

"You wouldn't understand," Lonergan said. He walked through the splatter of lights thrown on the carpet by the big buildings beyond the glass in the night, and carefully he picked up the telephone.

Whether he is writing under the pseudonyms Michael Collins, Mark Sadler, William Arden, or John Crowe, or under his real name, Dennis Lynds is one of today's finest purveyors of intelligent and thought-provoking crime fiction. His earliest accomplishment in the field was a series of offbeat stories in MSMM in the 1960s about a character named Slot-Machine Kelly; later he contributed a variety of other stories to EQMM, AHMM, and MSMM, among them several featuring his Michael Collins series character, one-armed New York private investigator Dan Fortune. "Homecoming," a nonseries tale, is Lynds at his most evocative and profound.

HOMECOMING

Michael Collins

(1964)

Sarah Williams did not open her eyes. But she knew they had come for her. She could feel them there in the room, hovering all around her bed.

She knew she was awake, but she lay on the bed with her eyes closed, her body motionless, her slow breathing the only movement in the room. She knew the bedroom was dark, the venetian blinds shut tight as always behind the heavy green curtains because she could not abide light when she was in bed. It was not the fear of light that made her lie there with her eyes closed long after it was time for her to be up and working.

It was the dream.

The memory of the cruel, horrible dream had rushed

over her like a speeding car from the night the moment she awoke.

In the dream, Peter had come home. Her only son Peter who had died in Korea. They had told her. Only nineteen, Peter, and he had been killed in the hills of Korea. There had not even been a grave for her to find and weep over.

Of course, they had always told her that Peter might not be dead. Peter could be a prisoner. The Chinese were strange people, and Peter could be a prisoner the Chinese had decided to keep and hide. She had told them to stop trying to make her build castles in the air. She was not a weak woman. Peter had died bravely for his country, and she could be brave, too.

Last night Peter had come home.

In the dream, of course. After five years of being dead, Peter had come home. Without even a telegram to warn her! Peter had come home like a thief in the night. Or was there a telegram? She seemed to remember Peter had said he had sent a telegram. She was sure, though, that she had never received one.

"Hello, Mother."

Like a thief in the night! Older, much older, with the horrible scars on his delicate face. Not the Peter she had remembered—the memory she had each time she stood and looked at his name on the monument. A scarred face, his thick hair not even combed, his uniform wrinkled and dirty, and the smile on his face was somehow evil.

"It's me, Mother. I'm here."

She had been alone in the kitchen. Late at night, because she had wanted to work a little longer on the speech she was to deliver to the Gold Star Mothers meeting. The bottle of whiskey on the table for her small nightcap. He had come in without even knocking.

"I'm home, Mother."

"You're dead," she had said.

Then Peter had sat down at the kitchen table. He had poured a long drink of whiskey for himself. He drained the glass in a single gulp. The dream, of course; her son never drank.

"You know I never allowed you to drink," she said.

"That was a long time ago," Peter said. "I've changed."

It had been all wrong, of course. His grin, the whiskey, the way he just sat there looking at her. All false. The way she herself had sat there without kissing him, without throwing her arms around him. Dreams were so false, so unreal. That was how you knew they were dreams.

"I've changed," Peter said. "There was a girl. After they captured me I met this Chinese girl, so I stayed. I brought her home."

He sat there in her immaculate kitchen; with the scars on his face, his tie loose, his shirt dirty and open at the neck, his army boots raised on a second chair, his thick hair matted. This was not her son! She was so annoyed by his appearance that she barely heard his ridiculous story of capture, prison camp, a Chinese girl, and final release only weeks ago.

"It's been a long time," Peter said. "What have you done?"

Behind her closed eyes in the bed, she shook her head. All wrong. Peter would have rushed to her, cried on her breast. They would have cried for joy. Her son would not have sat there drinking whiskey and asking questions.

"Tell me what you've been doing?" Peter said.

Such a stupid dream. Peter drinking all that whiskey and asking questions in a cold, changed voice.

"Oh, Peter, I've done so much," she said. "After you left I worked for the Red Cross, it was the least a mother could do with her boy in the service. We started a Soldier's Canteen, I wish you could have come to it. It was my idea. It's closed now, of course."

"The war's over," Peter said.

"I work now for the Ladies Aid, and I'm Director of the Legion Auxiliary. There's the League of Women Voters, we did a lot of work in the last election. Of course, I'm chairman of The Gold Star Mothers.''

"You've sure been busy," Peter said.

There! There! The horrible dream. Peter just sat there with a glass of whiskey in his dirty hand. He smiled that awful smile, and said only: *You've sure been busy*.

"It was the monument that got me started," she explained. "As chairman of The Gold Star Mothers I started the campaign for the monument. It was my idea, my campaign, my choice of design. Oh, I had to battle for it, let me tell you. A lot of them didn't want a monument. It's a Monument To All Wars.''

"I saw it," Peter said. "It sure is big."

"We took down all the old ones," she said. "It stands for the Civil War, the Spanish-American, the First World War, the Second World War, Korea, and all of them. It's for all of you poor dead boys.''

"What good would it do us?" Peter said.

Behind her eyes, she covered her ears. How evil his smile seemed as he said that. A cruel, cruel dream. Poor Peter. It was not right to even dream of him like that. So cold, so unfeeling. Peter could never be like that man last night, no matter what had happened to him. Not her Peter.

"War changes people, Ma," Peter said. "I'm home now.''

"It's our tribute, Peter!" she said. "Don't you see? Your name is on it. Your name in gold. The Gold Star Mothers did it for you. We've done a great deal for you. We're powerful, and I'm the chairman. That's how I started, you see? They listen to me, now. I even help your father in his work. I can help you a lot.''

"I brought her back," Peter said. "The Chinese girl. She's my wife. What can you do for me? I'm not dead. I didn't die in Korea. I'm home . . . I'm home . . . I'm . . .''

And he was laughing! Behind her closed eyes, Peter laughed and laughed and laughed. The high, animal laughter echoed in the dark room behind her closed eyes. It seemed to leap out at her, bounce from the dark walls, wind cold and tight about her rigid body.

War changes people . . . war changes people . . . I'm home . . . I'm home . . . war changes . . .

She clenched her eyes, covered her ears, curled tight around herself to shut out the endless laughter that bounced and leaped. She tried to open her eyes to end the horrible dream. Peter's voice was in her ear, hissing in her ear.

"You're not even a Gold Star Mother!"

She opened her eyes. There he was. Peter sat and grinned at her.

"I'm not dead. You're not a Gold Star Mother."

There he was. Peter. *You're not a Gold Star Mother.*

In the kitchen she sat and stared at her son. Her poor dead boy buried in an unmarked grave. *You're not a Gold Star Mother.* He smiled that evil smile.

She sat in the kitchen. And, of course, he was home. It had not been a dream. He had really come home, and she was not a Gold Star Mother, not even a member—a nothing. That Mrs. Tomlinson would take her position, do her work, leave her with nothing, nothing . . .

"Stop it!" she shouted.

Not a dream at all. She lay in the big bed in her dark bedroom, and she had to face it. It had not been a dream. None of it. Real, very real, and soon they would come for her. All the details of her bedroom seemed to stare at her with wide eyes, like the eyes of her son. Soon they would come for her.

"Stop it!" she shouted.

Not a dream, and she must soon get up, brush her hair, dress in her best dress, look her best when they came for her. She had to get up and walk down the stairs to where they would be waiting with David, poor David, her shocked husband with the tears in his eyes.

"Stop it! I hate you!" she shouted.

If only he had not smiled when he said it, *You're not even a Gold Star Mother!* Changed. He was so changed. If he had not smiled there in the kitchen, where the knife lay on the table. The long, shining, steel-sharp knife that she raised and plunged into his chest.

"I hate you!"

She plunged the knife deep into him. He staggered back, she saw it clearly, his eyes already glazing.

"You're dead!"

She plunged and stabbed and slashed. He fell against the table. He screamed. His blood spilled across the table. He fell, twisted, to the kitchen floor.

In the kitchen she stood with the knife in her hand.

Peter lay in a pool of spreading blood.

She listened. There was only silence in the house. David, her husband, lay asleep upstairs. David was a deep sleeper. She listened but there was no sound in the night, now. Her son was dead.

She picked up his feet, and dragged him out into the back yard. She dragged him down to the far end of the yard. In the tool shed she found a shovel. She dug a deep grave and dropped him into it. No one knew he was home. She covered the body and returned to the kitchen.

In the kitchen she washed the blood from the table and the floor. She wiped the blood from the whiskey bottle. She wiped the knife. Then she washed her hands and sat down at the table and began to giggle. They would never find him.

In her bed she lay behind her eyes and knew that it had not been a dream. Peter had come home. Peter was home. In the garden. With the long, shining, steel-sharp knife that had been near her hand there on the kitchen table. Her dead son.

She had killed him, and now they would come for her.

Not a dream. Behind her closed eyes, she clearly remembered how she had buried him in the garden. She remembered putting the knife away in its proper place. She liked things to be neat.

She remembered that almost-empty whiskey bottle. He

had drunk so much, not at all like her poor dead son. Her Peter, with his name in gold on her beautiful monument. It was her tribute to her son, the monument.

Now Peter was dead. She had killed him with the long, shining knife that had been there beside the whiskey bottle on the table.

"Stop it! I hate you! I hate you!"

And awake, Sarah Williams did not open her eyes. She knew she was awake now, but she lay on the narrow bed with her eyes closed, her body rigid, her slow breathing the only movement in the room.

But she knew they were there. They hovered above her in the dark room. They had come for her.

"You're dead," Sarah Williams said aloud.

Above where Sarah Williams lay on the narrow bed in the bare room with the barred windows, the three men looked down at her rigid form.

"She seems to dream," the doctor said. "Sometimes her eyes open and she mentions your name, Peter. From time to time she even speaks. Mostly she says, 'You're dead,' and 'I'm home.' "

"Poor Mother," Peter Williams said as he looked down at Sarah, rigid on the bed.

"Nothing else, Doctor?" David Williams said. "She just lies there?"

David Williams watched the still form of his wife where she lay on the narrow bed with her eyes closed tight in the dark and barren room.

"Sometimes she mumbles, things like 'stop it,' and 'you're dead,' " the doctor said. "And sometimes her hands move a little."

"Ten years," David Williams said sadly. "Peter was missing for five years, and now she's been like this for five years. How much longer? Will she ever be herself again?"

"There is some hope," the doctor said. "The problem

is to get through the shock, whatever it was. The shock must have been massive.''

Peter Williams looked down at his mother. There was a faint touch of gray in his neat brown hair as he brushed it back from his boyish face. He was a handsome man with an open, unlined, unmarked face.

"It was my homecoming," Peter said. "I remember when Dad and I walked into the kitchen, she was sitting there at the table like this. My telegram was on the floor. The whiskey bottle was almost completely empty."

"When you sent that telegram saying you were alive, she was afraid to believe it after all the years. The happiness was too much for her."

On the narrow bed, Sarah Williams moved. Her clenched right hand moved up and down, up and down. Her mouth opened. Her flat, toneless voice seemed to move up and down with the stabbing motion of her hand.

" . . . you're dead . . . you're dead . . . you're dead . . ."

Peter Williams sighed. "Poor Mother, she wanted me alive so much."

Early in 1957, two of the major mystery digests—AHMM and Manhunt—*underwent an experimental change to a large, flat-size format. The experiment lasted slightly more than a year in* Manhunt's *case, and less than a year in* AHMM's; *newsstand operators could not find proper space for these unwieldy issues, and buyers tended to overlook them. As a result, copies are extremely difficult to find today, and many fine stories that appeared in them have never been reprinted. "The Deadly Mrs. Haversham" is one such story, from a 1957 issue of AHMM—a magazine to which Helen Nielsen was a regular contributor in the 1950s and 1960s. (Her name could also often be found on the contents pages of the hard-boiled* Manhunt.) *A few of her short stories from this period were collected in the 1961 paperback* Woman Missing. *Among her expert suspense novels are such titles as* Detour, Sing Me a Murder, *and* A Killer in the Street, *and among her many TV screenplays are episodes of* Perry Mason *and* Alfred Hitchcock Presents.

THE DEADLY MRS. HAVERSHAM

Helen Nielsen

(1957)

The lettering on the door was clear and black: LT. O'KONSKY—HOMICIDE. The woman outside the door hesitated, one neatly gloved hand resting on the doorknob, while her eyes studied the words as carefully as if she were silently spelling out each letter. She was a small woman—slender, smartly dressed in black, and with a certain poise that suggested she might have been a debutante—and a lovely one—some thirty years earlier. Her face was soft, her eyes were sad, and a ghost of a smile touched her lips as she turned the knob with a determined gesture.

Detective Lieutenant O'Konsky sat at his desk reading a newspaper with a lurid headline: HAMMER SLAYER SOUGHT. The door opened quietly, but O'Konsky was suddenly aware of the incongruous aroma of expensive cologne. He looked up and stared at the woman, a mixture of surprise and apprehension struggling with the long-practiced objectivity in his eyes. The newspaper dropped to the desk as he came slowly to his feet. There were occasions when O'Konsky subconsciously remembered that a gentleman was required to rise in the presence of a lady, in spite of the scarcity of ladies encountered on his job.

There was over six feet of O'Konsky standing, but he might have been invisible. The woman came to the desk and looked down at the headline on the abandoned newspaper.

"A terrible thing," she said in a barely audible voice. "A wicked thing!"

O'Konsky inhaled the cologne.

"Yes ma'am," he said.

"Murder is such a wicked thing—and this one with a hammer." She shuddered inwardly. "So untidy."

O'Konsky hadn't taken his eyes from the woman, and his eyes weren't happy. She raised her head and gave him a faint smile.

"Do you remember me, Lieutenant?"

O'Konsky nodded.

"The fireplace poker murder last June," she said brightly.

O'Konsky cleared his throat.

"And the rat poison in July," he added.

"July? Was it really July?" The woman frowned over the thought—then nodded. "Yes, you're right. It was July—but it wasn't rat poison. It was insecticide. Nasty fluid. I've warned our gardener time and time again—" Her voice faded as she looked around the room. A side chair stood on the far side of the lieutenant's desk. "Do you mind if I sit down?"

O'Konsky remembered the rest of his manners. He bounded around the corner of the desk and came back with the chair. He even held it in place for her while she sat down.

"Excuse me," he said. "I was just surprised, Mrs. Haversham—"

"To see me again? Thank you, Lieutenant. Yes, that's much better. I'm a little tired. The stairs—"

"And the heat," O'Konsky suggested.

"Yes, it is warm for September, isn't it? I remarked to my brother only yesterday—"

O'Konsky was back in his own chair by this time. One hand furtively pressed the buzzer on his desk. The woman's eyes caught the action and clouded momentarily, but her voice remained unchanged.

"Do you remember my brother, Lieutenant?"

O'Konsky's eyebrows huddled over the question.

"Brother—," he mused. "Thin chap—pale moustache—not much hair."

The woman nodded.

"Charles began losing his hair when he was a very young man. It upset him terribly. He never mentioned it to me, of course. Charles isn't the communicative type—but I could tell. I've often wondered if he might not have married and been quite different if only he hadn't lost his hair. Men are so sensitive about such things."

The woman paused—suddenly embarrassed.

"Oh, I'm sorry. No offense, Lieutenant."

O'Konsky's hand came back from the receding hairline he'd unconsciously caressed.

"Don't worry about me," he said. "I gave up this battle long ago."

"But you're a married man—and a police officer. I don't suppose police officers are troubled by a sense of inferiority. But poor Charles—and his sister married to such a handsome and successful man!"

A door at the back of the room opened and a man came over to O'Konsky's desk. O'Konsky turned in his chair to greet him.

"Sergeant Peters, you remember Mrs. Haversham, don't you? Mrs. Harlan Haversham—widow of the late Harlan Haversham."

There was a note of pleading in O'Konsky's voice. Peters stared hard at the woman on the chair, and then his gaze dropped momentarily to the headline on the newspaper spread across O'Konsky's desk.

"Oh, *that* Mrs. Haversham!" he said.

O'Konsky sighed as if he'd just made the last payment on the mortgage, and then he scribbled something on a slip of paper and handed it to the man.

"This is why I buzzed you," he said. "Mrs. Haversham and I are having a little chat just now, so I thought maybe you could take care of this for me."

Peters scanned the paper and then shoved it into his coat pocket.

"Right away," he said. But at the doorway he paused to cast one long look back at Mrs. Haversham. He didn't appear any happier than O'Konsky.

Mrs. Haversham endured the interruption in patient but observing silence. When it was over, she continued the conversation as if nothing had taken place.

"Did you know my husband, Lieutenant?"

"I never had the pleasure," O'Konsky answered.

"That's a pity. You would have admired him—everyone did. He was so intelligent and kind, but his heart . . ."

Her voice broke off huskily. In the brief silence that followed she seemed almost at the verge of tears, and then, as if remembering that grief was a private matter not to be aired in a police detective's office, her back stiffened and her chin came up higher.

"But then," she continued, "I believe I asked you if

you knew my husband the first time we met. Let's see now, that was the time when—"

"A man fell down an elevator shaft," O'Konsky broke in. "Accidental death."

A fleeting smile crossed Mrs. Haversham's lips.

"According to the police," she said.

"Now, Mrs. Haversham—"

"Oh—" One gloved hand drifted up in protest. "I won't argue the point, Lieutenant—not now. After all, the case is closed."

"And the poker case is closed," O'Konsky said, "—and the rat poison."

"Insecticide," Mrs. Haversham corrected. Her glance fell to the headline again. "But not the hammer murder," she added. "There were no fingerprints, of course."

"No fingerprints," O'Konsky sighed.

Mrs. Haversham spread her hands out on her lap—palms up and then palms down. She wore extremely smart gloves. Black.

"So few women wear gloves any more," she said quietly, "but I always have—even before Mr. Haversham's tragic death. It's a matter of the way in which one has been reared, I suppose."

O'Konsky took a handkerchief out of his breast pocket and patted his neck. He was beginning to squirm in his chair.

"There were no fingerprints on the poker, either," Mrs. Haversham reflected.

"The case was open and shut—" O'Konsky began.

"—or on the bottle of insecticide."

"Mrs. Haversham—" O'Konsky's voice was troubled. The handkerchief was now a wadded ball in his hand. "—I know that you must have read all about this new murder in the newspapers."

She smiled vaguely.

"Oh, I have, Lieutenant, but they haven't reported all of it right. Newspapers never do."

"Then—" O'Konsky's face was haggard. "—I don't need to ask why you've come to see me."

"I always try to cooperate with the police," she said quietly.

"That you do, Mrs. Haversham. That you most certainly do!"

At that very moment the door opened and Sergeant Peters returned with another man—older, taller, dressed in an expensively tailored suit. The newcomer smiled at Mrs. Haversham, and she returned the smile in recognition.

"Dr. Armstrong! How well you're looking!"

"Thank you," the doctor said.

"And your wife? She's well, too?"

"Never better."

"That's nice. I've been meaning to drop a card, but I've been so busy."

"I'll bet you have, Mrs. Haversham. Do you want to tell us about it now?"

The woman hesitated. She looked at the doctor; she looked at O'Konsky. For the first time, her eyes were anxious.

"Where's the other one—with the notebook?" she asked.

"I don't think that will be necessary this time," the doctor said.

"Oh, yes. Things must be done in an efficient manner. That's one of the things my late husband taught me. I didn't learn too well, I'm afraid. But then, I have Charles. He's so very efficient about everything."

Mrs. Haversham paused. One hand went to her forehead in a meaningless gesture; then she noticed the sergeant and smiled again.

"Oh, you do have a notebook," she said. "That's better, now we can proceed." She wriggled straight in her chair while O'Konsky wriggled down in his. Then she began to dictate in a calm, clear voice:

"I, Lydia Haversham, being of sound mind and under no duress whatsoever, do hereby confess to the hammer murder . . ."

•   •   •

The lettering on the door was bright gold: DR. J. M. ARMSTRONG—PSYCHIATRIST. Behind the door, a thin, middle-aged man with a pale moustache and little hair on his head sat nervously on the edge of a chair. His light blue eyes, worried but attentive, were focused on the doctor's face. Only occasionally did he cast a quick, apprehensive glance in the direction of his sister—deep in a leather armchair alongside the doctor's desk. The conversation was about Lydia Haversham, although it seemed hardly to concern her.

"It all goes back to the shock of your brother-in-law's tragic death, Mr. Lacy," the doctor explained. "The implication of violence—"

Charles Lacy reacted in immediate protest.

"But there was no violence. Harlan Haversham suffered a heart attack. My sister knows that. He'd had these attacks several times prior to his death. We all knew—"

Dr. Armstrong's voice remained calm. "I said the *implication* of violence, Mr. Lacy. Unfortunately, this last attack occurred on a staircase. Mr. Haversham collapsed and fell over the balustrade, plunging a possible eight floors—"

The doctor raised the clip-end of his gold-plated pen in a gesture of silence as Charles Lacy opened his mouth to protest again.

"No, we do not run away from things any more. We do not pretend this horror hasn't occurred. Your sister and I have been having some very frank talks these past few days, and she's a much stronger person now."

Charles Lacy looked toward his sister for reassurance. She sat very small in the huge chair, an expression of tired resignation on her face.

"Harlan plunged eight floors," she repeated dully. "He was crushed and bleeding. It was because the elevators weren't running and he had to take the stairs."

"The elevators," Dr. Armstrong repeated. "Do you see the significance? A few months after her husband's tragic death, your sister came to the police and confessed to having pushed a man down an elevator shaft. There was no murder at all—it was merely an accident—but she'd read the account in her newspaper and a subconscious feeling of guilt compelled her to that ridiculous confession.''

"For better or for worse, in sickness and in health—" Lydia murmured.

The doctor nodded sympathetically.

"A wife always feels an exaggerated responsibility for her husband—especially a wife who loves deeply. The confession was ridiculous, and your sister knew that, but it fulfilled—temporarily—her need for punishment stemming from this mistaken sense of guilt.''

"It was Saturday," Lydia recalled. "The repair men were working on the elevators because it was Saturday. Harlan shouldn't have been in his office when they started working, but I had asked him to go—"

She spoke slowly and deliberately—like a child talking to herself. Dr. Armstrong caught Charles Lacy's eye and nodded. A signal of understanding passed between them.

"A month later a second confession," the doctor continued. "This time to a crime of a violent nature. A brutal slaying with a poker—"

Eight floors, Lydia repeated. "Crushed and bleeding."

"—and then, a month later, another confession. Unfortunately, Lt. O'Konsky didn't call me in for consultation until this third disturbance. He thought then—and I concurred as you will recall—that the confessions were merely a manifestation of loneliness—an attempt to draw attention to herself.''

Charles Lacy fidgeted on the edge of his chair. Lydia was watching him. She'd been watching him all this time. He'd just become aware of that.

"I've tried to follow your suggestions," he said defensively. "I've tried to get Lydia to go out more—and to have friends in. I've made sacrifices, too. I'm a busy man, doctor. Since my brother-in-law's death, the business keeps me working all hours."

"Charles always worked all hours," Lydia remarked, "—even before Harlan's death. He was Harlan's secretary— his right hand man. Harlan used to tell me that he wouldn't know how to find anything in the office if it weren't for Charles."

Nobody noticed her. Dr. Armstrong didn't so much as turn his head.

"I'm not blaming you, Mr. Lacy," he insisted. "If anyone's to blame it's myself for not going into this matter more thoroughly at the time of the last confession. I took too much for granted. I've worked with the police on such cases before, but never—" He hesitated. "—never with one of your sister's sensibilities. I should have probed deeper." And then he smiled and leaned back in his chair.

"But I believe we've gotten to the very root of the trouble this time," he added. "We understand it all now, don't we, Mrs. Haversham?"

Lydia Haversham smiled vaguely.

"Yes, I'm sure we do," she said.

"And you realize that you couldn't possibly have committed that hammer murder any more than you could have committed any of the other crimes to which you have confessed. You didn't even know the victim."

"It's all preposterous!" Charles exploded. "My sister was at home the entire evening the crime occurred. I telephoned her from the office at ten o'clock sharp. I always telephone when I work late."

Lydia nodded.

"Charles always telephones," she said. "He never forgets. It was only that he forgot to get his passport out of the safe—"

Charles swung about and faced his sister, but his words were for the doctor.

"She should forget about that!" he said. "Now that you've probed the past—or however you put it, Doctor, she should forget—shouldn't she?"

"She should—and will," the doctor answered, "—now

that she really understands why she felt compelled to
confess to crimes her nature would never have allowed her
to commit. You see, Mrs. Haversham—'' and now the
doctor faced Lydia for the first time ''—you aren't guilty
of anything. Your husband suffered a fatal heart attack on
the stairway—that was all. It was no one's fault. It could
have happened to you—or to your brother—or to myself,
for that matter. Many people have no warning whatsoever
about such things. It so happens that your husband did
have a medical record. You are completely absolved.''

Lydia Haversham's eyes didn't leave the doctor's face
while he spoke. She might have been memorizing every
word.

"It could have happened to anyone," she repeated softly.

"Anyone," the doctor agreed. "It's unfortunate that the
workman came to service the elevators while your husband
was still in his office. It's unfortunate they didn't know he
was there. It's unfortunate that he had to make an unexpected trip to his office, but none of these things are
conclusive. His heart might have stopped that day anyway.
You're not responsible.''

His voice was firm and persuasive. Lydia listened atten-
tively, but she didn't seem quite convinced.

"I asked him to get the passport—" she began.

"For me," Charles cut in. "You see, Dr. Armstrong, I
received a wire late Friday night—an important business
matter in our South American branch. My brother-in-law
couldn't get away, so I offered to make the trip myself.
But it all happened so quickly, and there were so many
things to do. Packing—tickets—In the rush, I forgot my
passport in the safe, and only Harlan and myself knew the
combination. If anyone is to blame for what happened, I'm
the guilty party—but I don't crucify myself, Lydia. I can't
afford to. I have to carry on the business, as I know Harlan
would want me to do. He'd want you to carry on, too.
You know that.''

It was a long speech for Charles. He'd put a lot into it.
He was a bit out of breath at the finish.

Lydia nodded, her eyes far away.

"South America," she said. "You never did go, did you, Charles?"

"How could I? When Harlan was found—"

"I've never been to South America. Why don't we go, Charles? Why don't we just forget everything and take a holiday?"

Charles seemed startled. He looked at the doctor. The doctor smiled.

"I think that's an excellent idea, Mrs. Haversham."

"But the business—" Charles began.

"Your brother-in-law left you his wife to care for as well as his business, Mr. Lacy. Speaking professionally, I'd heartily recommend a holiday. It should make a good beginning for a newer and fuller life."

The doctor came to his feet as he spoke. His words were like a benediction, to which he added one thought as he helped Lydia from her chair.

"And I don't want to ever find you in Lieutenant O'Konsky's office again, Mrs. Haversham."

Lydia smiled as she took her brother's arm.

"You won't, Dr. Armstrong," she promised. "You won't."

The lettering above the entrance stood twenty feet high: HAVERSHAM INDUSTRIES, INC. The ancient building was qualified to serve as a museum piece, an example of the rococo. Eight stories up, the door to the executive suite opened and a man and a woman came out into the hall. It was late. The hall lights cut a path through the darkness; the stairwell was a black hole with a small bright path at the bottom. Lydia Haversham advanced to the balustrade and looked down.

"How far it is," she said softly, "—and how empty. Are we really so alone, Charles? Is there no one else in the building?"

Charles Lacy, topcoat over his arm, scanned a pair of small green books held in his free hand.

"Our passports seem to be in order," he remarked. "We'd better get going if you still want to catch that midnight plane. . . . I'll say this for you, Lydia, when you decide to do a thing you don't waste any time."

"No more than necessary," Lydia murmured.

Charles stuffed the passports into a pocket of the topcoat, and then, for the first time, became aware of his sister's position at the balustrade.

"Lydia! Come away from there!"

But Lydia didn't move.

"It is a terrible fall, isn't it?" she said.

"You're not to think of that any more. It's all over. We're going away on a holiday and forget everything."

"Is it really that easy, Charles? Have you forgotten? Don't you ever hear his scream as he fell? Surely, he must have screamed . . ."

Lydia turned slowly as she spoke. Her eyes weren't sad any more. Her eyes were hard. She looked at Charles—a thin man with a pale moustache and a face that had gone chalk-white.

"Lydia—"

"But that wouldn't bother you, would it? You hated him. You were jealous of everything he had—everything he was. But you knew how to use him. You made yourself valuable to him with your great efficiency. That's what made me suspicious, Charles. After it was all over—the shock, and the funeral—I found myself wondering why my efficient brother made so many mistakes on one day. Why you forgot your passport in the office safe so Harlan had to go for it—why you forgot to tell him the men were coming to service the elevators that morning—*why you neglected to reserve the ticket you supposedly had to pick up at the airline office.*"

A thin man with a chalk-white face. Charles's mouth chewed at words that wouldn't come. Lydia's wouldn't stop.

"Yes, I checked on that. I discovered there was no

record of a reservation for Charles Lacy on any airline in the city that morning.''

Now Charles spewed out his words.

"You're talking nonsense! Airlines make mistakes. No record of a reservation isn't proof that none was made.''

Lydia smiled.

"I knew you'd say that—that's why I didn't tell the police. You're so much more clever than I. You would have explained everything—even the wire from South America—if there was a wire.''

She stood with her back against the balustrade, her hands grasping the railing at either side. She started to move slowly along the balustrade. She reached the first step . . . the second . . .

"This is the way it was, wasn't it?'' she said.

"Harlan here—starting down the stairs—and you behind him.''

"You don't know what you're saying!'' Charles cried. "You're imagining things again!''

"But I never imagine things, Charles. I've only been playing a game. Don't you remember the story of the shepherd boy who cried 'wolf' so many times when there was no wolf, that nobody believed him when the wolf did come? I've been crying 'murder' . . .''

"But why, Lydia? Why?''

Lydia looked at her brother. He was only a step away—a step that seemed to make him tower above her. She leaned back against the railing and looked at him long and hard.

"You wouldn't ask such a question if you could see your face, Charles. I've been watching it through all those confessions—watching, waiting for you to break. But not you! Not a man so wrapped up in hate! I think I might have forgiven you if you'd shown even a sign of regret—but it's too late now. I've played my game well. I could confess to a dozen crimes and nobody would believe me. But someday, somewhere—on a stairway, on the deck of a ship, on the mountain trail of some scenic tour, perhaps—someday I'll pay you back for killing my husband.''

Lydia's voice was calm and deliberate. Then the quiet came, the hollow, empty quiet of the blazing hall and the black gulf behind her. Her hands tightened on the rail.

"You tell me that," Charles said. "You idiot! Do you think I'm going to wait for you to kill me? Do you think I'm as big a fool as Harlan?"

She didn't think he'd wait, of course. Her weight shifted as he lunged toward her. Afterward, she wasn't sure if her foot had come out in a school-day trip, or if Charles had stumbled because his legs had become entangled in his topcoat. She never forgot how he plunged forward, how he started tumbling wildly down the stairs, until he struck the fragile supports of the balustrade and went through . . .

When the scream died away, Lydia Haversham opened her eyes. Charles's topcoat still dangled on the railing. She extended one gloved hand and pushed it over.

Her face was soft, her eyes were sad, and a ghost of a smile touched her lips.

"It could have happened to anybody," she whispered.

Edward D. Hoch has published well over 600 detective and mystery stories over the past thirty-odd years, including at least one in every issue of EQMM since 1973. Among his other accomplishments is editorship of the critically acclaimed annual Year's Best Mystery and Suspense Stories, *published by Walker. Perhaps the most appealing among the many series characters he has created for EQMM is Dr. Sam Hawthorne, a folksy country physician and amateur sleuth who reminisces about all sorts of "impossible" crimes in the 1920s to which he provided the solution. None of Dr. Sam's cases is more baffling than "The Problem of the County Fair," in which a dead body just could not—and yet somehow did—turn up inside a recently buried time capsule.*

THE PROBLEM OF THE COUNTY FAIR

Edward D. Hoch

(1977)

"Say now, I was gonna tell you about the county fair this time, wasn't I? Pull up a chair while I pour us a small—ah—libation. Close to the fire, where it's warm. This here's a summer story, but it's liable to chill you to the bone . . ."

It was in the summer of '27 (Dr. Sam Hawthorne went on), and I was settling into my medical practice nice and steady. We hadn't had a killing in Northmont since that election day mystery the year before, and for the first time I was thinkin' the Grim Reaper had gone and forgotten about us. Even my nurse, April, remarked on it as we were leavin' for the county fair that warm August morning.

"It's almost a year since the last killing, Dr. Sam. You think law an' order has finally come to Northmont?"

"I try not to think about it at all," I told her. "Afraid I might break the spell."

She piled into the yellow Pierce-Arrow Runabout, and I took the wheel. It was a short drive down Main Street and out the River Road to the fairgrounds. Usually it was a deserted place, on a slight hill not far from the river. The first thing we saw as it came into view was the grandstand surrounded by a high board fence painted a bright yellow. That and the little Ferris wheel off in the distance.

We parked the Runabout in a great, dusty field at the rear of the grandstand, and I could see from the number of cars that as usual the fair was attractin' visitors from all the surrounding counties. It was a big fair, a good fair, with lots of crowd-pleasing attractions. Though April shied away from the sideshow—the snake charmer, the fat lady, the scantily clad dancing girls, and the two-headed calf—they were popular with the men and boys who always found a way to separate themselves from the womenfolk.

There were gamblers, too, working their seedy con games, and they seemed to mostly prey on the young who knew no better. The older men, perhaps tired of the hootchy-kootchy girls after all these years, generally drifted down to the cattle show to inspect the animals. There, they stood around while their women went to the sheds where the cakes and pies and needlework were on display. The smaller children, tired and dusty-faced, usually accompanied the women—unless they could be palmed off on some willing older brother or sister.

"It's just so wonderful, Dr. Sam!" April exclaimed, her face alight with childish joy. "I wish the fair lasted the whole year long."

"But then it wouldn't be so wonderful," I argued logically. "In fact, I expect we'd all get bored with it quite soon."

"Look, there's Mayor Chadwick."

I never saw Felix Chadwick without remembering how his predecessor had been murdered at a Fourth o' July celebration three summers earlier. But it was doubtful that the same fate would ever befall Mayor Chadwick. He was a chicken farmer who had little use for even the ceremonial aspects of politics. I was surprised he'd even shown up—until I remembered about the time capsule.

The time capsule was Emma Thane's idea. She was the closest thing we had to a town historian, and she'd come up with some obscure evidence that in 1627 merchants and adventurers from William Bradford's Plymouth Colony had set up a trading post near the present site of Northmont. "In a way, it's our tercentennial," she'd announced at a meeting of the town council early that year, "and it should be celebrated properly."

Since Northmont had always been eager to fill the sky with fireworks on the Fourth o' July, there was some debate as to what form our tercentennial celebration should take. More fireworks? Bigger ones?

"No," said Emma Thane, pounding her knobby walking stick to be heard above the others. "We should bury a time capsule, to be opened a hundred years from now."

Well, the idea caught on right away, especially after Gus Antwerp from the Metal Works said he could make us a capsule out of sheet steel and even bury it for us, all at no cost to the town. It would be his contribution to the celebration and Mayor Chadwick was quick to accept the offer.

So here was the mayor himself bearin' down on April and me, trying to put aside chickens for a day of politics and pageantry. "Don't mean to horn in on you two. Mighty fine day, ain't it? Beamin' sun, not a cloud in the sky! It would be really goin' some to top a day like this."

"A fine day," I agreed. "And there's a goodly turnout for the fair. I see a lot of cars from outside the county."

"The bettin' attracts 'em," he confided, as if he was revealing some dark secret known only to the town council. "Are you ridin' in the afternoon races, Doc?"

It was a custom of our county fair to hold harness races on the oval track in front of the grandstand, with local citizens driving the sulkies. But it was not a sport that had ever appealed to me. "Not this year, Felix," I replied. I just never could bring myself to address him as Mayor.

"Well, I'll see you later at the time capsule. You brung somethin' to put in it?"

"Oh, sure."

He smiled at April and moved on, immediately swallowed up by the crowd headin' for the sideshow attractions. "That man!" April exploded when he was out of earshot. "I wonder if he'll go around passin' out free chickens again next election day. That's the only way he won last time."

"Oh, Felix isn't so bad. He's not up to the job, but does Northmont really need a mayor who's up to the job?"

April ran into some young women she knew, and they went off to the needlework exhibit. I wandered toward the sideshows, promising to meet her at the grandstand in an hour for the time-capsule ceremonies.

I was lingering near one of the gambling tables, watching a quick-fingered three-card monte operator, when a voice behind me said, "Dr. Hawthorne, I've had the most wonderful news!"

I recognized her voice even before I turned to accept the peck on the cheek with which she always greeted me. Gert Friar was a good friend, one of the livelier and more intelligent of Northmont's eligible young women. I'd made an effort to court her myself the previous summer, but it was obvious even then that her heart belonged to a fellow named Max McNear.

"The news must be about Max," I said at once, looking into her laughing blue eyes and hiding my disappointment that she still refused to even call me by my first name.

"He's coming home! He telephoned me from Cleveland three days ago. He should be here today."

"It'll be good seein' him again," I lied, smilin' all the time. Max McNear was something of an itinerant musician and troublemaker. He'd organized a small group to play country music for local square dances, and Gert had even sung with them a few times. That was how she met Max in the first place. But after a few dances where he'd gotten drunk on bootleg hooch and beaten up some local lads, he found himself pretty much ostracized by the community. By the end of last summer, Gert Friar was the only defender he had left. His return to Northmont now would bring a few grimaces to some of the townsfolk.

"I told him about the time-capsule ceremony and he said he'd be here in time for it."

"That's fine, Gert."

She fell into step beside me, the smile suddenly faded. "You've never really liked Max, have you, Dr. Hawthorne?"

"When you call me that I feel like your father. Please call me Sam."

"All right." The smile returned fleetingly. "Sam."

"Good! You know, I'm really not much older than you are."

"It seems you've been here forever, though. I remember you nursing me through the measles."

"I was right out of medical school then. It was the winter of '22 when I came here."

"Only five and a half years?"

"They were important years to you, Gert. You grew into a woman."

"I'm only twenty."

"And Max is—how old?"

"Thirty-one. I know—I've heard it all from my folks plenty of times. He's too old for me. He's no good. He drinks." Her voice grew softer. "But I love him, Sam."

"I remember you were pretty broken up when he left town."

"I guess it was the suddenness of it. One day he was here, the next day he was gone. He didn't even leave me a note."

"The police were after him. Sheriff Lens was going to throw him in jail after he beat up Mayor Chadwick's boy."

"I know. The drinking was no good for him. But he told me on the telephone that he's reformed now. He hasn't had a drink in months."

"Good for him!"

"You will be friendly to him, won't you, Sam? He has so few friends here. It would mean a lot to me."

"For you I'll be friendly to him." I glanced at my pocket watch and saw that it was almost noon. "But we'd better be gettin' over to the grandstand for the ceremonies or you might lose your job." Gert worked as a secretary for Gus Antwerp, and it seemed likely he'd want her on hand for the burying of his sheet-metal time capsule.

We joined the flow of the crowd toward the yellow-walled grandstand as the barkers made one last effort to lure folks into the hootchy-kootchy tent. But even the kids were deserting temporarily the pleasures and thrills of the Ferris wheel and the other rides to witness this moment of history. The first person we saw as we entered the grandstand was old Emma Thane, leanin' on her knobby walking stick and breathin' fire. She spotted Gert at once and blocked our path.

"Well, young lady, your man is back, I see."

"Max! He's here?"

"Darn near ran me off the road with that truck o' his! You tell him to be more considerate to people. If he's back in Northmont to make more trouble, you tell him we'd just as soon he stayed away."

"I'm sure he wasn't trying to harm you," Gert Friar

murmured. I could see she was mainly interested in gettin' past this woman and flyin' into Max NcNear's arms.

But Emma Thane wasn't yet ready to release us. "Folks hereabouts got to have the gumption to stand up to the likes of Max McNear. They got to tell him he has to live as part of the community. The law says we don't drink intoxicatin' beverages, and that law is the same for you and me and Max McNear."

"I'm sure he understands that, Miss Thane."

"Don't know that he does! Drove all over that road like he was drunk again. Just like the old days." But now she'd stepped aside and we were finally able to get by her. I made a parting comment on the beautiful weather and we entered the grandstand, where I got my first look at Gus Antwerp's time capsule.

He'd dug a hole for it in the very center of the oval field, around which ran the harness-racing track that would be put to use later in the afternoon. From my angle the capsule looked like a great silver cigar suspended upright from a block and tackle, its bottom already hidden by the piles of dirt around the hole. At the top of its eight-foot length, a hinged metal door stood open to receive the mementos of the community.

Mayor Chadwick, still tryin' to shake off his chicken-farmer's image, stood up and said a few appropriate words through a static-filled loudspeaker just purchased at county expense. Then Emma Thane came forward to be honored for her idea. The mayor helped her up the dirt pile so she could reach the door in the top of the erect capsule and deposit her memento—the day's newspaper. A line of schoolchildren followed. Some of the smaller ones had to be held in the mayor's arms to reach the door of the time capsule, where they deposited a selection of their textbooks.

I left Gert Friar in the stands, still searching for Max's familiar face, and made my way onto the field. Gus Antwerp, looking almost clean in his neatly pressed suit, shook my hand with vigor. "Good to see you here, Doc! Got a smidge o' something for my capsule?"

I pulled a booklet from my inside pocket. "Medical records for last year from the grammar school. A hundred years from now they might be interested in what made our kids sick."

"Great!"

I stared up at the sheet-metal capsule. "How long did it take you to build this thing?"

"Just part o' one night is all. I rolled the sheet and welded the seam, then fixed a flat piece to the bottom and put the door in the top."

Mayor Chadwick motioned me forward, announcing my name almost inaudibly over the faulty loudspeaker. It didn't matter, though. Just about everyone knew me, and a little cheer went up. I could see April at the edge of the crowd, waving to me.

I climbed up the dirt pile with my record book, taking time to peer down into the time capsule, inspectin' the thing out of sheer curiosity. The hinged door itself was round like the top of the capsule, and about two feet in diameter. With the sunlight from overhead I could see all the way to the bottom of the capsule, where the papers and books and other mementos were beginning to form a small pile. The capsule seemed too big for what little we were putting into it, but I was never one to criticize another man's labors. Besides, the thing looked great hangin' there from its ropes—almost like one of those spaceships on the cover of *Amazing Stories* magazine, pointed toward the stars.

I tapped the thin metal wall with my knuckles, wondering if it would really last a whole century, then I dropped my record book in among the other things and climbed down. A few small kitchen and farm implements went in next, together with some prizewinning recipes from the fair's baking contest. A picture of a prize bull, a Sears

Roebuck Catalogue, and Mayor Chadwick's copy of the town charter completed the collection.

As we all watched, the mayor closed the top of the capsule and Gus Antwerp sealed it with his bulky welding equipment. Then, like a ship's captain guiding his vessel through a narrow strait, Gus pulled out the metal support beneath the upright capsule and signaled for it to be lowered the rest of the way into the earth. There was a screeching of metal as it disappeared from view. Then the mayor handed Emma Thane a shovel decorated with a red ribbon and helped her throw in the first symbolic bit of earth.

I went to join April. "You were fine, Dr. Sam," she announced. "The whole thing was so moving! I wish I could be here a hundred years from now to see it dug up."

Before I could reply, Gert Friar joined us. Her deep blue eyes were wide with fright. "Dr. Haw—Sam, you've got to help me!"

"What is it?"

"I've been looking all over for Max and I finally found his truck. But he's not in it!"

"He's probably in the crowd somewhere."

"Sam, I think there are bloodstains on the front seat of the truck."

April and I exchanged glances. "I'll go look," I said quietly.

The truck was a Ford, and its canvas sides were painted with the words *Max's Music Makers*. It had been a familiar sight on the back roads of Northmont during the previous summer, before Max McNear's sudden disappearance. Now it had brought him back here—to what end?

"They're bloodstains," I confirmed. "But there could be lots of explanations. He might have cut his finger. Or it could even be animal blood."

"Do you believe that?" Gert asked.

I didn't answer directly. "We'll go look for him."

"I *have* looked. I've looked everywhere."

I tried to make a joke of it. "Bet you didn't look in the hootchy-kootchy tent."

"Sam, please."

"All right, I'll help you. April, you know Max McNear, don't you? We'll fan out over the fairgrounds and meet back at this truck in thirty minutes."

I took the sideshow route, checking the dancing girls' tent and the fat lady's booth. But there was no sign of the missing Max McNear. Near the end of the half hour I came upon Emma Thane, and I questioned her about the truck. "You said it nearly hit you, Miss Thane. What time was that?"

"Mebbe about eleven. Or a bit earlier. Did you see him?"

"We're looking. He seems to have disappeared again."

Just like a year ago, I couldn't help thinking.

Back at the truck, I learned that April and Gert had been no more successful. "I have to find him," Gert insisted. "Those bloodstains mean he's hurt."

Or dead, I added silently. But then another thought came to me. "Gert, are you sure it was Max you talked to on the telephone the other night? Long-distance lines can sound garbled at times, you know."

I saw her hesitate. "Well, of course it was Max. Why would he say he was if he wasn't."

"I don't know," I admitted.

"I'd be in a sorry state if I couldn't recognize Max's voice."

I watched some children running in and out of the crowd by the cake booth. Off in the distance the men were assembling for the afternoon's weight-hauling contest with teams of draft horses. Everything seemed as it should be, except for Max McNear's bloodstained truck. "Look," I said, "maybe Max didn't come back today."

"Didn't come back? Of course he came back!"

"Only Emma Thane saw him, and in truth she really saw just the truck. Gert, this is going to be very hard on you, but I have to say it. Maybe Max never came back because he never went away. He had a lot of enemies a year ago. Maybe one of them killed him."

Her sharp intake of breath was almost like a scream. "No, no, it was Max on the phone, I tell you!"

"All right," I agreed with a sigh. "Let's keep looking."

This time we agreed to meet at the grandstand for the harness races. April stayed with me, and as soon as we were alone she asked, "Do you really think he's dead, Dr. Sam?"

"I don't know what to think, April. Can you remember how things were a year ago? Who were Max's enemies?"

"All I know is what the talk was at the time. He beat up Mayor Chadwick's son awfully bad, you know."

"I remember that."

"Heck, anybody he met might have disliked Max McNear. He was that sort. Even Gert Friar mighta disliked him lf she caught him with some nineteen-year-old behind somebody's barn."

"Some gal was hornin' in on Gert?"

"No one gal, but I know there were some. With Max McNear you could tell by just lookin' at him."

"Gert was already out of high school then. Was she working for Gus Antwerp?"

April shook her head. "Remember? Gus didn't move here till the fall, after Max was long gone. Gert was at loose ends, and Gus needed a girl around the place, so he hired her."

I had one more place to look—the stables where the trotters were being prepared for the afternoon races. April came with me and we went through the stalls—but there was no Max McNear.

"Change your mind 'bout racin'?" Mayor Chadwick asked, encountering us there.

"No chance," I said. "I don't even drive buggies any more. Horseless carriages for me."

He walked with us out to the grandstand, where most of the people at the fair were once again assembled. Even the gamblers and con artists had closed up their games and were busy taking bets on the races. Out in the center of the oval, Gus Antwerp and a few others were finishing the burial of the time capsule. The block and tackle still hung over them—like an empty scaffold awaiting its next victim.

A cheer went up from the crowd as the first of the sulkies appeared on the oval track. But somethin' else had caught my eye—something white that fluttered in the afternoon breeze on the ground near the buried capsule. "Go find Gert," I told April. "I'll be right back."

I dashed across the dirt track and onto the grassy oval, headin' toward the men with their shovels. Gus Antwerp waved as he saw me approaching.

The thing on the ground was a book, its white pages flappin' open. It was one of the books the schoolchildren had brought to deposit in the time capsule—a seventh-grade arithmetic book.

Its pages were splattered with blood.

I found Mayor Chadwick in the reviewing stand, watchin' the parade of the sulkies. "You're just in time, Doc. Got your bets down? You know Sheriff Lens is drivin' one o' them things?"

"Mayor, I want you to order the time capsule dug up."

"The—what did you say?"

"The time capsule. You have to dig it up."

"What in tarnation for? You forget to put some love letters in it? Ha, ha!"

"I'm serious, Mayor. Max McNear has disappeared."

His face hardened. "McNear disappeared a year ago."

"And now he's disappeared again."

"Well, he sure ain't in that time capsule!"

I held out the blood-splattered arithmetic book. "*This* is supposed to be in the capsule and I found it out in the field. I think the capsule was opened again after it was buried."

"Impossible!"

"I know it's impossible, but impossible things have happened in Northmont before this. I should know—I'm becoming something of an expert on them."

"You're serious, ain't you, Doc?" he asked, squinting at me.

"Damned serious."

He sighed and started for the steps. "Let's see what Sheriff Lens thinks."

The sheriff was sitting in his sulky, trying to button the checkered silk shirt over his ample stomach. "I agreed to this in a weak moment," he rumbled as he saw us approaching. "I don't need none o' your jokes, Doc."

"Doc's not tellin' jokes today," Chadwick said. "He wants us to dig up the time capsule 'cause Max McNear's disappeared again."

"What are you talkin' about?"

I explained quickly, telling Sheriff Lens exactly what had happened. When I'd finished he snorted and climbed down off the sulky. "I think you got a screw loose, Doc, but to tell the truth I'd welcome any excuse not to have to drive this fool thing. Come on, let's dig."

Gus Antwerp put down his shovel as we approached and listened to our request. "We just got it buried and you want us to dig it up again?"

"That's right," I said.

"And when we get it dug up?"

"We want to open it and take a look inside."

"You're crazy! You're all crazy!"

I held out the bloodstained book. "This is crazy too, but it's a fact. There's blood in McNear's truck and blood on this book from the time capsule. I want it opened."

"But he *couldn't* be in there!" Antwerp insisted.

"I want to look all the same."

The balding man shrugged and handed me his shovel. "You got ten years on me, Doc. Go ahead and dig."

I started digging and the others joined in. When Antwerp saw we were serious he helped uncover the upper part of the capsule and got the ropes back around it. "The earth is still loose," he said. "We can probably pull it out with the block an' tackle."

A few of us got at the end of the rope but the capsule wouldn't budge. "Get a team of them draft horses," Sheriff Lens suggested. "They'll have it out in jigtime."

Someone went to get a team while the rest of us dug a little more. Up in the stands a low hum of conversation had grown into shouts of inquiry. They wanted to know what was going on and when the races would start. None of us answered them.

When the team was hooked up they pulled the metal cylinder free of the earth in less than a minute. We lowered it to the ground on its side and Gus Antwerp went to work with a chisel, knocking off the spot welds he'd made. Watchin' him work, I began to feel a little foolish.

Gert Friar and April had come out to watch as the time capsule was reopened. I tried to keep Gert back but she insisted on looking. And I heard her scream even before I could see inside myself.

Then April was holdin' her, and I was pushin' past the white-faced Sheriff Lens to peer in at the impossible. There, among the scattered books and tools consigned to the twenty-first century, was the body of Max McNear.

We tried to look at it logically.

Someone had built an underground tunnel to the capsule and gotten the body in that way.

Except that we dug all the loose earth out of the hole and found no tunnel. Found nothing but dirt.

Or maybe Gus Antwerp had the body hidden inside the capsule all the time.

Except that Gus didn't even know McNear, and I'd looked into the capsule myself and saw there was no body inside.

Or maybe the capsule had been dug up between noon and the time I found the bloodstained book.

Except that Antwerp and a couple of others were there filling in the hole. "I left for maybe ten minutes to get a hot dog," Gus said, "but there were people in the grandstand all the time, eatin' their lunches and watchin' us. That capsule never budged from the ground once it was buried."

We looked at it logically.

And logically it couldn't have happened.

"What killed him, Doc?" Sheriff Lens asked when we'd pulled the body out of the metal cylinder and I'd had a chance to examine it.

"Blow to the head with some sort of blunt instrument."

"He been dead long?"

"Hard to say in this hot weather, but he's been dead a good many hours. All bleeding's stopped and rigor mortis's pretty far advanced. I'd say he was already dead when Emma saw his truck this morning."

"Which means?"

"Which means he wasn't drivin' it. Maybe he was dead on the front seat and the killer was driving."

Sheriff Lens just grunted at that. "But look, Doc, if the bleedin' had stopped, how'd the blood get all over the arithmetic book you found? That looked like pretty fresh blood to me."

"I don't know," I admitted.

"Do dead bodies bleed?"

"Not as a rule. But the blood drains to the lowest point, and if there's a large wound at that point the blood could still be oozing out some time after death." I saw April coming and went to meet her. "How's Gert taking it?"

"Not very good, I'm afraid. You might have to give her a sleepin' powder. It's a terrible shock having him come back after a year, only to get killed."

"A shock and a damned shame. Who'd hold a grudge that long?"

April led me to the needlework tent, where Gert was resting on a cot. Old Emma Thane hovered over her, pressing a damp cloth to her forehead, and Gus Antwerp was holdin' her hand. "I keep tellin' her it'll be all right," he said. "But she's just not comin' around."

"It's been a shock," I said. "She'll be all right after a good rest. Why don't you all go away now?"

When Gert was alone with April and me, she opened her eyes and said, "I saw the top of his head when that door opened, Sam. His hair was all bloody."

She shuddered at her own words.

"Gert, I have to ask you some questions. It's either Sheriff Lens or me, and I thought you'd rather talk to me."

"What is it, Doc?"

"Who knew about that phone call from Cleveland? Who knew he was coming back today?"

"No one."

"Think harder, Gert. You told me when you saw me today. Maybe you told someone else, too. Did your boss know?"

She shook her head. "Gus never knew Max, so there was no reason for me to tell him. Oh, he'd probably heard me mention Max, but he never met him."

"How about Emma Thane?"

"Why would I tell her?"

"I don't know. She just didn't seem too surprised when she saw his truck this morning."

She sat up with a little jerk. "There was one person I told. He saw me yesterday and asked if I'd be at the ceremony for burying the time capsule. I said yes, and then I mentioned that Max would be back for it, too."

"Who was it you told?"

"Mayor Chadwick."

I found the mayor out by the grandstand, staring at the time capsule that still lay on its side by the dirt piles. He glanced at me with a bleak expression and said, "Damned clever way to get rid of a body, I do say that! Can you imagine their faces a hundred years from now if they opened it up an' found a skeleton?"

"About like our faces this afternoon," I suggested. The sun was low beyond the yellow fence. It was almost evening.

"Yeah," he agreed. "But who killed him, Doc?"

"It had to be someone who knew he was coming back. You knew, didn't you, Felix?"

"What's that?"

"Gert told you he was coming back today."

"She may have mentioned it. I didn't pay much attention."

"Whatever happened to that son of yours? The one Max beat up so bad."

"Joe's away at college," he answered stiffly.

"In the summer?"

He was silent for a moment. Then he said, "I might as well tell you. My wife would, if you asked her. Joe's never been right in the head since that beating. He's away at a hospital. He had to drop out of college."

I stared at where the sun had been, above the yellow fence. "Enough to drive a father to murder?"

He took a plug of chewing tobacco from his pocket. "Hell, I'd of just killed him and let him lay! The business of hidin' the body in a time capsule is beyond my imagination."

I tried to remember he was only a chicken farmer posing as a mayor. Maybe a murder scheme like this was beyond him.

"All right," I said at last. "I'll see you later, Felix."

"Findin' that body sure shot the hell out of our fair," he complained, more to himself than to me. "Had to cancel the harness racing, and a lot of the sideshow attractions people are packin' up. They don't want no truck with the police."

"It was a fine fair while it lasted," I told him.

I went off, anxious to reach the sideshow attractions before they'd all vanished. I found the barker at the girlie show and motioned him aside. "I need some information," I said.

He scowled. "Not from me, you don't."

"I'm not with the police. I'm a doctor."

"We didn't see a thing. Me an' the girls are clean."

"Sure you are. Look, sometimes sideshows do the stunt of burying someone alive—right?"

"Yeah," he said with a shrug. "I know a guy does it. Stays buried for the whole run of the fair. Folks pay a quarter to look down a tube an' see him resting in his coffin."

"How's it done?" I asked.

"Huh?"

"What's the trick?" I took a bill from my wallet and held it suggestively.

He grabbed the bill. "Don't say I told you."

"I won't."

"The body in the coffin is a wax dummy. As soon as he's buried he crawls out through a tunnel. Indian fakirs been doin' it for centuries."

"A tunnel . . ."

"Sure, what'd you think?"

I thanked him and went away. He hadn't helped me at all. There was no tunnel to the time capsule, and even if there had been, how could the body have passed through the solid metal sides of the cylinder itself?

I went back to the grandstand, deciding to have a final look at the capsule. Mayor Chadwick was gone, and dusk had settled over the field. A few kids playing on the mounds of dirt scattered as I approached.

For a long time I just stood and stared.

Suppose there were *two* capsules, and we'd dug up the second one. No, the books and papers and tools had all been there. Even my school medical log was there with the body. It was the same capsule.

But with a body inside.

I tapped my knuckles against the metal cylinder, as I'd done earlier.

Then I tapped again.

There wasn't the same ringing sound I'd heard this afternoon. Now the sound was different, more solid.

Then I remembered something else. I remembered the screeching of metal . . .

"So you know how it was done?" a voice behind me asked.

I turned and saw Emma Thane standing there in the dusk, her knobby walking stick held firmly in one hand.

For an instant I almost leaped at her, thinkin' to disarm her. But then she coughed gently and repeated her question, and I relaxed. I even smiled. "I think I do, Miss Thane. I think it's just come to me."

"He should never have come back. He wasn't wanted here. The past simply caught up with him."

"Oddly enough, I think it was the future that caught up with him."

"How's that?"

I tapped her walking stick with my finger. "You should be careful of this thing, Miss Thane. Someone might mistake it for a blunt instrument."

I walked away, leaving her standing by the time capsule that was part of her dream.

April was standing with Sheriff Lens by the needlework displays when I returned. "Where's Gert?" I asked.

"Her boss is drivin' her home," April replied.

I was done takin' chances with people's lives. "Come on, we've got to stop them! There could be another murder!" Already I was running toward my car.

April came after me. "You can't mean you think Gert killed Max!"

"Of course not."

The sheriff and April piled into the two-passenger front seat with me. "But Gus never even *knew* the dead man," Sheriff Lens argued.

"That's why he killed him," I replied, sounding like one of those paradoxes in G. K. Chesterton's stories. "Didn't you notice Gus holdin' Gert's hand earlier? It's not so strange for a middle-aged man like Gus Antwerp to imagine himself in love with his pretty twenty-year-old secretary. He never knew Max McNear, but he'd heard plenty about him from Gert and others. He imagined Gert would be swept off her feet by the return of her lover, before he could do anything about it. It wasn't Max's past but Gus Antwerp's future that supplied the motive."

Up ahead we could see the lights of Antwerp's truck. I beeped the horn and made as if I intended to pass him. Then I cut in front of the truck, forcing it to stop. Gus tried to yank Gert from the seat, but when he saw Sheriff Lens he let go and ran off toward the nearby woods. The sheriff took off after him.

"Are you all right?" I asked Gert.

She was rubbing her bruised wrist. "I—I guess so. He's gone crazy, Sam. He wanted me to run off with him tonight!"

"I was afraid he'd decide to run and take you with him. Once we found the body he knew it was only a matter of time before we figured it all out."

Sheriff Lens reappeared, alone. "Antwerp went into the river," he said. "I don't think he made it across."

We drove back to town, with the sheriff following at the wheel of Gus Antwerp's truck. He notified the state police to watch for Gus, just in case he'd survived the river. Then, back in the sheriff's office, it was my turn to talk some more.

"It was an odd, impossible crime—but once I figured how the body got into that time capsule, Gus was the only possible killer. You see, the body wasn't put in before the capsule was sealed, or after it was opened. So it passed through those sheet-metal walls somehow while the capsule was buried."

"You're makin' it sound even more impossible," the sheriff complained.

"Not really. When I tapped my knuckles on the capsule this evening it sounded different than before. More solid. And I remembered that screeching of metal as it was bein' lowered into the ground. If you examine it closely you'll see there are now *two* thicknesses of metal instead of one. Gus Antwerp put Max's body in a second cylinder, maybe an inch narrower than the one we saw. It was already in the ground, directly beneath the upright time capsule.

"After our mementos were in place, Gus pulled out the metal support—which was also the bottom of the time capsule. Everything fell through to the lower cylinder, which was open at the top, and where Max McNear's body was already hidden. Then Gus guided the larger top cylinder down so it fitted completely over the smaller bottom one beneath the ground. I suppose he greased the sides, but there was still that screeching of metal as they slid together. It was such a tight fit that when the capsule was dug up it looked like a single metal cylinder."

"How'd he do all that without being seen?" Sheriff Lens asked.

"It would have been easy last night, with no one around the fairgrounds. If anyone did see him unloading the second cylinder from his truck he could have said it was a spare. And once the narrower cylinder, containing the body, was beneath the ground there was no danger of its being seen. You'll remember the dirt was piled around the rim of the hole, and the top cylinder was partly in already, actually resting over the bottom one.''

"But how'd Antwerp know Max was comin' back?'' April asked. "Gert says she never told him.''

"We can make a good guess at that. Max was due back today, but he must have come a day early in order for Gus to have killed him and planted the body last night. It's logical to believe Max tried to phone Gert again about his change in plans. She was out and her boss took the call. Instead of givin' Gert the message, Gus Antwerp's love-crazed brain devised this scheme. He told me himself he made the capsule in less than one night. It was a simple job for him to make a second, slightly narrower, cylinder that would slide inside the first one.

"Gus waited for Max's arrival last night and probably killed him with a blow to the head in the front seat of Max's truck, leaving those bloodstains. Then he took the body and the cylinders to the fairground in his own truck. This morning he drove Max's truck to the fairground, nearly hittin' Emma Thane, so it would look as if Max arrived today on schedule and then disappeared again.''

Sheriff Lens grunted. "I've heard'a killers burying the bodies in some pretty clever places, but this is the first one I know who tried to bury a body in the next century!''

Dr. Sam Hawthorne took a sip of his drink as he concluded the story. "They found Antwerp's body in the river the next morning, and that was the end of it. Another small—ah—libation before you go? What's that? You're not satisfied? I didn't explain about the bloodstained arithmetic book?

"Well, April settled that the next day. One of the boys in line at the time capsule had a sudden nosebleed all over his book. He couldn't put it in the capsule like that, so he just dropped it on the ground, behind some dirt. It had nothing to do with the killing, except that it got me to dig up the capsule and find the body. I like to leave that part out of the story, 'cause it makes me look sort of foolish. I wish you hadn't asked.

"Next time? Well, 1927 was the year of the first talking movie. Northmont was a long way from Hollywood, but when a film company came there to shoot an early talking picture it had unexpected and deadly results. But that's for next time. Come now, let me refill your glass."

Loren D. Estleman writes contemporary detective fiction and historical Westerns with equal facility. One of his novels featuring Chandleresque and Detroit-based private eye Amos Walker, Sugartown, *was the recipient of a 1985 Private Eye Writers of America Shamus; and one of his Westerns,* Aces and Eights *(a chronicle of the life and death of Wild Bill Hickok) won a Western Writers of America Spur in 1982. "The Tree on Execution Hill," which appeared in AHMM and was Estleman's first published short story, is an effective blend of the two genres—a tale of mystery and history set in the modern West.*

THE TREE ON EXECUTION HILL

Loren D. Estleman

(1979)

It seemed as if everybody in Good Advice had turned out for the meeting that night in the town hall. Every seat was taken, and the dark oaken rafters hewn and fit in place by the ancestors of a good share of those present resounded with a steady hum of conversation, while the broad pine planks that made up the floor creaked beneath the tread of many feet.

Up in front, his plaid jacket thrown back to expose a generous paunch, Carl Lathrop, the town's leading store-keeper and senior member of the council, stood talking with Birdie Flatt from the switchboard. His glasses flashed a Morse code in the bright overhead lights as he settled and resettled them on his fleshy nose. I recognized the gesture from the numerous interviews I had conducted with him as a sign that he was feeling very satisfied with himself, and so I knew what was coming long before most of my neighbors suspected it.

I was something of a freak in the eyes of the citizenry of Good Advice, New Mexico. This was partly because I had been the first person to settle in the area since before 1951, when the aircraft plant had moved on to greener pastures, and partly because, at forty-two, I was at least ten years younger than anyone else in town. Most people supposed I stayed on out of despair after my wife Sylvia left me to return to civilization, but that wasn't strictly true. We'd originally planned to lay over for a week or two while I collected information for my book and then move on. But then the owner of the town newspaper had died and the paper was put up for sale, and I bought it with the money we'd saved up for the trip. It had been an act of impulse, perhaps a foolish one—certainly it had seemed so to my wife, who had no intention of living so far away from her beloved beauty parlors—but my chief fear in life had always been that I'd miss the big opportunity when it came along. So now I had a newspaper but no Sylvia, which, all things considered, seemed like a pretty fair trade.

The buzz of voices died out as Lathrop took his place behind the lectern. I flipped open my notebook and sat with pencil poised to capture any pearls of wisdom he might have been about to drop.

"We all know why we're here, so we'll dispense with the long-winded introductions." A murmur of approval rippled through the audience. "You've all heard the rumor that the state may build a superhighway near Good Advice," he went on. "Well, it's my pleasant duty to announce that it's no longer a rumor."

Cheers and applause greeted this statement, and it was some minutes before the room grew quiet enough for Lathrop to continue.

"Getting information out of these government fellows is

like pulling teeth," he said. "But after about a dozen phone calls to the capital, I finally got hold of the head of the contracting firm that's going to do the job. He told me they plan to start building sometime next fall." He waited until the fresh applause faded, then went on. "Now, this doesn't mean that Good Advice is going to become another Tombstone overnight. When those tourists come streaming in here, we're going to have to be ready for them. That means rezoning for tourist facilities, fixing up our historic landmarks, and so on. The reason we called this meeting is to decide on ways to make this town appealing to visitors. The floor is open to suggestions."

I spent the next twenty minutes jotting down some of the ideas that came from the enthusiastic citizens. Birdie Flatt was first, with a suggestion that the telephone service be updated, but others disagreed, maintaining that the old upright phones and wall installations found in many of the downtown shops added to the charm of the town. "Uncle Ned" Scoffield, at ninety-seven, Good Advice's oldest resident, offered to clean out and fix up the old trading post at the end of Main Street in return for permission to sell his wood carvings and his collection of hand-woven Navajo rugs. Carl Lathrop pledged to turn the old jail, which he had been using as a storeroom, into a tourist attraction. The fact that outlaw Ford Harper had spent his last days there before his hanging, he said, could only add to its popularity. Then, amidst a chorus of groans from scattered parts of the room, Avery Sharecross stood up.

Sharecross was a spindly scarecrow of a man, with an unkempt mane of lusterless black hair spilling over the collar of his frayed sweater and a permanent stoop that made him appear much older than he was. Nobody in town could say how he made his living. Certainly not from the bookstore he had been operating on the corner of Main and Maple for thirty years; there were never any more than two customers in the store at a time, and the prices he charged

were so ridiculously low that it was difficult to believe that
he managed to break even, let alone show a profit. Everyone was aware of the monthly pension he received from an
address in Santa Fe, but no one knew how much it was or
why he got it. His bowed shoulders and shuffling gait, the
myopia that forced him to squint through the thick, tinted
lenses of his eyeglasses, the hollows in his pale cheeks
were as much a part of the permanent scenery in Good
Advice as the burned-out shell of the old flour mill north
of town. I closed my notebook and put away my pencil,
knowing what he was going to talk about before he opened
his mouth. It was all he ever talked about.

Lathrop sighed. "What is it, Avery? As if I didn't
know." He rested his chin on one pudgy hand, bracing
himself for the ordeal.

"Mr. Chairman, I have a petition." The old bookseller
rustled the well-thumbed sheaf of papers he held in one
talonlike hand. "I have twenty-six signatures demanding
that the citizens of Good Advice vote on whether the tree
on Execution Hill be removed."

There was an excited buzz among the spectators. I sat
bolt upright in my chair, flipping my notebook back open.
How had the old geezer got twenty-five people to agree
with him?

For 125 years the tree in question had dominated the
high-domed hill two miles outside of town, its skeletal
limbs stretching naked against the sky. Of eighteen trials
that had been held in the town hall during the last century,
eleven of those tried had ended up swinging from the
tree's stoutest limb. It was a favorite spot of mine, an
excellent place to sit and meditate. Avery Sharecross, for
reasons known only to himself, had been trying to get the
council to destroy it for five years. This was the first time
he had not stood alone.

Lathrop cleared his throat loudly, probably to cover up
his own astonishment. "Now, Avery, you know as well as

I do that it takes fifty-five signatures on a petition to raise a vote. You've read the charter."

Sharecross was unperturbed. "When that charter was drafted, Mr. Chairman, this town boasted a population of over fourteen hundred. In the light of our present count, I believe that provision can be waived." He struck the pages with his fingertips. "These signatures represent nearly one-tenth of the local voting public. They have a right to be heard."

"How come you're so fired up to see that tree reduced to kindling, anyway? What's the difference to you?"

"That tree"—Sharecross flung a scrawny arm in the direction of the nearest window—"represents a time in this town's history when lynch law reigned and pompous hypocrites sentenced their peers to death regardless of their innocence or guilt." His cheeks were flushed now, his eyes ablaze behind the bottle-glass spectacles. "That snarl of dead limbs has been a blemish on the smooth face of this community for over a hundred years, and it's about time we got rid of it."

It was an impressive performance, and he sounded sincere, but I wasn't buying it. Good Advice, after all, had not been my first exposure to journalism. After you've been in this business awhile, you get a feeling for when someone is telling the truth, and Sharecross wasn't. Whatever reasons he had for wishing to destroy the town's oldest landmark, they had nothing to do with any sense of injustice. Of that I was certain.

Lathrop sighed. "All right, Avery, let's see your petition. If the signatures check out, we'll vote." Once the papers were in his hands, Lathrop called the other members of the town council around him to look them over. Finally, he motioned them back to their seats and turned back toward the lectern. For the next half hour he read off the names on the petition—many of which surprised me, for they included some of the town's leading citizens—to make sure the signatures were genuine. Every one of those mentioned spoke up to assure him that they were. At length the storekeeper laid the pages down.

"Before we vote," he said, "the floor is open to dissenting opinions.—Mr. Macklin?"

My hand had gone up before he finished speaking. I got to my feet, conscious of all the eyes upon me.

"No one is arguing what Mr. Sharecross said about the injustices done in the past," I began haltingly. "But tearing down something that's a large part of our history won't change anything." I paused, searching for words. I was a lot more eloquent behind a typewriter. "Mr. Sharecross says the tree reminds us of the sordid past. I think that's as it should be. A nagging reminder of a time when we weren't so noble is a healthy thing to have in our midst. I wouldn't want to live in a society that kicked its mistakes under the rug."

The words were coming easier now. "There's been a lot of talk here tonight about promoting tourist trade. Well, destroying a spot where eleven infamous badmen met their rewards is one sure way of aborting any claims we might have had upon shutter-happy visitors." I shook my head emphatically, a gesture left over from my college debating-club days. "History is too precious for us to turn our backs on it, for whatever reason. Sharecross and his sympathizers would do well to realize that our true course calls for us to turn our gaze forward and forget about rewriting the past."

There was some applause as I sat down, but it died out when Sharecross seized the floor again. "I'm not a philistine, Mr. Chairman," he said calmly. "Subject to the will of the council, I hereby pledge the sum of five thousand dollars for the erection of a statue of Enoch Howard, Good Advice's founder, atop Execution Hill once the tree has been removed. I, too, have some feeling for history." His eyes slid in my direction.

That was dirty pool, I thought as he took his seat amid thunderous cheering from those present. In one way or another, Enoch Howard's blood flowed in the veins of over a third of the population of Good Advice. Now I knew how he had obtained those signatures. But why? What did he hope to gain?

"What about expense?" someone said.

"No problem," countered Sharecross, on his feet again. "Floyd Kramer there has offered to bulldoze down the tree and cart it away at cost."

"That's true, Floyd?" Lathrop asked.

A heavy jowled man in a blue work shirt buttoned to the neck gave him the high sign from his standing position near the door.

I shot out of my chair again, but this time my eyes were directed upon my skeletal opponent and not the crowd. "I've fought you in print and on the floor of the town hall over this issue," I told him, "and if necessary I'll keep on fighting you right to the top of Execution Hill. I don't care how many statues you pull out of your hat, you won't get away with whatever it is you're trying to do."

The old bookseller made no reply. His eyes were blank behind his spectacles. I sat back down.

I could see that Lathrop's attitude had changed, for he had again taken to raising and lowering his eyeglasses confidently upon the bridge of his nose. Enoch Howard was his great-grandfather on his mother's side. "Now we'll vote," he said. "All those in favor of removing the tree on Execution Hill to make room for a statue of Enoch Howard signify by saying aye."

Rain was hissing on the grass when I parked my battered pickup truck at the bottom of the hill and got out to fetch the shovel out of the back. It was a long climb to the top and I was out of shape, but I didn't want to risk leaving telltale ruts behind by driving up the slope. Halfway up, my feet began to feel like lead and the blood was pounding in my ears like a pneumatic hammer; by the time I found myself at the base of the deformed tree I had barely enough energy left to find the spot I wanted and begin digging. It was dark, and the soil was soaked just enough so that each time I took out a shovelful the hole filled up again, with the result that it was ten mintutes before I made any progress at all. After half an hour I stopped to rest. That's when all the lights came on and turned night into day.

The headlights of half a dozen automobiles were trained full upon me. For a fraction of a second I stood unmoving, frozen with shock. Then I hurled the shovel like a javelin at the nearest light and started to run. The first step I took landed in the hole. I fell headlong to the ground, emptying my lungs and twisting my ankle painfully. When I looked up, I was surrounded by people.

"I've waited five years for this." The voice belonged to Avery Sharecross.

"How did you know?" I said when I found my breath.

"I never did. Not for sure." Sharecross was standing over me now, an avenging angel wearing a threadbare coat and scarf. "I once heard that you spent all the money you had on the newspaper. If that was true, I wondered what your wife used for bus fare back to Santa Fe when she left you. Everyone knew you argued with her bitterly over your decision to stay. That you lost control and murdered her seemed obvious to me.

"I decided you buried her at the foot of the hanging tree, which was the reason you spent more time here than anyone else. The odds weren't in favor of my obtaining permission to dig up the hill because of a mere supposition, so it became necessary to catch you in the act of unearthing her yourself. That's when I got the idea to propose removing the tree and force you to find someplace else to dispose of the body."

He turned to a tall man whose Stetson glistened wetly in the unnatural illumination of the headlights at his back. "Sheriff, if your men will resume digging where Mr. Macklin left off, it's my guess you'll find the corpse of Sylvia Macklin before morning. I retired from the Santa Fe Police Department long before they felt the need to teach us anything about reading rights to those we arrested, so perhaps you'll oblige."

From 1966—when his first short story, "You Don't Know What It's Like," appeared in Shell Scott Mystery Magazine—*to the early 1980s, Bill Pronzini contributed nearly 200 criminous tales to the crime-fiction digests. Among these were the first recorded cases of his popular series sleuth, the "Nameless Detective," several of which were gathered together in the 1983 "Nameless" collection,* Casefile. *"Bank Job," a nonseries short published in EQMM, was said by Ellery Queen (Frederic Dannay) to be "an ingenious crime story whose unfolding will be one step ahead of your anticipations—because of a protagonist who is a master of improvisation . . ."*

BANK JOB

Bill Pronzini

(1978)

I was standing beside the tellers' cages, in the railed-off section where the branch manager's desk was located, when the knocking began on the bank's rear door.

Frowning, I looked over in that direction. Now, who the devil could that be? It was four o'clock and the Fairfield branch of the Midland National Bank had been closed for an hour; it seemed unlikely that a customer would arrive at this late time.

The knocking continued—a rather curious sort of summons, I thought. It was both urgent and hesitant, alternately loud and soft in an odd spasmodic way. I glanced a bit uneasily at the suitcase on the floor beside the desk. But I could not just ignore the rapping. Judging from its insistence, whoever it was seemed to know that the bank was still occupied.

I went out through the grate in the rail divider and walked slowly down the short corridor to the door. The shade was drawn over the glass there—I had drawn it myself earlier—and I could not see out into the private parking area at the rear. The knocking, I realized as I stepped up to the door, was coming from down low on the wood panel, beneath the glass. A child? Still frowning, I drew back the edge of the shade and peered out.

The person out there was a man, not a child—a medium-sized man wearing a mustache, modishly styled hair, and a business suit and tie. He was down on one knee, with his right hand stretched out to the door; his left hand was pressed against the side of his head, and his temple and the tips of his fingers were stained with what appeared to be blood.

He saw me looking out at about the same time I saw him. We blinked at each other. He made an effort to rise, sank back onto his knee again, and said in a pained voice that barely carried through the door, "Accident . . . over in the driveway . . . I need a doctor."

I peered past him. As much of the parking area as I could see was deserted, but from my vantage point I could not make out the driveway on the south side of the bank. I hesitated, but when the man said plaintively, "Please . . . I need help," I reacted on impulse: I reached down, unlocked the door, and started to pull it open.

The man came upright in one fluid motion, drove a shoulder against the door, and crowded inside. The door edge cracked into my forehead and threw me backward, off-balance. My vision blurred for a moment, and when it cleared and I had my equilibrium again, I was looking not at one man but at two.

I was also looking at a gun, held competently in the hand of the first man.

The second one, who seemed to have materialized out

of nowhere, closed and relocked the door. Then he too produced a handgun and pointed it at me. He looked enough like the first man to be his brother—medium-sized, mustache, modishly styled hair, business suit, and tie. The only appreciable difference between them was that One was wearing a blue shirt and Two a white shirt.

I stared at them incredulously. "Who are you? What do you want?"

"Unnecessary questions," One said. He had a soft, well-modulated voice, calm and reasonable. "It should be obvious who we are and what we want."

"My God," I said, "bank robbers."

"Bingo," Two said. His voice was scratchy, like sand rubbing on glass.

One took a handkerchief from his coat pocket and wiped the blood—or whatever the crimson stuff was—off his fingers and his temple. I realized as he did so that his mustache and hair, and those of the other man, were of the theatrical-makeup variety.

"You just do what you're told," One said, "and everything will be fine. Turn around, walk up the hall."

I did that. By the time I stopped again in front of the rail divider, the incredulity had vanished and I had regained my composure. I turned once more to face them.

"I'm afraid you're going to be disappointed," I said.

"Is that right?" One said. "Why?"

"You're not going to be able to rob this bank."

"Why aren't we?"

"Because all the money has been put inside the vault for the weekend," I said. "And I've already set the time locks; the vault doors can't be opened by hand and the time locks won't release until nine o'clock Monday morning."

They exchanged a look. Their faces were expressionless, but their eyes, I saw, were narrowed and cold. One said to Two, "Check out the tellers' cages."

Two nodded and hurried through the divider gate.

One looked at me again. "What's your name?"

"Luther Baysinger," I said.

"You do what here, Luther?"

"I'm the Fairfield branch manager."

"You lock up the money this early every Friday?"

"Yes."

"How come you don't stay open until six o'clock?"

I gestured at the cramped old-fashioned room. "We're a small branch bank in a rural community," I said. "We do a limited business; there has been no need for us to expand our hours."

"Where're the other employees now?"

"I gave them permission to leave early for the weekend."

From inside the second of the two tellers' cages Two called, "Cash drawers are empty."

One said to me, "Let's go back to the vault."

I pivoted immediately, stepped through the gate, entered the cages, and led the two of them down the walkway to the outer vault door. One examined it, tugged on the wheel. When it failed to yield he turned back to me.

"No way to open this door before Monday morning?"

"None at all."

"You're *sure* of that?"

"Of course I'm sure. As I told you, I've set the time locks—here, and on the door to the inner vault as well. The inner vault is where all the bank's assets are kept."

Two said, "Damn. I knew we should have waited when we saw the place close up. Now what do we do?"

One ignored him. "How much is in that inner vault?" he asked me. "Round numbers."

"A few thousand, that's all," I said carefully.

"Come on, Luther. How much is in there?"

His voice was still calm and reasonable, but he managed nonetheless to imply a threat to the words. If I continued to lie to him, he was saying tacitly, he would do unpleasant things to me.

I sighed. "Around twenty thousand," I said. "We have no need for more than that on hand. We're—"

"I know," One said, "you're a small branch bank in a rural community. How many other people work here?"

"Just two."

"Both tellers?"

"Yes."

"What time do they come in on Monday morning?"

"Nine o'clock."

"Just when the vault locks release."

"Yes. But—"

"Suppose you were to call up those two tellers and tell them to come in at nine-thirty on Monday, instead of nine o'clock. Make up some kind of excuse. They wouldn't question that, would they?"

It came to me then, all too clearly, what he was getting at. A coldness settled on my neck and melted down along my back. "It won't work," I said.

He raised an eyebrow. "What won't work?"

"Kidnapping me and holding me hostage for the weekend."

"No? Why not?"

"The tellers *would* know something was wrong if I asked them to come in late on Monday."

"I doubt that."

"Besides," I lied, "I have a wife, three children, and a mother-in-law living in my house. You couldn't control all of them for an entire weekend."

"So we won't take you to your house. We'll take you somewhere else and have you call your family and tell them you've been called out of town unexpectedly."

"They wouldn't believe it—"

"I think they would. Look, Luther, we don't want to hurt you. All we're interested in is that twenty thousand. We're a little short of cash right now; we need operating capital." He shrugged and looked at Two. "How about it?"

"Sure," Two said. "Okay by me."

"Let's go out front again, Luther."

A bit numbly I led them away from the vault. When we passed out of the tellers' cages, my eyes went to the suitcase beside the desk and lingered on it for a couple of seconds. I pulled my gaze away then—but not soon enough.

One said, "Hold up right there."

I stopped, half-turning, and when I saw him looking past me at the suitcase I grimaced.

One noticed that, too. "Planning a trip somewhere?" he asked.

"Ah . . . yes," I said. "A trip, yes. To the state capital—a bankers' convention. I'm expected there tonight and if I don't show up people will know something is wrong—"

"Nuts," One said. He glanced at Two. "Take a look inside that suitcase."

"Wait," I said, "I—"

"Shut up, Luther."

I shut up and watched Two lift the suitcase to the top of the desk, next to the nameplate there that read *Luther Baysinger, Branch Manager*. He snapped open the catches and swung up the lid.

Surprise registered on his face. "Hey," he said, "money. It's filled with *money*."

One stepped away from me and went over to stand beside Two, who was rifling through the packets of currency inside the suitcase. A moment later Two hesitated, then said, "What the hell?" and lifted out my .22 Colt Woodsman, which was also inside the case.

Both of them looked at me. I stared back defiantly. For several seconds it was very quiet in there; then, because there was nothing else to be done, I lowered my gaze and leaned against the divider.

"All right," I said, "the masquerade is over."

One said, "Masquerade? What's that supposed to mean, Luther?"

"My name isn't Luther," I said.

"What?"

"The real Luther Baysinger is locked inside the vault."

"What?"

"Along with both tellers."

Two said it this time, "What?"

"There's around eight thousand dollars in the suitcase," I said. "I cleaned it out of the cash room in the outer vault not long before you showed up."

"What the hell are you telling us?" One said. "Are you saying you're—"

"The same thing you are, that's right. I'm a bank robber."

They looked at each other. Both of them appeared confused now, no longer quite so sure of themselves.

One said, "I don't believe it."

I shrugged. "It's the truth. We both seem to have picked the same day to knock over the same bank, only I got here first. I've been casing this place for a week; I doubt if you cased it at all. A spur-of-the-moment job, am I right?"

"Hell," Two said to One, "he *is* right. We only just—"

"Be quiet," One said, "let me think." He gave me a long, searching look. "What's your name?"

"John Smith."

"Yeah, sure."

"Look," I said, "I'm not going to give you my right name. Why should I? You're not going to tell me yours."

One gestured to Two. "Frisk him," he said. "See if he's carrying any identification."

Two came over to me and ran his hands over my clothing, checked inside all the pockets of my suit. "No wallet," he said.

"Of course not," I said. "I'm a professional, same as you are. I'm not stupid enough to carry identification on a job."

Two went back to where One was standing and they held

a whispered conference, giving me sidewise looks all the while. At the end of two minutes, One faced me again.

"Let's get this straight," he said. "When did you come in here?"

"Just before three o'clock."

"And then what?"

"I waited until I was the last person in the place except for Baysinger and the two tellers. Then I threw down on them with the Woodsman. The inner vault was already time-locked, so I cleaned out the tellers' drawers and the cash room, and locked them in the outer vault."

"All of that took you an hour, huh?"

"Not quite. It was almost quarter-past three before the last customer left, and I spent some time talking to Baysinger about the inner vault before I was convinced he couldn't open it. I was just getting ready to leave when you got here." I gave him a rueful smile. "It was a damned foolish move, going to the door without the gun and then opening up for you. But you caught me off-guard. That accident ploy is pretty clever."

"It's a good thing for you that you didn't have the gun," Two said. "You'd be dead now."

"Or you'd be," I said.

We exchanged more silent stares.

"Anyhow," I said at length, "I thought I could bluff you into leaving by pretending to be Baysinger and telling you about the time locks. But then you started that kidnapping business. I didn't want you to take me out of here because it meant leaving the suitcase; and if you did kidnap me, and I was forced to tell you the truth, you'd dump me somewhere and come back for the money yourselves. Now you've got it anyway—the game's up."

"That's for sure," One said.

I cleared my throat. "Tell you what," I said. "I'll split the eight thousand with you, half and half. That way, we all come out of this with something."

"I've got a better idea."

I knew what was coming, but I said, "What's that?"

"We take the whole boodle."

"Now wait a minute—"

"We've got the guns, and that means we make the rules. You're out of luck, Smith, or whatever your name is. You may have gotten here first, but we got here at the right time."

"Honor among thieves," I said. "Hah."

"Easy come, easy go," Two said. "You know how it is."

"All right, you're taking all the money. What about me?"

"What about you?"

"Do I get to walk out of here?"

"Well, we're sure as hell not going to call the cops on you."

"You did us sort of a favor," One said, "taking care of all the details before we got here. So we'll do you one. We'll tie you up in one of these chairs—not too tight, just tight enough to keep you here for ten or fifteen minutes. When you work yourself loose you're on your own."

"Why can't I just leave when you do?"

One gave me a faint smile. "Because you might get a bright idea to follow us and try to take the money back. We wouldn't like that."

I shook my head resignedly. "Some bank job this turned out to be."

They tied me up in the chair behind the desk, using my necktie and my belt to bind my hands and feet. After which they took the suitcase, and my Colt Woodsman, and went out through the rear door and left me alone.

It took me almost twenty minutes to work my hands loose. When they were free I leaned over to untie my feet and stood up wearily to work the kinks out of my arms and legs. Then I sat down again, pulled the phone over in front of me, and dialed a number.

A moment later a familiar voice said, "Police Chief Roberts speaking."

"This is Luther Baysinger, George," I said. "You'd better get over here to the bank right away. I've just been held up."

Chief Roberts was a tall wiry man in his early sixties, a competent law officer in his own ponderous way; I had known him for nearly thirty years. While his two underlings, Burt Young and Frank Dawes—the sum total of Fairfield's police force—hurried in and out, making radio calls and looking for fingerprints or clues or whatever, Roberts listened intently to my account of what had happened with the two bank robbers. When I finished he leaned back in the chair across the desk from me and wagged his head in an admiring way.

"Luther," he said, "you always did have more gall than any man in the county. But this business sure does take the cake for pure nerve."

"Am I to take that as a compliment, George?" I said a bit stiffly.

"Sure," he said. "Don't get your back up."

"The fact of the matter is, I had little choice. It was either pretend to be a bank robber myself or spend the weekend at the mercy of those two men. And have them steal all the money inside the vault on Monday morning—approximately forty thousand dollars, not twenty thousand as I told them."

"Lucky thing you had that Woodsman of yours along. That was probably the clincher."

"That, and the fact that I wasn't carrying my wallet. I was in such a hurry this morning that I left it on my dresser at home."

"How come you happened to have the .22?"

"It has been jamming on me in target practice lately," I said. "I intended to drop it off at Ben Ogilvie's gunsmith shop tonight for repairs."

"How'd you know those two hadn't cased the bank beforehand?"

"It was a simple deduction. If they had cased the bank, they would have known who I was; they wouldn't have had to ask."

Roberts wagged his head again. "You're something else, Luther. You really are."

"Mmm," I said. "Do you think you'll be able to apprehend them?"

"Oh, we'll get them, all right. The descriptions you gave us are pretty detailed; Burt's already sent them out to the county and state people and to the FBI."

"Fine." I massaged my temples. "I had better begin making an exact count of how much money they got away with. I've called the main branch in the capital and they're sending an official over as soon as possible. I imagine he'll be coming with the local FBI agent."

Roberts rose ponderously. "We'll leave you to it, then." He gathered Young and Dawes and prepared to leave. At the door he paused to grin at me. "Yes, sir," he said, "more damned gall—and more damned luck—than any man in this county."

I returned to my desk after they were gone and allowed myself a cigar. I felt vastly relieved. Fate, for once, had chosen to smile on me; I had, indeed, been lucky.

But for more reasons than Roberts thought.

I recalled his assurance that the bank robbers would soon be apprehended. Unfortunately—or fortunately, depending on the point of view—I did not believe they would be apprehended at all. Mainly because the description of them I had given Roberts was totally inaccurate.

I had also altered my story in a number of other ways. I had told him the outer vault door had not only been unlocked—which was the truth; despite my lie to the two robbers, I had not set any of the time locks—but that it had been open and the money they'd stolen was from the cash room. I had said the robbers brought the suitcase with them, not that it belonged to me, and that the Woodsman had been in my overcoat pocket when they discovered it. I had omitted mention of the fact that I'd supposedly called their attention to the suitcase in order to carry out my bank-robber ruse.

And I had also lied about the reasons I was not carrying my wallet and why I had the Woodsman with me. In truth, I had willfully left the wallet at home and put the gun into the suitcase because of an impulsive, foolish, and half-formed idea that, later tonight, I *would* attempt to hold up a business establishment or two somewhere in the next county.

I would almost certainly *not* have gone through with that scheme, but the point was that I had got myself into a rather desperate situation. The bank examiners were due on Monday for their annual audit—a month earlier than usual in a surprise announcement—and I had not been able to replace all of the $14,425.00 that I had "borrowed" during the past ten months to support my regrettable penchant for betting on losing horses.

I had, however, managed on short notice to raise $8,370.00 by selling my car and my small boat and disposing of certain semi-valuable heirlooms. The very same $8,370.00 that had been in the suitcase, and that I had been about to *put back* into the cash room when the two robbers arrived.

As things had turned out, I no longer had to worry about replacing the money or about the bank examiners discovering my peccadillo. Of course, I would have to be considerably more prudent in the future where my predilection for the Sport of Kings was concerned. And I would be; I am not one to make the same mistake twice. I may have a lot of gall, as Roberts had phrased it, and I may be something of a rogue, but for all that I'm neither a bad nor an unwise fellow. After all, I *had* saved most of the bank's money, hadn't I?

I relaxed with my cigar. Because I had done my "borrowing" from the vault assets without falsifying bank records, I had nothing to do now except to wait patiently for the official and the FBI agent to arrive from the state capital. And when they did, I would tell them the literal truth.

"The exact total of the theft," I would say, "is $14,425.00."

Missourian John Lutz has been a frequent contributor to the digest-size mystery magazines for more than twenty years. His stories run the gamut of criminous types—detective tales featuring St. Louis private eye Alo Nudger (two of which, both published in AHMM, have been the recipients of an MWA Edgar and a Private Eye Writers of America Shamus); psychological suspense; the Hitchcockian twist; offbeat humor. No one writing today does the reductio ad absurdum *story better than Lutz, and ''Discount Fare'' is one of his best of this type.*

DISCOUNT FARE

John Lutz

(1979)

Milner hurried through the bustling terminal building, clutching his scuffed, brown two-suiter suitcase. Around him fellow travelers were striding purposefully in the same direction, some of them carrying attaché cases or carry-on garment bags. A nasal voice on the airport's public-address system droned in the background announcing departing and arriving flights.

As Milner approached the Small World Airways reservation counter, he was glad to see that there was only a short line. The trip to New York on business had come up unexpectedly, and his secretary had phoned for his reservation. He had only to pick up his boarding pass, check his luggage, and walk to the departure gate on the lower concourse.

The line moved quickly, and when Milner reached the

counter a blue-vested SWA reservations clerk smiled prettily at him. He smiled back and told her his name and that he had a reservation.

After punching some buttons and scanning the screen of a small gray computer, the girl glanced up at him, no longer smiling.

"This line is for full-fare passengers, sir. I'm afraid you'll have to join that line." She pointed to a long line at the other end of the counter.

"Don't I have a full-fare ticket? My secretary made the reservation."

"You have our Small World Airways Cheap-Chargers Six-City discount ticket, sir."

"Well, couldn't I—"

"I'm sorry, sir, it's too late to change your reservation. The flight leaves in twenty minutes."

A small man with a sharply receding hairline and mild blue eyes, Milner knew from experience that he wasn't the persuasive type. Besides, there was no time to argue. He nodded to the girl and joined the longer line.

Milner found himself standing behind a heavyset woman carrying a child of about three. The child—Milner couldn't be sure of its sex—glared over the woman's shoulder at him with absolute hostility.

Ten minutes later, when Milner was halfway to the counter, the child spat at him. Milner backed up a step and looked around to see if anyone else had witnessed this extraordinary breach of etiquette. When he turned back he found that a large man carrying a black sample case had crowded into line ahead of him. Milner cursed silently but said nothing.

Finally he reached the counter. A squat woman with acne and a huge nose soberly filled out his boarding pass.

"I have one suitcase to check," Milner told her.

"Discount-fare passengers must carry on luggage under twenty-four by seven by twenty inches," she informed him, squinting over the counter at his suitcase.

"I've never measured—"

"You'll have to carry that one on with you, sir." She handed him his boarding pass.

"But I've always checked this suitcase."

"Gate twenty-nine," she said.

An elbow jabbed into Milner's ribs and he was forced aside. He lifted his suitcase and began walking toward the gate.

When he reached the departure gate, he was surprised to see that there were few people in line waiting to board the plane. He handed his boarding pass to the attendant to process. He was not asked for a seat preference. Careful to avoid the fat woman with the hateful child, he joined the line several passengers behind her.

When they boarded the plane, Milner saw that the first-class and full-fare passengers had already boarded and were drinking complimentary cocktails. The plane was going to be full. A sign proclaimed that the rear of the plane was where discount-fare passengers were to sit. There was a mild scramble for seats. Milner found himself beside the fat woman with the malevolent child.

"I'm sorry," she said as the child kicked Milner. "He's a problem, Damon is. Probably always will be."

"I hope not," Milner told her, and fastened his seat belt.

His suitcase wouldn't quite fit beneath the seat, and when he pointed this out to a stewardess she informed him that he would have to hold it on his lap.

"I thought that was against safety regulations," Milner said.

"The regulations have been waived for discount-fare passengers, sir," she said, hurrying off.

It would only be for a few hours, Milner assured himself, squeezing the heavy suitcase onto his lap, then he would be off the plane and in the comparatively courteous atmosphere of a New York taxi. The plane took off smoothly. A small clenched fist began to beat on Milner's suitcase as if it were a drum.

Shortly after they reached cruising altitude, the stewardesses began rolling their service tray along the aisle as they handed out SWA lunches and beverages. Milner watched the two attractive women bend gracefully and smile, not once spilling a drop of coffee or soda.

By the time they reached the tail section, the plane was flying through rough air. Milner could feel every bump against the firm upholstery as his body was compressed by the heavy suitcase.

A stewardess handed him a watercress sandwich and a bag of cheese snacks. This didn't look at all like the food served to the full-fare passengers.

"I'll have a cup of coffee," Milner told the stewardess.

She poured it dutifully and handed Milner the scalding paper cup. "That will be one dollar."

Milner looked up at her in surprise, balancing the lunch and the hot cup on his suitcase. "I thought meals were complimentary."

"They are, sir, but not the beverages—for discount-fare passengers."

Milner contorted himself beneath his burden and extracted a dollar from his wallet.

When the stewardess had gone, he looked at his meal. At least the lettuce in the sandwich was fresh. He'd skipped lunch, so he was hungry enough to settle for anything. He peered closely. There was a small bear-shaped cookie floating in his coffee. As he watched, the hot liquid disintegrated it.

Milner ate the sandwich and cheese snacks but skipped the coffee. Next to him a tiny voice began to complain about the missing cookie.

When they'd been airborne for over an hour, the captain's voice came over the speaker system announcing that they would soon put down in Pittsburgh and that the weather there was fine.

Pittsburgh? Milner was going to New York! He began signaling frantically for the stewardess, who was adjusting the seat of a full-fare passenger. Pinned as he was in his own seat, Milner waved both arms and a leg violently until the stewardess glanced in his direction. A moustached man across the aisle shook his head and pretended to read a paperback novel, obviously disdainful of Milner.

When the petite blonde stewardess arrived, Milner asked why they were landing in Pittsburgh.

She arched elongated, penciled eyebrows. "Why, it's our destination, sir."

"But I'm going to New York. My ticket says New York!"

She produced an SWA smile. "Yes, sir. But there's a two-hour layover in Pittsburgh."

"My ticket doesn't say that!"

"It must, sir."

Shifting the weight of his suitcase, Milner withdrew his ticket and examined it. The stewardess was right.

"Full-fare passengers are booked on the through flight to New York, sir. All discount-fare passengers change planes at Pittsburgh."

"But I don't *want* to stop at Pittsburgh!"

She looked at him oddly—"I'm sorry, sir"—and moved smartly up the aisle.

"I have to be in New York before three o'clock," Milner said to the woman beside him. "On business."

She nodded unconcernedly. The child in her lap glared at Milner.

The plane flew through a sharp downdraft and the tail section lurched crazily, its motion exaggerated by its distance from the wings. Milner had forgotten about his coffee. The now-icy liquid spilled over his suitcase and down onto his pants. He was wearing a new suit, and the coffee would stain unless he could dilute it with water. Milner reached beneath the sopping suitcase and worked to unbuckle his seat belt. He attempted to smile at the woman but couldn't. "Pardon me," he said, "I have to go to the rest room."

She stared ahead as if he'd suggested something vulgar.

When his seat belt was unbuckled, he tried to swivel in his seat so he could stand, and in the process drove a corner of the suitcase into Damon's chubby side. Finally upright in the aisle, Milner bent forward to apologize. That was when Damon grabbed a ballpoint pen from Milner's pocket and plunged it into Milner's left ear.

Milner retrieved his pen and, his hand clamped to his wounded ear, he teetered to the rear of the plane.

Inside the cold, confining rest room, he forgot about toweling the stain from his pants. The ringing in his horribly aching ear was maddening, causing him occasionally to shudder.

Pittsburgh! He didn't want to go to Pittsburgh!

Methodically, hardly conscious of what he was doing, he unwrapped several of the small bars of soap and held them under the water until they'd soaked and welded into one another. Then, with fingers possessed, he began to mold them into the form of a gun.

When the gun was finished he let it dry to firmness, then slipped it into his suit-coat pocket. If he covered it with a handkerchief it would seem real enough.

He left the rest room and made his way toward the blonde stewardess, who was standing near the door to the pilot's compartment. A few of the full-fare passengers glanced at him as he went by.

"This is a gun," he said softly to the stewardess. He saw her eyes widen, fooled by the carefully molded contour beneath the white handkerchief. "Into the pilot's compartment," he commanded.

"What is this?" the pilot asked as they entered. He'd been reading a news magazine while occasionally checking the automatic pilot. "Regulations forbid anyone unauthorized in the cockpit."

"He's got a gun," the stewardess whispered.

The copilot, who had been idly toying with an unlighted cigarette, glanced around quickly and began to stand.

"Steady, Harry," the pilot said. Harry settled back down in his seat. "What do you want?" the pilot asked.

The ringing in Milner's ear was almost gone now, but it was of higher pitch. "We're going where I say."

"Cuba?"

"New York. And not Newark Airport. La Guardia. It costs a fortune to take a cab from Newark."

"But you have a connecting flight to New York from Pittsburgh," the stewardess said impatiently.

"Change course," Milner told the pilot, who nodded resignedly.

The plane banked sharply and began its turn.

The stewardess stumbled into Milner and the copilot stood up and grabbed at the gun. As the two men struggled, the soap flew out from between them onto the floor beneath the copilot's seat. The stewardess and the pilot scrambled for it. The stewardess found it, straightened, and tried to point it at Milner, but it slipped from her grasp.

"It's not a real gun!" the pilot cried, and, standing, he struck Milner with his fist. Milner sank to the cockpit floor and pretended to be unconscious.

"The controls!" the copilot said in alarm. "We're losing altitude!"

"There's no cause for concern," the pilot said. "I can set us down." The smooth tailoring of his uniform lent confidence.

There was a hurried conference between the pilot, copilot, and stewardess and Milner could hear the passengers in a turmoil on the other side of the closed door. The stewardess went out to calm them.

"We're having mechanical difficulties," she said in an almost-cheerful voice, "but don't worry. Our captain is going to land the plane in the Monongahela River."

"I'll put her down so gently you'll hardly know it," the pilot broke in over the speaker system.

There was near-panic among the passengers as they felt the plane descend. Seizing the moment, Milner crept from the pilot's compartment and lost himself among the frightened passengers. Then suddenly, as smoothly as the pilot had promised, the plane was down. There had been only an unexpected series of jolts.

"Don't be alarmed," the pilot advised the passengers. "The aircraft will float long enough for everyone to disembark through the emergency exits." Indeed, passengers were already disembarking as Milner felt the cold waters of the Monongahela lap at his shins.

Making himself as inconspicuous as possible, he stood and got into line for what was so far a remarkably calm and orderly deplaning. Once away from the plane, he would make his escape and somehow try to make amends for his temporary madness.

The blonde stewardess was standing alongside the nearest emergency door, directing people as they left the plane. The cold water was now above Milner's knees.

He reached the door. The stewardess had a bump on her forehead and her eyes were slightly glazed. She was in mild shock, Milner imagined, and didn't recognize him when she moved him aside with her arm and said, "Full-fare passengers deplane first in emergency procedures, sir." As the water rose, people rushed quickly past Milner and out the door.

"Full-fare passengers deplane first," the stewardess repeated as the water rose faster.

When the water was nearly to Milner's neck, "Full-fare passengers first," the stewardess announced for the final time, and she swam out the door with a flick of her shapely ankles.

Milner tried to protest, but the icy water reached his mouth, his nose, and swirled over his head.

As the aircraft settled nose up on the bottom of the Monongahela River, Milner's body sank slowly to the rear of the plane.

In the early 1950s, the contents pages of Manhunt *and such other hard-boiled mystery digests as* Verdict, Pursuit, Hunted, *and* Accused *regularly carried stories by-lined Evan Hunter, Richard Marsten, and Hunt Collins. It was in these magazines, with these stories, that Hunter learned his craft—learned it so well that he was able, in 1956, to launch with immediate success his 87th Precinct series of police procedures under his most famous pseudonym, Ed McBain. The best of Hunter's crime stories from those early years can be found in his collections* The Jungle Kids *and* The Last Spin *(as by Hunter), and* The McBain Brief *(as by McBain), as well as in numerous anthologies. "Consolation," which appeared in* Mystery Monthly, *is one of his more recent tales; this powerful, uncompromising, and sexually explicit story of two small-time criminals named Colley and Jocko was later revised and incorporated into the McBain novel* Guns, *published that same year.*

CONSOLATION

Ed McBain

(1976)

They were worried that the lady in the basement had seen the blood.

They had parked the car behind Jocko's building, and then had come in through the back door, into the basement, carrying Jocko between them. There was a lady there, near the washing machines, but she was busy putting in detergent and they went right by her, hoping she'd think it was some guys bringing home a drunken buddy. She hardly looked at them as they went past her to the elevator. But now they were worrying she had maybe seen the blood.

Jocko was still bleeding.

The blood had slowed to a steady seep, but it was still coming from under the sleeve of his poplin windbreaker and dropping onto the floor of the elevator. There was no one in the elevator with them; they were grateful for that. They had driven past the front stoop of the building first, and had almost lost heart when they saw all those people sitting there on the steps talking; this was ten o'clock on a hot night in August, and nobody was eager to go upstairs to apartments like furnaces. It was Teddy who got the idea to drive around to the big, open parking lot behind the building, then go in the door to the basement. The sleeve of Jocko's jacket was covered with blood, and his pants were covered with blood, and there was almost as much blood on Teddy and Colley from carrying him.

"You think she seen the blood?" Teddy asked again.

"No," Colley said, "she didn't see it, stop worrying about it, will you?" But he was worried himself.

The elevator stopped on the fifth floor, and they eased Jocko out into the hallway, and then belatedly looked around to see if anybody was there. Without a word they turned to their right and started toward the end of the hall. Behind them, the doors to the elevator closed, and it began whining down the shaft again. Outside apartment 5G, Colley rang the doorbell.

"Just like Jeanine to have gone to a movie," Teddy said.

"No, she'll be home. Night of a job, she'll be home," Colley said, and rang the bell again. They could hear chimes sounding inside the apartment. Colley thought he heard a television set going, but that might have been in the apartment next door. He pressed the bell button again. The peephole flap suddenly went up, and then fell again an instant later. They heard the door being unlocked—first the deadbolt, then the Fox lock, then the night chain. The door opened wide.

Jeanine stood slightly to the side to let them past. She didn't scream, she didn't say a word. She'd already seen them through the peephole, so she knew something had gone wrong. She just watched them silently now as they moved past her into the living room, and then she closed and locked the door behind them—first the deadbolt, then the Fox lock, and then the chain. They were standing in the middle of the living room waiting for her to tell them where to take her husband, who was dripping blood all over the rug. She didn't ask what happened, she didn't ask how bad it was, she didn't say a word. She began walking toward the rear of the apartment instead, and they followed her without being told to follow her. Jocko was beginning to weigh a ton. He was a big man to begin with, and now they were practically dragging him across the floor, his feet trailing, his two hundred and twenty pounds multiplying with each step they took.

"In the bathroom," Jeanine said.

They managed to squeeze him through the narrow bathroom door by going through it sideways, and then they sat him down on the toilet bowl, and Jeanine began undressing him. She was wearing white shorts cut high on the leg, an orange halter top, no shoes. Her long, blond hair was hanging loose around her face as she took off the blue windbreaker and then began unbuttoning the white shirt under it. Both the shirt and the jacket were soaked with blood, and each time she brushed her hair away from her face, she got blood on her cheek and in the hair itself.

She had good features going a bit fleshy; Colley guessed she was in her late thirties, maybe closer to forty. Her eyes were dark green, not that pale jade you saw on most light-complexioned women, but a deeper green—like an emerald a burglar had once showed him, thing big enough to choke a horse. She had a good, sensible nose with a tiny scar on the bridge that made it look like she'd lived with the nose a long time, had sniffed around with it a little, had maybe stuck it in places where it didn't belong, and had it broken or slashed. The nose and the eyes and the mouth, those were what gave her face definition. The mouth was full, the upper lip lifting gently away from her teeth, so that you always saw a flash of white and got the impression she was parting her lips and about to say something. Her skin was very white; he imagined she turned lobster red in the sun. Years ago, she'd been a stripper down in Dallas, Jocko told him, and she still had a stripper's body, heavy breasts in the halter top, generous hips, good legs showing below the brief shorts, thighs a bit fleshy like her face, but the calves firm, tapering to slender ankles. Her feet were big. Her feet were peasant's feet. They didn't seem to go with that face and that body.

She lowered Jocko's shirt off one shoulder and then gently tugged the sodden material away from the wound, and slid the sleeve off his arm. Colley caught his breath as she exposed the wound, but it wasn't all that bad, the slug seemed to have ripped away only a small piece of flesh just below the biceps, hadn't even entered the arm really. Colley'd been expecting something much worse; the cops had both been carrying .38-caliber pistols.

He realizes all at once that both of them are left-handed, they are holding their pieces in their left hands as they come down a narrow aisle formed by two standing racks. The racks are made of metal, they are green, they are maybe eight or ten feet high, and they are neatly stacked with whiskey bottles. The detectives are each at least six feet tall, they come charging down the narrow aisle like bulls coming into an arena. At the far end of the aisle, Colley sees an open door. There's a room back there, he can see cartons piled on the floor. That's where the cops were staked out, in the room back there . . .

". . . shoes and socks," Jeanine said.

"What?"

"Where the hell are you?" she said.

"I'm sorry, I—"

"Take off his shoes and socks. Teddy, run the tub."

Colley stooped at Jocko's feet and began unlacing his shoes. There was blood even on the shoes—*Jesus,* what a mess! He got off the shoes and socks and then he helped Jeanine pull down Jocko's pants and take off his undershorts. Jocko had red crotch hair, same as the hair on his head. He had a very small pecker. Colley was surprised. Big man like that, you expected . . .

"Help me lift him," Jeanine said.

Together, the three of them lifted him over the edge of the tub and lowered him gently into the water. The water immediately turned a murky pink. "Could stand it a trifle hotter," Jeanine said, and turned the hot water tap open full. Jocko looked enormous lying there in the water. Massive head, red hair curling on it, eyelids closed over those pale blue eyes, menacing eyes hidden now by the closed lids; his face looked almost cherubic except for the curl of his lip betraying the meanness, even when he was unconscious. Power in the wide shoulders and huge chest—must've lifted weights as a kid. Pink water rippling over bulging pectorals, tiny contradictory penis hidden now, just a blush of deeper red where his crotch hair peeked through the pink water. He was still unconscious, but he twitched now, and grunted something, and Jeanine giggled unexpectedly.

"What is it?" she said. "Don't you want your Saturday-night bath?" and giggled again.

Colley couldn't see anything funny about their present situation. He wanted to tell her to quit making dumb jokes. But there was something even more frightening about Jocko naked in the tub there and lying on his back than when he was dressed and standing on his own two feet. Even unconscious, Colley was afraid Jocko might overhear something he said to Jeanine and get up out of the water and . . . well . . . hurt him. There'd been a big guy like Jocko in prison, and he had hurt Colley.

"You going to need me?" Teddy said. "I want to get rid of the car. Hot car sitting out there with blood all over the front seat."

"Go ahead," Jeanine said.

"Okay to call my wife? She's gonna be wondering."

"Phone's in the bedroom," Jeanine said, and turned off the hot water. Teddy went down the hallway to the bedroom. In the bathtub, Jocko sighed. Jeanine was soaping the wound now, gently using a sponge on it. Down the hall, Teddy began dialing the phone. The apartment was silent except for the tiny splashing sounds of Jeanine dipping the sponge and lifting it from the water and dipping it again. There was blood on her white shorts. Blood on her thigh, too. Down the hall, they could hear Teddy's muffled voice. Jeanine pulled the stopper from the tub, and then turned on the hot and cold water faucets and tested the stream of water with her hand. With a clean wash cloth, she began rinsing off Jocko. Teddy came back up the hallway and leaned in the bathroom doorway.

"I'm gonna split," he said, "get rid of the car." He hesitated. "Were they both dead, Colley?"

"I don't know," Colley said. "Two cops sitting the store," he explained to Jeanine. "In the back room, there."

"Him and Jocko walked into a stakeout," Teddy said.

"Minute Jocko threw down on the old man, the two of them came out the back yelling fuzz."

"You shot two cops?" Jeanine said.

"I only shot one of them. Jocko—"

"Never mind *who* shot them," Jeanine said. "I'm asking—"

"Yeah, two cops got shot."

"They both looked dead," Teddy said. "Colley, they really looked dead to me. That one lying closest to the door, his brains were all over the floor."

"Great," Jeanine said.

"They surprised us," Colley said.

"Great," she said again. "Two dead cops."

"I ain't so sure about them being dead," Colley said. "I ain't even sure about the one Teddy says had his brains—"

"It'll be on television later," Teddy said. "I'll bet it's on television. Two cops getting killed."

"Look, we don't know for sure—"

"They're dead all right," Teddy said. He looked very owlish and wise and sad behind his glasses. He also looked exhausted. He had been busy since early that morning, boosting the car in Brooklyn, and he still had to get rid of it. Before the holdup, it had only been a stolen car. Now it was a car that had been used in a felony murder . . . well, Colley wasn't sure either *one* of them was dead. Man could *look* dead without *being* dead. Hell, Jocko'd been bleeding like a pig all the way over here, but now he looked fine. Might be the same with those cops in the liquor store. Even the one Colley had shot might not . . .

"I'll call you in the morning," Teddy said.

"You going outside like that?" Colley said.

"Huh?"

"All that blood on your clothes?"

"Shit," Teddy said. "You got something I can put on, Jeanine? Just something to—"

"Jocko's clothes'd be too big for you," she said. "Maybe my raincoat."

Together, they went out of the bathroom. Colley could hear them rummaging around in one of the closets. In the tub, Jocko mumbled something, and then fell silent. Colley heard them in the hallway again, heard the front door opening and closing, heard Jeanine relocking it. Teddy had left without saying good night. He heard Jeanine padding barefooted toward the bathroom again. She came in, went directly to the tub, and said, "Give me a hand, here."

Colley leaned over the tub and put his arm under Jocko's

right arm and across his slippery back. Jeanine grabbed
Jocko's legs, and together they half lifted him, half rolled
him out of the tub. Colley got a better grip on him then,
and they moved him over to the toilet bowl, and sat him
down again. Jocko was still unconscious; his head lolled to
one side as Jeanine began drying him with a big, white
towel. Watching her, Colley was reminded of something—
though he couldn't tell what. He was completely absorbed
watching her. Down the hallway, he could hear a clock
ticking someplace. He kept watching her. The wound had
stopped bleeding completely. She patted it dry carefully,
and then took some stuff from the medicine cabinet over
the sink, and squeezed something from a tube onto the
wound, and then put a gauze pad over it, and wrapped it
with bandage and adhesive tape.

"Help me get him in the bedroom," she said.

Colley took him from behind, like before, but grabbing
him under both arms now, and Jeanine lifted his legs
again, and they carried him down the hall to the bedroom.
He got heavier each time they moved him; Colley was
beginning to think this was what Hell must be like—lifting
and carrying Jocko Wyatt through eternity.

In the bedroom, Jeanine let his legs go while she pulled
back the spread and then the blanket. Colley stood there
supporting Jocko, the weight of the man pulling on his
arms and his shoulders and his back. His own legs were
beginning to tremble.

"Come on," he said.

"Yes," she said, and nodded.

He had the feeling she wasn't even talking to him. She
had pulled the blanket to the foot of the bed, and was
coming around to where Colley stood with Jocko collapsed
against him. She seemed completely involved with her
own thoughts. She picked up Jocko's legs as if she were
picking up the handles of a wheelbarrow. Together they
moved him onto the bed.

"You better cover him," Colley said.

She pulled the sheet up over his waist, and stood there looking down at him for a moment. He was breathing evenly and regularly. In the hallway outside, a light was burning; they turned it off before they went into the living room. There was a television set against one wall. Colley instantly looked at his watch. It was ten-thirty. If either of those cops was dead, the eleven o'clock news would surely carry the story.

"Place looks like a slaughterhouse," Jeanine said, and shook her head. "Do we have to worry about cleaning up right this minute?"

"What do you mean?"

"Are you expecting *company* is what I mean."

"Cops, you mean?"

"Cops, I mean."

"No, no."

"You sure?"

"Well, I'm not sure. But even if the old guy—"

"What old guy?"

"Behind the counter."

"Great, did you shoot *him*, too?"

"No, no. Come on, Jeanine, it couldn't be helped."

"What about him?"

"I'm saying even if he gives them a good description of us, well, it takes time, you know, to check files, you know, and come up with mug shots and fingerprints and like that. They might *never* get to us. I mean, even if the old guy remembers what we look like—"

"Colley," she said, "if those cops are dead, they'll get to you."

"Well," he said.

"Even if only *one* of those cops is dead—"

"Who said anybody's dead? Teddy was only in the store there a minute, when he come in to help me with Jocko. Whyn't you ask *me*, huh? I was the one in there with Jocko when the shooting started. I'm the one ought to know what happened in there."

"All right," she said, "what *did* happen in there, Colley?"

"They surprised us, that's all. Jocko threw down on the guy behind the counter, and next thing you know there was fuzz."

The cop is about to say, "Police officers!" again. He gets only part of the word out. He says "Po—" and then the bullet takes him in the mouth. It's as if the bullet rams the rest of the word back in his throat and breaks it up into a thousand red and yellow and white globules that come flying out the back of his head and splatter all over a Seagram's poster behind him. He does an almost comic skid, the force of the bullet knocking him backwards, his feet still moving forward and flying out from under him. He goes into the air backwards, hangs there for an instant in an upside-down swan dive, his arms thrown wide, the shield in one hand, the gun in the other, his back arched, his head thrown back and spurting blood. Then he crashes suddenly. . . .

". . . started shooting?"

"What?"

"Who was the one started shooting?"

"The one coming at me," he said. "Holding out his badge. He was left-handed, Jeanine, both of them were left-handed. They had their pieces in their left hands, how you like that?" he said, and shook his head in amazement. "Listen," he said, "you got anything to drink around here? I could really use a drink."

"There's booze in the kitchen," she said.

"You want one?" he said.

"Mix me a light Scotch and water."

"I'm not moving in," he said, "I just want to see the news. I'll go right after the news, you don't have to worry."

"Who's worrying?" Jeanine said, and looked at him.

"Well, I didn't mean actually *worrying.*"

"What *did* you mean?" she said.

She was still watching him. He couldn't read the look on her face. He knew she was angry because of the shooting in the liquor store, and Jocko getting hurt. But there was something else mixed in with the anger.

"What I meant is I know you're upset right now," he said, and got up quickly and went out into the kitchen. On the counter, near the refrigerator, there was an almost full bottle of Scotch and an unopened bottle of bourbon. He pried an ice-cube tray loose from the freezer compartment and put a few cubes in each of two glasses. He was pouring Scotch liberally into both glasses when he remembered she'd asked for a light one, so he poured more heavily into his glass, which made hers light by comparison. "Did you say water in this?" he called to the living room, but she either didn't hear him or didn't care to answer him. He himself wanted soda, but there wasn't any in the refrigerator, so he put a little water in both glasses and then carried them out to the living room. The living room was empty. Down the hall, he heard the shower going. He looked at his watch again. It was quarter to eleven, plenty of time before the news came on.

He turned on the set, and then sat on the sofa and took a good heavy gulp of his drink, and then another heavy gulp, and then just began sipping at it slowly. Down the hall, the shower was still going. The apartment was still except for the steady drumming of the water and the drone of the television set. A movie was on, he watched it only because he did not want to think about what had happened in the liquor store. He did not want to believe that either of those two cops were dead.

He could accept them being hurt bad, but he didn't want to believe they were dead because then he might just as well admit he himself was dead. You kill a fuckin' cop in this city—*any* city, for that matter—that was it, Charlie. So he didn't want to believe he had killed that cop. Until he knew otherwise, why then he chose to believe the man was only hurt bad. Stupid bastard, running at him that way, holding out the badge as if it was a shield could protect him from harm. Like people hanging St. Christopher medals in their car. All those crazy bastards on the highway, you needed more than a St. Christopher medal to survive.

The sound of the water stopped. He kept watching the movie. He had no idea what the movie was about, no idea who the actors were. Down the hallway, he heard the bathroom door opening. Silence. The ticking of the clock. On the street outside, filtering up to the open windows, the distinctive laughter of a black woman. In the distance, the sound of an approaching train rattling along the elevated tracks on Westchester Avenue. Summertime. It was summertime in that apartment and beyond those open windows. Summertime. And he had shot a cop.

When she came back into the room she was wearing faded blue jeans and a white cotton T-shirt. No bra, her breasts moved fluidly beneath the thin fabric as she came barefooted into the room. She looked clean and cool and she brought the scent of soap with her. She looked younger, too, possibly because the narrow jeans hid the fleshiness of her thighs and gave her a long, slender look. Stopping just inside the door to the living room, she put her hands on her hips, and stood there watching the television screen. The movie was ending. Another train went roaring past on the avenue a block away, smothering all sound. Jeanine looked for her drink, saw it on the coffee table and leaned over to pick it up.

The anchorman came on just then to give a quick summary of the news. They both turned to watch the screen, Jeanine standing to Colley's left, the drink in one hand, the other hand still on her hip. The anchorman was saying something about a demonstration outside the U.N. building. Jeanine sipped at the drink, her eyes on the screen. Now the anchorman was talking about a three-alarm fire in the Wall Street area. Colley was hoping there wouldn't be anything about the robbery. If they didn't report it on television, that would mean neither of the two cops had been hurt bad. But then the anchorman said, "In the Bronx tonight, one detective was killed and another was seriously injured when a pair of armed men attempted to hold up a liquor store on White Plains Avenue. And in—"

"There it is," Jeanine said.

"Shhh," Colley said.

". . . the Brooklyn Battery Tunnel, a three-hour traffic jam caused tempers to flare while temperatures soared. Details on these in a moment."

"One of them's dead," Jeanine said.

"I heard."

"Great," she said.

"Shhh, I want to hear if they—"

"Just great."

She seemed about to say something more, but instead she angrily plucked a cigarette from the box on the coffee table, and struck a match with the same angry, impatient motion, and then walked to the easy chair across from the sofa and was about to sit in it when she saw she still had the burnt match in her hand. She pulled a face and came back to the coffee table and put the burnt match in the ashtray there. Then, instead of going back to the easy chair, she sat crosslegged on the floor in front of the couch, and silently and sulkily watched the screen. The commercial was over, the news team came back to elaborate on the events the anchorman had earlier summarized. Jeanine dragged on the cigarette and let out a streak of smoke. They were showing footage of the Wall Street fire now, it was really fascinating, fires fascinated Colley. They began interviewing a fireman, he was telling all about the people they'd rescued from the top floor of the office building. Then, suddenly, the liquor store appeared on the screen.

There it was all right, it was really funny seeing it there on a television screen. Earlier tonight, Colley had felt the job itself was like a goddamned movie, and now it really *was* a movie, right there on television. Only thing missing was the actors. Camera was roving around outside the store, showing the lettering on the plate-glass window, Carlisle Liquors, and the bottles in the window, focusing on a sign that was advertising something for $3.99, and then moving away to the front door, the door was opening, the camera was moving into the store itself, going in through the door, showing the bloodstains on the floor, and then continuing to move deeper into the store, toward the cash register, to show where the second cop had been shot.

It was just like all the newsreel movies Colley had ever seen on television, with bad lighting, most of the scene dark except for the area right near the lights, camera jogging and bouncing, reporter explaining what had happened earlier and hoping the audience would be able to reconstruct the action. This time, Colley had no trouble at all reconstructing the action; Colley had been *part* of the action. The reporter finished by saying the second cop had been taken to Fordham Hospital, where he was still in critical condition. Then he smiled and said, "What's the weather for tomorrow, Frank?"

Colley got up and turned off the set just as the weatherman appeared in front of his map. He went back to the sofa then, picked up his drink, drained the glass, and set it down on the coffee table.

"Now what?" Jeanine said.

"I don't know what."

"He's dead, you killed a cop."

"I ain't so sure I'm the one who killed him," Colley said.

"You just heard—"

"It could've been Jocko. It could've been the one *he* shot."

"What difference does it make?" Jeanine said. "You were in there together, you're accomplices—"

"All right."

". . . you killed a man!"

"All *right*, I said!"

"Great," Jeanine said.

"I want another drink," he said, and went out into the kitchen. As he mixed the drink he thought what a lousy break it was, the cop dying. He was beginning to convince himself the cop had really fired first, that if only the cop had played it cool, if only everybody had kept their heads inside the store there, the cop would still be alive. As he took ice cubes from where they were melting in the tray, he became aware of how hot the apartment was. He'd been so busy carrying Jocko in, and then watching the news, he hadn't had time to concentrate on anything else. But now he felt the heat, and felt the bloodstained clothing sticking to his flesh, and called from the kitchen, "What's the matter with the air conditioner?"

"Nothing," she said.

"Whyn't you turn it on?" he said.

"What for?"

"Cause it's hot as hell in here."

"I don't feel hot," she said, and he remembered Jocko telling him how much she liked the heat, how she'd been born in Florida someplace—where had he said? He went back into the living room and said, "Where you from in Florida?"

"Fort Myers."

"Yeah, Fort Myers, that's what Jocko said. You like it when it's suffocating like this, huh?"

"Right, let's talk about the weather," she said. "We just heard the cop is dead—"

"Yeah, that's a lousy break," Colley said.

"But let's talk about the weather, okay? You think it's going to rain tomorrow? Maybe if it rains the cops won't come looking for you."

"They probably won't come looking for us anyway," Colley said. "I doubt the old man will finger us." He drank from his glass, nodded thoughtfully, and then said, "He was scared, you know? When Jocko threw down on him. He might figure if he fingers us, we'll go back and hurt him."

"He might also figure you won't be *able* to go back and hurt him," Jeanine said.

"What do you mean?"

"He might figure you'll be in jail a long, long time."

"Well, you always get *out* of jail, you know."

"They bust Jocko for this one, it's his third offense. They'll throw away the key."

"Yeah," Colley said. "I forgot about that."

"He could get a maximum of life."

"Yeah. But, you see, the old man don't know that. The old man in the liquor store. He don't know us from a hole in the wall. So he'll be afraid to finger us, you see."

"You *hope*," Jeanine said.

"Well, sure, I *hope*. I mean, who the hell can say for sure what *anybody'll* do nowadays? Who can figure that cop starting to shoot there in the liquor store? Comes running at me holding out his badge and shooting before he hardly has the words out of his mouth."

"What words?"

"He yells 'Police officers!' and starts shooting."

They were silent for several moments, drinking. Outside, another train roared past. The windows were wide open, but not a breeze came through into the apartment. Colley debated asking her again to turn on the air conditioner. Instead, he finished his drink, sucked on one of the ice cubes for a moment, and then said, "You mind if I fix myself another one of these?"

"Go ahead," she said.

"You want another one?"

"Just freshen this a little," she said, and handed him her glass.

He carried both glasses out into the kitchen. The Scotch bottle was almost empty. He poured some of what was left into Jeanine's glass and the remainder in his, and then he added a little water to both glasses and carried them back into the living room.

"What it is," he said, handing Jeanine her glass, "you get lots of cops, they're trigger-happy. They'll shoot little kids carrying water pistols, you know that?"

"Yeah, they're bastards," Jeanine said, and sipped at her drink.

"Not that we were carrying water pistols," he said, and laughed.

"That's for sure," Jeanine said.

"This is really something, ain't it?" Colley said, and took a long swallow of the drink. The booze was beginning to reach him. This was his third, and he'd poured all of them with a heavy hand, just the way he'd have poured them if the job had gone off okay. Always drank after a job, man had to celebrate, didn't he? This one hadn't come off, but it was the first one that hadn't since they'd been working together, so what the hell, have a little drink anyway. He was beginning to feel a little hazy, and very comfortable and cozy here in the living room. Safe. He was beginning to feel safe.

"Thing *I'm* worried about," she said.

"Yeah?"

"Is I hope we won't need a doctor for him."

"I don't think we'll need a doctor."

"You know anybody?"

"No."

"Who'd come, I mean. If we needed him."

"I don't know anybody."

"So what do we do if he starts bleeding again?"

"I don't know. I think he'll be okay, though. He's a strong guy."

"Oh, yeah, he's strong all right," she said. "Take more'n a bullet to kill old Jocko. Take a stake in his *heart*, you want to know," she said, and laughed, and then sobered immediately and glanced past Colley toward the hallway, as though afraid the laughter might have disturbed Jocko.

"How long you been married?" Colley asked.

"Three years."

"You were a stripper when you met him, huh?"

"No, who told you that?"

"Jocko said you used to be a stripper."

"Yeah, but that was before I met him. I haven't been stripping for seven, eight years now. This is August, ain't it?"

"Yeah, August."

"I quit stripping eight years ago November."

"I didn't realize that."

"Yeah, I've been out of it a long time."

"How come you quit?"

"Getting old, sonny," she said, and smiled.

"Yeah, sure," he said.

"How old do you think I am?" she asked.

"Thirty-two, thirty-three."

"Come on," she said.

"Okay, thirty-seven, okay?"

"I'm forty-four," she said. "I was thirty-six when I quit. Girl gets to be thirty-six, even if she takes good care of herself, she starts looking it, you know what I mean? Starts getting a little flabby."

"You don't look flabby to me," Colley said.

"Thanks. Guys coming to strip joints, they don't want to look at somebody who's over the hill, they want to see firm young bodies."

"You got a great body," Colley said.

"Thanks."

"I mean it."

"I said thanks. Also, I was getting static from my husband. Not Jocko, this was my first husband. He said it was wrong what I was doing, shaking my ass and getting guys all hot and bothered. *He* turned out to be a junkie with a habit long as Southern California, but he was always bugging *me* about being a stripper, can you imagine? Those were the days, all right," she said, and rolled her eyes and sighed.

"Did you like being a stripper?" he asked.

"It wasn't bad," she said. "Actually, it was exciting sometimes."

"How do you mean?"

"Turning guys on," she said. "I'd go out there, you know, and the drums'd be banging, and the lights'd be on me, and I'd start throwing myself around, and it would reach me sometimes." She shrugged. "You know what I mean?"

"Sure," he said.

She shrugged again, tossed her head slightly, and then took another cigarette from the box on the table. He watched her while she lighted it. She shook out the match, and he watched her breasts moving under the T-shirt, and then she walked to the window and he watched the motion of her hips in the tight blue jeans, and he kept watching her as she stood by the window with one hand cradling her elbow, hip jutting, the other hand holding the cigarette and bringing it to her mouth. The sky outside was filled with stars. There wasn't a chance of it raining anytime soon, not with all those stars in the sky. Heat would probably last another day or two. He kept watching her.

"They're all the same, actually," she said. "I told Jocko I was thinking about taking a job in a massage parlor, they get good money those girls. He hit the ceiling, said that was nothing but whoring. I don't happen to think it's whoring. A massage ain't the same as whoring."

"Well, lots of massage parlors, it's more than just a massage," Colley said.

"You ever been in one of those massage parlors?"

"Oh, sure."

"What do they do in there?"

"Well, they do a lot more than just massage a man."

"What do they do?"

"Let's just say I can see why Jocko hit the ceiling. If you were my wife, I wouldn't like the idea of you working in a massage parlor."

"How about my being a stripper?"

"That might be different," Colley said. "I don't know how I'd feel about that."

"Uh-huh," Jeanine said, and nodded.

"You're thinking I'd hit the ceiling, right?"

"How'd you guess?" she said.

"Maybe I would. Good-looking woman like you," he said, and quickly picked up his glass, and discovered it was empty, booze sure went fast around here. He tried to remember whether the bottle in the kitchen was Scotch or bourbon, the bottle that hadn't been opened yet; he suspected it was bourbon, wasn't good to mix Scotch with bourbon. He was feeling exceedingly content now, sitting there in the living room watching Jeanine. The job had gone wrong, true enough, but there was something very pleasant about being here with Jeanine, something reassuring about her standing there at the window looking out, though he wondered just what the hell she found so fascinating out there.

•   •   •

He debated complimenting her on her body again, a woman didn't tell you how old she was unless she wanted you to say she looked terrific. But just then another train went by outside, and she turned toward the sound of it, probably wanted to read that terribly interesting graffiti sprayed on the side of the cars, "Spider 107" or "Shadow 49" or "Spic 32," dumb bastards scribbling all over the city. If she ever turned away from that window, maybe he'd look her straight in the eye and tell her she had great knockers. You've got great knockers, Jeanine, did you realize that? No, of course she didn't realize it. She'd only been a stripper for Christ knew how long, only had guys yelling and hollering every time she took off her bra and twirled it in the air, but no, she didn't realize she had great knockers. I'm stoned, he thought. I killed a fuckin' cop, this is my third drink, my fourth drink, who the hell's counting. I don't know what the fuck I'm doing, and don't give a shit besides.

"You've got great knockers," he said.

"Thanks," she said.

"What are you doing there by the window?"

"I was just thinking," she said.

"What about?"

"I was wishing something, actually."

"What were you wishing?"

"That Jocko would die."

He was not sure he had heard her correctly. He reasoned that she could not have said what she'd just said because he'd seen her a little while ago giving tender loving care to Jocko in the bathtub, even though Jocko had a very small pecker, very tender loving care indeed, washing out his wound and gentling him, yes. You did not wash away a man's wound and then wish he was, *wish* he was dead.

"You want to know something about your friend Jocko?" she asked.

He shook his head. No, he did not want to know something about his friend Jocko. Jocko was his fall part-

ner and you did not go around looking at your fall partner's wife and thinking she had great knockers . . . had he
said it out loud? No, he did not want to hear nothing more
about Jocko.

"Your friend Jocko beats me," she said.

"No, no," Colley said, and shook his head.

"Yes, yes," Jeanine said. "He hasn't missed a day
since I came up to New York. How long've I been in New
York now? When did I come up from Dallas?"

"I don't know," Colley said. "Two months ago? Five?"

"I came up on the twentieth of May. What's today?"

"Saturday."

"The date, I mean."

"I don't know," he said.

"August sixteenth, ain't it?"

"Yeah," he said.

"That's three months," she said.

"Yeah."

"Look at this," she said, and seized the bottom of the
T-shirt in both hands and pulled it up over her breasts. Her
rib cage, her chest, the slopes and undersides of her breasts
were covered with angry black and blue marks. "*That's*
your friend," she said, and lowered the shirt again.

"Listen," Colley said, "you shouldn't be saying such
things about Jocko."

"Why not?"

"He's my fall partner, we work together. It's not right
to say such things."

"You still think you've got a little gang going, don't
you?" Jeanine said. "You killed a cop tonight—"

"No, no," he said, and shook his head.

"Yes, yes, and for all you know the *other* cop might
die, too. But you still think you've got a little holdup gang
going. *Jesus*!" she said.

"I just don't want to hear nothing more about Jocko,"
he said.

"Are you afraid of him?"

"No."

"Sure you are."

"No, I am not afraid of Jocko," he said.

"Sure you are," she said again, and smiled.

"Fine," he said, "have it your way. Fine. You got something I can wear out of here? I think I better leave."

"Are you drunk?" she asked suddenly.

"No, sir, I am not drunk," he said.

"Jesus, how did you get so drunk?"

"I am not drunk," he said.

"You'd better get in the shower," she said.

"Wash off the blood," he said.

"Wash off the *booze*. How'd you get so drunk, man? Go get in the shower. You know where the shower is?"

"Know where the shower is," he said.

"Right down the hall there."

"Right down the hall."

"Go ahead now."

"Thanks," he said, and went down the hall to the bathroom. He was surprised to discover that he had a big pistol, big .38 Detective Special in his waistband. He pulled the gun out and placed it on top of the toilet tank, and then was further surprised to learn that his pants, his jacket, and his shirt were stained with blood, where'd he get all this blood on him? He took off his pants and saw that his undershorts were soaked with blood, too. There was dried and crusted blood on his left arm, and on both hands, and all over his face. He wondered if he should get in the shower with his clothes in his arms, and then dropped them in a bundle instead. He got into the shower, drew the curtain closed, opened it again to make sure his gun was still there on the toilet tank, and then closed the curtain and turned on the water and almost scalded himself. He backed away swearing, adjusted the water gingerly, and then looked around for the soap.

He soaped his crotch and the hair on his chest and under his arms, and remembered that when he was in prison first thing anybody soaped when they got in the shower was their crotch. Not that he looked. Guy in prison saw you looking, he figures you were ready to be turned out as his punk, next thing you knew, he was making a heavy play for you. This was nice soap, it smelled nice, he guessed it was Jeanine's. Big guy like Jocko wouldn't use sweet-smelling soap like this. He wondered if Jeanine had seen him looking Jocko over. He didn't want her to think he was, you know, *looking* at it. Nothing wrong with a little curiosity, though. Guy's sitting there, nothing wrong with checking him out, see how you shape up in the world. Nothing wrong with using Jeanine's soap, either. Besides, it was the only soap here in the bathroom, so what the hell. So he'd smell like a bed of roses, so what? Dig *me*, girls. I'm the Queen of the Roses, he thought.

There was a guy in prison, his name was Kruger, he was as big as Jocko. They all called him the Kraut, he had a scar on his cheek, they said he'd been in the German Army during World War II before coming to New York, where he got busted. What he got busted for, he took a thirteen-year-old girl up to a hotel room, burned her with cigarettes, raped her, broke both arms and legs, dislocated her jaw, blackened her eyes, knocked out seven of her teeth. He left her for dead, she sure as hell *looked* dead. But the girl was still alive, and she identified him by name, the stupid bastard had given her his real name when he'd picked her up in Central Park. Why she'd gone up to that hotel with him was anybody's guess, guy old enough to be her father, take one look at him you *had* to know he was a mean bastard. First time Colley saw him in prison . . .

Listen, how'd we get on *this?* he thought. Listen, let's get off this, okay? You start thinkin' about that fuckin' Kruger, you'll take the nice fine edge off this fuckin' high, who the hell wants to think about *that* bastard? Standing in the yard there, smoking his cigarette. Standing there. Cool gray eyes, that scar on his face. He turned his eyes to

Colley, and he grinned, and a chill went up Colley's spine.
He came over, then, and stuck out his hand, and Colley
shrank away from him, terrified, and he grabbed Colley's
hand in his own and squeezed it, squeezed it so hard it felt
like he was going to break all the bones in it, and he kept
grinning all the time, grinning.

In the shower now, Colley shivered. The water was hot,
the water was pouring down on him in a steady, sobering,
hot stream, but he shivered thinking of Kruger. He hadn't
known what Kruger wanted from him then, and he still
didn't know. It wasn't sex. Kruger had his steady punk, a
slender, blond kid who'd been busted for pushing dope
and who Kruger had turned out two days after the kid
drove up. So it wasn't sex, he didn't want sex from
Colley. Colley didn't know *what* the hell he wanted. Followed him around all over the joint. Colley'd get in the
shower, he'd check six ways from tomorrow to make sure
the Kraut wasn't anywhere around. Then, minute he turned
on the water and started soaping himself, the Kraut would
suddenly appear, grinning, and he'd step behind Colley
and grab his ass in both hands, and squeeze the cheeks so
hard Colley thought he would faint from the pain. Rotten
son of a bitch bastard! Three and a half years in prison,
and the Kraut dogging him day and night, hurting him.
Just hurting him for the sheer fucking pleasure of it. Like
Jocko, he supposed. Like Jocko putting those black and
blue marks all over Jeanine, what the hell was wrong with
a man like that? He thought of Jeanine. He thought of
Jeanine lifting the T-shirt up over her breasts. He thought
of her stripping for a roomful of men. He soaped himself
and he thought of her.
    There was a knock on the bathroom door, he almost
didn't hear it over the sound of the water. His hand
stopped.
    "Yeah?" he said.
    "You okay in there?" Jeanine said.

"Yeah," he said.

"All right to come in? I've got some clothes for you."

"What?"

"You can't leave here in your own clothes, all that blood on them."

"Oh, sure. Come on in."

The door opened. The shower curtain billowed in toward him, the plastic sticking to his legs. The water was drumming against his groin, his prick was standing up stiff with the water drilling it and the soap running off him in long white streams.

"I'll put them here on the counter," she said.

"Thanks."

"I hope the pants fit you."

"Yeah," he said. He did not hear the door opening and closing again. "Jeanine?"

"Yeah?"

"You still in here?"

"I'm still in here," she said.

"I'm coming out now," he said.

"Come on out," she said.

"Jeanine?"

"Yeah."

"I want to come out now."

"So come on," she said.

He poked his head and one shoulder around the edge of the shower curtain. Jeanine was leaning against the sink.

"Hey," he said.

Her eyes met his.

"Get out of here," he said.

"Why?"

"Jeanine, you're looking for trouble," he said, and realized all at once that they were both whispering.

"No," she said, "I'm looking for consolation. I'm looking to be soothed, Colley. I'm looking to be comforted."

He hesitated a moment, and then he pushed the curtain

back on the rod, and stepped out of the tub. She did not move from the sink. She kept leaning against the sink, with her hands resting on her thighs, her legs stretched out in front of her, her shoulders back. Her eyes did not leave his face as he approached her. He stopped in front of her, and lifted the front of the T-shirt the way she had lifted it in the living room not ten minutes ago, took the bottom of it in both wet hands and pulled the shirt up over her breasts.

When he is committing a robbery, he sees every detail as if he is on dope, everything is slowed down, everything moves at a rhythmic pace slower than the beat of his heart. It is the same making love to her now. He tries to remember whether it has ever been like this before, whether everything ever slowed down for him with any other woman. He believes it is because Jocko is in the bedroom across the hall. The danger of Jocko across the hall—even though Jocko has a bullet wound in his arm and is lying bandaged and unconscious on the bed—the danger of Jocko is what makes this so exciting, causing time to hang suspended, forcing time to come to a near stop. Like on a job. The danger of going to prison again, the danger of someone like Kruger again, the gamble, the high excitement of going in there with a pistol, it is the same as this, the same as this with her in this steamy bathroom while Jocko lies across the hall unconscious.

The steam is dissipating, the mirror is running rivulets of water behind her blond head, he cannot see himself clearly in the mirror because it is completely steamed over except for the silvery rivulets. He is soaking wet, he stands before her dripping water onto the tile floor. She is still leaning against the sink. Her hands are still on her thighs, the fingers spread. He notices that she has long, slender hands, that the fingernails are painted red as bright as the blood that spurted from the dead cop's head, he does not want to think about that stupid bastard, he reaches up for her breasts. The T-shirt is bunched above them, she stands with her shoulders back, the breasts jutting, a faint smile on her face, her eyes slitted, a lazy, languid look in them, the steam is turning to a faint rain, it is raining in the bathroom as he reaches for her breasts, brings his open hands up to her breasts. She leans into his hands.

He touches her breasts lightly, he does not want to hurt her the way Jocko hurt her, he is almost afraid of causing fresh bruises on the white, her skin is so white. There is a sheen to her skin, the flesh is taut, the globes shimmer with secret pinks and lavenders, mother-of-pearl breasts, he touches them gently, his fingers explore. The skin around the nipples comes as a coarse reminder of sex, blatant and rude, the circles of darker flesh erupting in pinpoint mounds. The hardening nipples are a declaration, he responds to them wildly, seizing her breasts harshly, tightening his hands on them, cupping them to his mouth, kissing the freckled sloping tops and rounded sides, and then bringing his mouth up to hers, waiting wet and wide, and covering her lips with his.

She throws herself into him, she grinds her hips against him, he visualizes her on a small stage in a smoke-filled room. *I'd go out there, you know, and the drums'd be banging, and the lights'd be on me, and I'd start throwing myself around,* and he reaches for the front of the blue jeans and finds first the button, and then the zipper, which he begins to lower. She is naked under the jeans, her nakedness comes as a surprise, the smooth shock of her belly, the sudden deep navel, the crisp, tangled hair. He spreads his fingers onto her crotch and she pulls her mouth from his and whispers directly into his ear, a cannon shot in his ear, "He'll kill you." She is referring to Jocko, he knows she is referring to Jocko, but he can visualize only Kruger grabbing him in the shower, Kruger squeezing his cheeks in both hands, squeezing, squeezing, he will faint, and then stopping just in time, and grinning and walking out, the other cons pretending nothing has happened.

"He'll kill you," she says again, but she is stepping out of the blue jeans, she is kicking them away on the tile floor, she is reaching for him again, leaning back against the sink, hands coming up behind his neck, mouth open, grinding again even before their naked bodies touch. He reaches behind her and clasps her buttocks in both hands and lifts her up onto the sink. Then they hear the voice. The first thing he thinks is that it's the police, he does not know why he thinks it's the police. The next thing he thinks is, *The door, the bathroom door, is the door locked?*

"Jeanine," the voice says.

The voice is hoarse, he cannot recognize it at first. But Jeanine knows the voice immediately, and reacts to it at once. She closes her legs, she puts her hands against Colley's chest and shoves him away from her, she slides off the sink and onto the floor, she's putting on her jeans before the voice says again, slightly louder this time, "Jeanine." There is no question mark at the end of that voice, this is not someone used to calling her and not having her come, this is someone who beats her a lot, this is her Kruger, and his name is Jocko. She is pulling the T-shirt over her head now, Colley sees the swollen breasts for just an instant longer before she pulls the shirt down over them. The nipples are still hard, they poke through the thin cotton fabric, the nipples are the same but everything else is changing, everything is speeding up again, time is becoming real again, the bathroom was damp and time was becoming real.

She moved swiftly to the door. Her hand reached for the knob. She unlocked the door, and then turned to face him.

"Later," she whispered.

"No," he said, and shook his head.

"He's calling me."

"I hear him."

"We'll make it later."

"No, we won't make nothin' later," Colley said. "Go on, go take care of him." He felt foolish and white and soft standing there naked with her all dressed and ready to go to Jocko. He looked toward the toilet tank, where he'd put his gun before getting into the shower. The gun was still there. He felt better knowing the gun was there.

"Yes, later," she whispered, and went out of the bathroom.

He stood there feeling dumb. He looked down at himself. He looked around the room. He found a clean towel, and dried himself, and then found the clothes she'd brought him. Jocko's clothes. There was no underwear or socks, only a pair of pants and what looked like an old sweater. Just the thing he needed on a hot August night, one of Jocko's ratty old sweaters. He tried on the pants without any underwear, surprised that the waist fit him, big guy like Jocko, he expected the pants to swim on him. The pants had a button fly, and he was starting to button them when he realized something was wrong, same thing that was wrong in the liquor store when the two cops came running at him with their guns in their left hands. The pants were buttoning wrong. The buttons were on the wrong side. He realized then that they were women's pants, they were Jeanine's pants, and he started laughing because he'd finally got in her pants all right, but not the way he *thought* he'd get in them.

He debated putting on the bloodstained shirt again, and decided in favor of the sweater, no matter *how* damn hot it was. He still had to go down in the street, and all he needed was some cop stopping to ask about the blood on his shirt. There was only a little blood on one of his socks, so he put on the socks and shoes, and then he combed his hair with a comb he found on the counter top, lots of long, blond hair tangled in it, probably Jeanine's, like the pants. He still thought it was comical how he'd finally got in her pants. He didn't know how funny Jocko would think it was. He was a little afraid of going out there and looking Jocko in the eye. He lifted the gun from the toilet tank. He tucked the gun into the waistband of the pants. He pulled back his shoulders and opened the bathroom door.

Jeanine was standing in the doorway to the bedroom.

"He's out again," she said.

"Too bad," Colley said.

"He was okay two or three minutes, then he drifted off again. Clothes fit you, huh?" she said.

"Yeah. I'm gonna split now. I'll call you tomorrow, okay? See how Jocko is."

She walked him to the front door. He could hear the clock ticking. Time was with him again. She said, "I meant what I said about later."

"Sure," he said. "Later."

"I'd do it now, you wanted to."

"No, I got to get going."

"Well, good night then," she said, and unlocked the door for him.

"Good night," he said.

He stepped into the hallway. The door closed behind him. He heard her fastening all the locks again. He looked at his watch as he went down the hallway to the elevator. It was close to midnight, another day. He rang for the elevator and stood watching the indicator bar as the elevator crept up the shaft, these goddamned projects never put in quality merchandise.

When he reached the street, he began walking toward the train station on Westchester Avenue. He thought about the job as he walked, thought about how wrong the job had gone, couldn't have gone wronger—he'd killed one cop, Jocko had maybe killed another one. He thought about Jeanine, and how that had gone wrong, too, some consolation *that* had been; Jocko calling from the other room. Colley'd never made it with a stripper in his life, probably never would get another chance at her, no matter *what* she said about later. *Shit,* he thought, and kicked at something on the sidewalk, didn't even know what it was, something shiny. Times he wanted to quit this racket, get himself a nice girl, his mother was always telling him to get himself a nice Italian girl, settle down someplace. Times like tonight he was tempted to do it. Who the hell needs this kind of life?

He felt the gun in the waistband of the pants.

The gun was cool against his naked skin.

Colley took the steps up to the elevated platform two at a time. He waited for the train, feeling the gun, knowing the gun was there, feeling everything would work out fine, he had a gun, he knew how to use it, everything would be fine again.

He was whistling when the train pulled in.

3